EYE OF TRUTH

AGENTS OF THE CROWN BOOK I

LINDSAY BUROKER

Eye of Truth
Agents of the Crown, Book 1

by Lindsay Buroker

FOREWORD

Greetings, and welcome to the start of a new fantasy series. I'm glad you're here and willing to try a new world and a new set of characters. I promise action, adventure, romance, humor, and a good time if you call... er, wait. Not that last thing.

Eye of Truth was originally published on my blog in the summer of 2018. Many thanks to those who read along there and commented (and pointed out the occasional typo). I originally intended to write a single novel, but you know how those things go. By the time I was halfway into it, I decided this would be the start of a new series of fantasy mysteries. Now, I have plans to write five novels. Maybe six. These things have a tendency to expand!

Before you jump in, please let me thank the tireless folks who help me publish my books:

My editor, Shelley Holloway, who has helped me with dozens (no, really—*dozens!*) of novels over the years. My book buddies and frequent beta readers, Sarah Engelke, Rue Silver, and Cindy Wilkinson. My cover designers, the good folks at Deranged Doctor Design. My regular typo hunters who so often catch things the rest of us missed. And lastly, thank you, good reader. Whether this is the first book of mine that you've tried or you've read all my series, I thank you for your support, and I hope you enjoy this new adventure.

CHAPTER 1

INQUISITOR ZENIA CHAM CROUCHED ATOP a parked wagon, observing the brick square in front of the Temple of the Water Order. Observing and waiting.

Pedestrians ambled through the area, buying from vendors, ignoring beggars, and tossing pebbles into the dragon fountain for luck. Two boys waded through the water, scrambled up the statue, and giggled as they stuck their fingers into the dragon's nostrils in an attempt to plug the streams shooting out of them.

Zenia almost yelled for them to get off the fountain—that statue represented the Blue Dragon founder of the Water Order and deserved respect—but she had a greater criminal to catch.

"He's *not* going to come back here," her colleague whispered from behind her.

"You're doubting my ability to read a criminal's intentions in his actions?" Zenia arched her brows and smiled over her shoulder.

Rhi Lin leaned casually against the wagon's dormant smoke stack, but she also scrutinized the square from their elevated perch, her dark brown eyes missing little. "I'm doubting anyone would be stupid enough to return to the scene of his crime. Twenty minutes after committing it."

"Judging by the nervous way he kept glancing over his shoulder, he knew we were following him. And his hand strayed often to his purse full of stolen coins. Those were hesitant touches. I believe he knows he won't escape and that he's decided to return the offering to the temple charity plate in the hope that we'll let him go."

"Your rock tell you that?" Rhi glanced at the front of Zenia's robe.

Zenia's dragon-tear gem wasn't visible, but her colleague knew well that she kept it on a chain around her neck.

"I didn't need magic to deduce our criminal's motives."

"So, you're guessing." Despite the skeptical curve of Rhi's lips, she leaned forward onto the balls of her feet, her fingers curled around her bo staff. She was ready to spring into action.

"We'll see." Zenia smiled and turned her attention back to the square.

It *was* a guess, but after more than ten years as an inquisitor, and five years apprenticed to an inquisitor before that, she believed in her guesses. Her *deductions*. They typically proved correct.

One of the twin bronze-and-wood doors to the temple opened, their massive size and height making the blue-robed figure that stepped out appear diminutive. But the white-haired Archmage Sazshen was anything but diminutive, and when she yelled at the boys to get off the dragon, they leaped down and sprinted away so quickly they tripped over their own feet. Repeatedly.

Sazshen gazed calmly after them, then around the square. *Her* square.

Uncharacteristic nerves trotted through Zenia's belly as she realized the temple leader, who was also her employer and mentor, might witness her failing. What if she had guessed wrong? Sazshen would think it odd to find her protégé sunning herself atop a wagon for no reason.

Rhi touched Zenia's shoulder. "There he is."

Before Zenia spotted their target, Rhi sprang from the top of the wagon. She landed lightly on the brick pavers, her soft shoes not making a sound as she sprinted through the pedestrians with her bo in hand. People hurried out of the way, though she wouldn't have knocked anyone aside. Rhi was five and a half feet tall and as stocky as a dwarf, but she had the uncanny agility of an elf.

She weaved through the crowds like a dancer, the six-foot olive-wood staff a natural extension of her body rather than a clunky weapon, and if people hadn't made exclamations of surprise as she ran past, her target never would have heard her.

But the gaunt man in tattered clothing glanced back and jumped, spotting her sprinting toward him. Rhi had been circling as she ran, perhaps hoping to herd him up the steps and into the temple's great hall. But he took off down the street instead, heading toward the wagon where Zenia perched.

She hopped down, not with as much agility as her colleague, but she was ready when the man approached, bystanders scattering to get out of the way. Zenia lifted her arms and stepped toward him. She had no great magical attacks she could throw at him, since her gem only lent her powers that were useful in sussing out clues and tracking down criminals, but she prepared to shout a mental command into his mind, a compulsion to stop and surrender.

Before she sent it, he saw her and halted so quickly he tumbled to his knees in front of the dragon fountain. Sheer terror flashed in his eyes, making Zenia feel like some tyrannical troll that ate those who trespassed in its territory.

The man was so gaunt and clad in such tattered clothing that a part of her wished she could let him go, that she could look the other way and let him take the Order's donation money to buy some fish and flatbread. Times had been difficult for many these last years of the war, and Zenia hadn't forgotten what it was like to go hungry and to have hunger turn into desperation.

But she had sworn an oath long ago to do the Water Order's bidding, to protect the interests of the temple and all it employed. If the laws were ignored for one, they might as well be ignored for a thousand. Besides, she could never let a criminal go with Archmage Sazshen looking on.

As Zenia stepped forward, believing the man would give up, he threw another terror-filled look at her and leaped to his feet. He whirled to sprint in the other direction.

By now, Rhi had caught up with him. She launched a fist at his face. His nose crunched loudly enough that Zenia heard it from several paces away, even over the rumble of a nearby steam carriage and the gurgle of the fountain. The blow dropped the man to his back.

As Zenia approached, Rhi knelt to pat down the thief. Groaning and dazed, the man brought shaky hands to his nose but did not object to the search.

Rhi produced a jangling pouch and handed it up to Zenia. A witness in the temple had seen the man slip the donation coins into the pouch, so there was no question that they belonged to the Order.

"All those hours I spend sparring with Jagarr and throwing sandbags around in the gym," Rhi said, shaking her head, "and criminals are more terrified of you than they are of me."

She truly sounded disgusted.

"It's the pin that terrifies them." Zenia accepted the pouch and pointed to the dragon claw pin attached to the front of her robe, the pin that marked her as an inquisitor. "Those with sins staining their souls get nervous when an inquisitor of any of the Orders comes around."

"I'm not arguing that, but you've got a special reputation in the city. And don't tell me you don't know it."

Zenia grimaced as Rhi hefted the thief to his feet, tears streaming from the man's eyes. She *was* aware of her reputation and the fact that she was known as the Frost Mage—and occasionally the Frost Bitch, depending on who was listening.

She never knew how to feel about it. In the early years, she had been proud, because it had come about due to all the crimes she'd solved, all the underworld felons she'd located and brought in. She'd risen to her current level of fame—or perhaps infamy, at least in the eyes of guilty parties—three years ago after finding and defeating the elusive Dark Stalker, a man who'd raped and murdered his way up and down the kingdom coast.

She remained proud that she was good at her job, but her reputation did lead to a degree of isolation that she hadn't anticipated. Even within the temple, she had few friends, and she wasn't sure why that was. It had been years since a man had asked her out to dinner or for a walk on the beach. Even though she was focused on her career and told herself companionship wasn't important, she sometimes wondered if she would die without ever marrying and having children, without finding someone she loved and who loved her.

Her gaze drifted up the long marble steps to where Archmage Sazshen still stood, now gazing down at them. Sazshen was everything Zenia longed to be, with a career and power that nobody could take from her, but she'd also never married and she had no children. By choice? Or because she, too, had been feared by men rather than loved by them?

Realizing that Rhi was almost to the top of the stairs with the prisoner, Zenia trotted up after them. She hoped the gaunt man wouldn't be punished unduly for his crimes, especially since the money had been recovered before it could be spent.

Archmage Sazshen regarded him with cold eyes.

"Dungeon, Archmage?" Rhi asked.

"Dungeon." Sazshen nodded firmly. "Brakkor will drop a few lashes on his back to ensure he thinks twice about stealing again."

"Yes, ma'am." Rhi escorted her charge into the cool temple interior.

Zenia was glad the man would receive a whipping rather than the traditional punishment for theft, having his hand cut off. Thankfully, all the Orders had grown more lenient in dispensing justice these last few years. It was anything but a time of prosperity for the kingdom, and half the city would be without hands if punishments remained as harsh as they had been historically. Even so, Zenia was glad she was usually assigned tough cases, men and women who had done far more evil than swiping a few coins from the Order's coffers.

"How did you convince the thief to return to the temple?" Sazshen asked. "I'm sure your monk appreciates having such a short walk to the dungeon with her recalcitrant prisoner."

Your monk. As if Archmage Sazshen didn't know Rhi's name. A few dozen monks lived in or worked for the temple, but that wasn't so many that one couldn't learn their names. And Rhi, as one of only two female monks here, was memorable.

"He convinced himself, Archmage."

"Handy."

"I thought so." Zenia thought about mentioning that Rhi had wanted to head to the public market, believing the thief would rush to spend his ill-gotten coin there, and that it had been she who'd deduced the criminal's route. She shouldn't feel the need to brag, and it irritated her that she still had the urge to do so, to point out that she'd done something clever. She'd passed her thirty-second birthday, and she was established in her profession. Why did she still feel the need for praise?

"I sensed your approach and came out to meet you." Sazshen touched the tear-shaped gem that she wore openly on the outside of her robe, an intricate representation of the fountain in front of the temple carved into its surface. Most people who owned the valuable gems hid them, lest they tempt the desperate and the hungry.

"Do you need something more than thieves from me?" Zenia asked.

"I wish to take you to lunch."

"Ah." Zenia had hoped for more interesting news, but she was always willing to spend time with her mentor. "I would be happy to dine with you."

"I thought we would discuss my retirement."

"Again?" Zenia smiled.

Archmage Sazshen had been threatening to retire for years. More than once, she'd hinted that she might suggest Zenia to her colleagues at the other temples as a possible replacement, but Zenia hadn't been holding her breath. Even though she liked to think her work and dedication to the Order would make her ideal for the position, there were other mages and inquisitors who were more eligible. Older and more experienced. And from the nobility. Even though the temples supposedly promoted people equally these days, and ignored kingdom titles, the bias was there. And Zenia was... well, her father had never acknowledged her existence, so it didn't matter that she was technically half zyndar.

"Many have watched your work and your career with interest," Sazshen said. "Archmages are usually at least in their fifties before they're considered wise and mature enough for the position—if Archmage Xan's tendency to place noise-maker cushions on the chairs of his colleagues at meetings can be considered *mature*—but I've mentioned your name numerous times, and I believe they're considering you. If you were to complete one more high-profile task for the Order, I suspect they could be swayed."

Zenia clasped her hands behind her back. "I would certainly be honored to be chosen for the position, Archmage."

Was it possible a high-profile task was already on the horizon? Perhaps some new crafty criminal was at work right now, harming the Order or the subjects of the kingdom.

"As it happens, I have a challenging assignment for you right now."

"Oh?" Zenia leaned forward on her toes, not bothering to hide her eagerness. It had been weeks, if not months, since she'd had a truly demanding assignment. The capital city of Korvann had been unusually restful since news of the king's death and the end of the war had arrived, as if its one million residents believed a period of prosperity would return now that resources would no longer be funneled across the sea to the north.

"I find it encouraging that you appear more excited about an assignment than a promotion," Sazshen said, smiling slightly.

"You know I enjoy the challenge of my job, Archmage."

"Indeed I do. I suspect that would have to be one of the stipulations of the promotion, that you would continue to tackle difficult assignments as an inquisitor."

"Is that a possibility?" Zenia had dreamed often of rising all the way to archmage, not only the highest position in the Water Order Temple, but, because this temple presided over the capital city, one of the highest positions in the entire kingdom. Only the Fire, Earth, and Air Order archmages would be her equals. For a girl of her dubious origins... it was amazing to think that she might rise so far.

"You would be the boss over the whole temple. You would make the rules."

"That sounds encouraging."

Sazshen patted her on the shoulder. "Let's save that talk for the future and discuss this new assignment. You wouldn't mind arresting a zyndar, would you?"

Zenia imagined her eyes flaring with inner fire. Usually the kingdom's nobles were untouchable, above most of the laws of the land—and they knew it—but if a crime was grievous enough, they could be brought in for an inquisition and punishment. And she loved bringing in those arrogant entitled sots. Maybe it made her petty, but she couldn't help it. So many of them did not deserve all that they had.

"I would not mind," Zenia said calmly, hoping her feelings didn't show.

"Good. Good. Because an artifact was stolen from the temple several years ago. Now that the war is over, and the soldiers are returning home, we may be able to get it back. *You* may be able to get it back."

"I'm ready. Who has it?"

"Zyndar Jevlain Dharrow."

CHAPTER 2

ZYNDAR JEVLAIN DHARROW GRIPPED THE railing as the ship turned, knifing through the gleaming waves of the Anchor Sea, and Korvann came into sight. The war hadn't touched these shores, and the capital was as he remembered it, the whitewashed plaster walls, the red-clay tile roofs, and the four pillars to the four founding dragons rising up from the winter, spring, summer, and fall quarters of the city. The brown waters of the Jade River delta still marked Korvann's eastern border, with few attempting to build inland along the waterway, not with the dense mangrove swamps rising along the muddy shores for miles.

Claps, cheers, and shouts came from behind Jev as the ship sailed closer. All he felt like doing was throwing up.

He rubbed his face. The feeling in his stomach wasn't nerves, not exactly. He didn't know what it was, but it wasn't what he'd expected. He'd longed for an end to the war for so long, it had become a habit, but he wasn't sure what he was coming home to. His crusty old father? The woman who hadn't waited?

Someone walked up from behind and thumped Jev on the shoulder. "Is the city as wondrous a sight to you as it is to me, Captain?" the cheerful voice asked.

Jev attempted to arrange his face into an expression of good cheer as Second Lieutenant Targyon joined him at the rail.

"Korvann remains beautiful," Jev said, hoping the young officer wouldn't notice that he didn't quite answer the question.

Targyon, one of fallen King Abdor's nephews, hadn't earned a reputation as a great warrior or dauntless leader during his two years at the front, but his bookishness had lent itself toward craftiness. Despite the affable smile that made him seem simple rather than shrewd, the twenty-two-year-old man didn't miss much.

"I was beginning to wonder if I'd ever again see a settlement that wasn't full of death and booby traps. And I was only out there for two years. I can only imagine what this moment must be like to you after ten. That's almost half my lifetime." Targyon shook his head.

"Yes." Jev lowered his voice when he added, more to himself than to his young officer, "Long enough to grow jaded to death and fear and pain and to almost forget one's identity. But not quite long enough to forget... other things."

Targyon's brow furrowed.

Jev forced a smile onto his face. "I'm looking forward to getting smashing drunk and sleeping it off on the beach under one of those thatch umbrellas," he offered, both because that was what so many of the men had expressed longing for and because it *did* sound appealing right now.

"That's how you'll celebrate? You won't go home to see your father? Your mother has passed, hasn't she? You never mentioned if there was anyone else."

Jev locked that smile onto his face, though it wanted to drop off onto the deck of the ship.

Naysha, her name floated into his mind. He'd thought he had gotten over her, come to accept that she had moved on. It had been years now. But seeing the city he'd visited so often in his youth and knowing he would soon ride past the farms and vineyards of his family's estate brought all the memories back. Too many memories.

"No," Jev said. "There's no one else."

Oh, he had cousins, aunts, and uncles aplenty, but they weren't the ones occupying his thoughts.

Since Targyon looked like he might pry, Jev hurried to add, "What will you do, Lieutenant?"

"Go back to school and finish my classes. Become a professor of the sciences, as I'd always planned. This..." Targyon extended a hand backward, encompassing the hundred-odd men out on the deck, the soldiers who had survived countless battles, fighting for a king who'd never been able to see that the war was unwinnable. "This was a startling dose of reality and something I'll always remember, but I wasn't a soldier two years ago when I joined you in Taziira, and in my heart, I know I'm still not. I do appreciate you letting me tag along, letting me get myself into trouble even."

Targyon offered a lopsided grin, silently alluding to how few zyndar captains had wanted the king's scholarly nephew in their company. But he'd fit in well with the intelligence-gathering Gryphon Company, and Jev had never minded having him along. He hadn't been a burden.

"You're a soldier," Jev said. "Don't let anyone tell you differently. You became a soldier the day you stopped hiding under the table in the mess hall and started helping me ferret out the activities of the Taziir."

"Thought I saw the boy under the table last week," came a deep male voice from behind them, the timbre reminiscent of rocks grinding together.

"Only because I dropped my fig," Targyon said, turning toward Cutter, the only dwarf who'd fought with the kingdom army during the war.

Red-haired, red-bearded, and barefoot, Cutter wore a belt full of weapons and tools that would have brought most men to their knees with its weight. After almost five years, Jev still didn't know his real name. Cutter assured him it was too difficult for humans to pronounce, even though Jev spoke six languages in addition to a smattering of Preskabroton Dwarf.

"That wasn't a prize I was willing to let go easily," Targyon added. "Considering nothing but berries grow on the elves' benighted continent."

"So long as there was a reason your dusty butt was top-up like a dirt flower sprouting from a rock."

"A dirt flower? Is that an actual plant?" Targyon arched his eyebrows at Jev.

"Maybe," Jev said, "but dwarves have about fifty words for dirt. It's possible there wasn't a more apt translation."

"I hope you're not mocking my language, human." Cutter pointed the hook that replaced his missing right hand up at Jev's face. "I'd hate to have to break your nose when you've somehow managed to survive all these years of battles without a blow to crook it."

Cutter's own nose looked like a sculptor's drunken apprentice had battered at it for years with a hammer.

"You'd better treat my nose well," Jev said, "if you want that introduction to the city's master gem cutter."

"Arkura Grindmor," Cutter said, his tone managing to take on a wistful quality without losing any of its harshness. He faced the railing and the city. Their vessel had sailed close enough that the masts and smokestacks of docked ships blocked the view of the waterfront, but meandering streets climbed up the slope from the harbor with buildings visible as they stretched up and over the ridge. "Can we see the master today? Do you know where the workshop is located?"

"I do know where his shop is, assuming it hasn't moved in the last ten years." Jev looked to Targyon since he'd been in the city far more recently.

"I don't think *she's* moved in ten years," he said dryly.

"There's plenty of moving involved in bringing out the magic in a gem," Cutter said. "I'm sure she's as sound as a boulder."

"That's a compliment, right?" Targyon asked.

Jev nodded. "For a dwarf, yes. He's practically swooning. One wonders if his interest in our city's master gem cutter isn't more personal than professional. I hadn't realized Master Grindmor is a, er, woman." Considering he'd seen the dwarf a few times and even gone to the shop once, it was somewhat alarming that he hadn't known that.

"She does have that appealing beard." Targyon scraped his fingers through his own beard. It was on the clumpy and scraggly side, but Jev's wasn't much better. None of them had bathed, shaved, or had haircuts in he couldn't remember how long.

"Indeed," Jev said. "It's fuller and fluffier than the tail of a wolfhound."

Cutter squinted up at Jev's face, perhaps entertaining nose-breaking fantasies again. "I've never met her," was all he said. "But I've waited a long time to beg her to take me on and teach me."

Cutter touched one of the many leather pouches and kits attached to his belt, one that held his jewelry tools. He had often put those tools to use while assisting the army, repairing and improving the dragon-tear gems that some of the officers wielded. They were the only source of magical power in the world that humans could draw upon and use, and they'd been imperative in surviving against the magical Taziir. Jev didn't know what more the dwarf hoped to learn about carving, but he owed it to Cutter to help him gain an apprenticeship if he wanted one.

"King Alderoth?" a man asked as he approached Targyon. It was Lieutenant Morfan, one of the signal officers.

"What?" Targyon's brow furrowed at the incorrect address.

Jev wondered if they had both misheard it. The earnest Lieutenant Morfan wasn't known for telling jokes. Or laughing at the ones others told.

"Sire." Morfan dropped to one knee and bowed his head. "You may have noticed the flag message we received a short while ago."

Jev and Targyon glanced toward the high stone walls that stretched into the Anchor Sea, creating a protected harbor for the docks and swimming beaches. A semaphore soldier had been atop it earlier, waving his colored flags toward the *Fleet Stallion*. Since Jev was colorblind, he'd never tried to add the semaphore code to his repertoire of languages, but he did remember thinking the flags had been waving about more quickly than usual. More urgently?

"Uhm, yes, but whatever you think you saw must have been a mistake if…" Targyon spread a helpless hand and glanced to Jev, as if *he* had some idea what was going on.

He did not. As his father's eldest—and now only—son, Jev knew how the government and the succession worked, but he couldn't think of anything that would account for this. King Abdor was dead, but according to the last reports Jev's company had received, his three sons were alive with Crown Prince Dazron running the kingdom.

"It's not a mistake, Sire. I checked three times to be certain. I, too, was… surprised." The lieutenant lifted his head but only enough to glance up at Targyon. "The three princes died of a rare disease of the blood, all within weeks of each other and all quite suddenly. This left the kingdom without a named heir. The four archmages of the Orders came together and debated the merits of the children of the king's sisters."

Jev scratched his bearded jaw and watched Targyon's face as the story unfolded. His mouth hung open. No, it was frozen open. The expression stamped there held both horror and disbelief.

Horror for the deaths of the princes, Jev guessed. He didn't know how close Targyon was with his cousins, but unlike their warmongering father, they had been well-liked among the populace. And disbelief because—

"I'm the youngest," Targyon managed to blurt. "Of six boys. My mother is the oldest of my uncle's sisters, yes, but Himon, Dralyn, and—four hells, *all* of them would be before me."

"I don't claim to understand, Sire." The lieutenant was careful to use the royal honorific. Whether this proved to be a mistake or not, he wouldn't risk failing to respect the possibility. "I just know what I read in the flags. The ship's captain would like you to join him. We'll be docking shortly, and he's arranging a suitable bodyguard for you. Representatives of the Orders, including Archmage Petor, should be waiting to explain everything to you."

"Bodyguard," Targyon mouthed, then looked to Jev again.

"Sorry, Lieutenant," Jev said, figuring Targyon would appreciate a familiar title right now. "I don't know what to tell you, but I do know the oldest-is-considered-first rule is only for the king's direct descendants. In this situation, the precedent is for the archmages to decide among themselves which of the potential heirs that put themselves forward would be best for the kingdom."

"Put themselves forward?" Targyon brightened at this potential loophole. "I didn't do that. That makes this a mistake. Or maybe they assumed since I volunteered to serve in the army that I would—no, this must be a mistake. And I can get out of it, right?"

"You'll have to discuss it with the archmages," Jev said neutrally. He couldn't imagine young Targyon saying no or even arguing with those intimidating figures. Few did. On paper, the Orders and the kingdom government had equal power over the land, but the archmages tended to get what they wanted, especially in those rare incidents when all four Orders worked together toward a common goal.

"I will." Targyon nodded firmly and turned, almost tripping over the lieutenant who still knelt, his head bowed. "Where's the ship's captain, Morfan?"

"Permission to rise, Sire?"

"Uh, yeah."

Morfan stood. "I'll take you to him."

Jev felt numb as he watched them go, having a hard time envisioning Targyon as king. Even if he only dove under tables these days for figs.

How had this happened? A disease of the blood? That struck down all three princes in the prime of their lives? By the founders, that was as unlikely as a dragon cave without treasure in it. Jev hoped the Orders' inquisitors were crawling all over the castle looking for signs of foul play. He imagined every newspaper in the city speculating that the Taziir were behind it.

But why would they be? The elves had won the war. Their archers had found the cracks in Abdor's armor and taken him down, leaving no one else who cared to continue the assault. The kingdom was no further threat to Taziira.

"That boy is going to be a king?" Cutter asked. He'd been silent during the exchange, but he scratched his head vigorously with his hook now. If the metal appendage bit into his scalp, he didn't notice it. "He's barely out of diapers."

Jev didn't voice an objection to the observation since he was more than ten years older than Targyon and also had a tendency to think of him as a boy. What had the Orders been thinking?

A green-clad figure with pointed ears and silver hair walked toward Jev and Cutter, his pack slung over one shoulder and his longbow visible over the other. His elegant facial features were impossible to read as he glanced past them and toward the ships. The *Fleet Stallion* was only seconds from sliding into one of several vacant slips along the main dock—other troop transport ships trailed behind, waiting their turns.

The sailors scurrying about preparing the *Stallion* glanced uneasily at the elf.

"You decide to take me up on my offer, Lornysh?" Jev asked.

Lornysh arched a slender silver eyebrow, first at Jev, then at Cutter. "To share a guest room with a snoring dwarf?"

"My family has a *castle*. There's more than one guest room."

"Are there trees?" Lornysh's ice-blue eyes shifted, his gaze sweeping across the city.

Here and there, squat olive trees rose between buildings, and one could glimpse the dark mangroves stretching up the Jade River, but to an elf accustomed to the dense northern forests across the sea, Jev supposed the foliage seemed sparse.

"There are some trees. My father's land is fifteen miles that way." Jev pointed up the river and past the ridge. "Outside of the city. We have fields for the cows and sheep, but there are copses here and there near the water. We have a lovely bog where we grow lots of gort leaves."

"Hm." The single note held disapproval, for the paucity of trees rather than for the gort bog, Jev assumed. One didn't typically disapprove of gort until one had tasted it. Multiple times. Which didn't take long in Korvann where it was served with almost every meal. "Your people are such... assiduous loggers."

The pause did nothing to hide Lornysh's distaste of all things related to humans and their proclivities. That he'd worked so many years as a scout in Gryphon Company, and occasionally even an assassin, was a marvel. He'd never shared his reason for turning on his people, but a few omissions here and there led Jev to believe Lornysh had been cast out for some reason.

"We like to clear them so we can farm and eat, but I can find you some trees on our land," Jev said. "I would be happy to string you up a hammock outside the castle."

It would actually be easier for Jev to fulfill his promise of sanctuary to Lornysh if he opted to sleep outside. Perhaps his father need never know an elf was on his land. Not that Jev would lie if the subject came up. His honor wouldn't permit that.

"You going to live here among the humans, Lorn?" Cutter asked.

"For a few weeks. I wish to see some of their culture and art. I haven't decided yet what I'll do after that."

Jev hadn't either, and this was his home. Was that odd?

He was sure his father would be quick to put him to work again on the estate, which had to have been neglected since the king had required that Jev recruit eighty of their men to form up a company to join the army with him. So many women had been without their husbands for so long. And some of their husbands would never return.

Jev felt he owed something to the estate for that, especially since he hadn't been able to keep an eye on his men once he'd been transferred to Gryphon Company, but a job overseeing Dharrow farms, dairy, and craftsmen seemed far too tame to hold his interest after the action of war. All the other men spoke of plans, of all the delightful things they would enjoy now that they were free. And Jev had no idea beyond introducing a dwarf to a bearded woman and finding a hammock for Lornysh.

A blue robe on the docks caught his eye. A woman from the Water Order stood at the base of the recently extended gangplank, a space of several feet around her clear of people, even though soldiers, sailors, and vendors hawking their wares crowded the area. Only one person stood near the robed figure, another woman, this one in a blue monk's gi. She was as stout as a dwarf, one of their temple's enforcers, no doubt.

Jev saw the browns, reds, and whites of the other Orders farther up the dock and assumed the temple representatives were here to talk to

Targyon. Poor kid. Jev wasn't sure what was worse. Getting stuck with the job of king or having to deal with the Orders.

"I've heard you have to join some kind of criminal guild if you want to be an assassin in a human city," Cutter said.

"I will join nothing," Lornysh said.

"So, you're going to be as social here as you were in the company."

"There is nothing I wish to say to humans. Or dwarves."

"Or elves either, apparently," Cutter said, "seeing as how you're fine with poking them with arrows these days. Is it hard making friends when you'll stick pointy metal in anyone you meet?"

Lornysh looked at Jev, as if Jev were Cutter's handler and could silence him with a jerk of a leash.

"How far is the hammock tree from his room?" Lornysh asked.

"Nearly a mile," Jev said, waving toward the gangplank. Targyon and six soldiers pressed into bodyguard duty had already descended, and other men were crowding it, eager to escape into the city. "The grounds around the castle were cleared centuries ago, back when squabbles between the zyndar were as common within the kingdom's borders as battles with surrounding nations."

"A mile *should* suffice," Lornysh said.

"You're sure? Cutter snores loudly."

"Are the walls of your castle so thin?"

"The snore of a dwarf is a battering ram even thick walls cannot withstand," Jev said.

"True."

Jev walked down the gangplank ahead of his companions, hoping people would notice him first and not make trouble for Lornysh. Not even a half elf would be welcome in the capital these days. A full-blooded one? Jev wanted to get him past the city walls as quickly as possible.

As he walked, he made sure the gold wolf-head clasp securing his gray cloak to his shoulders was visible. The Dharrow family emblem marked him as zyndar, a noble from one of the oldest and most recognizable lines. Commoners here in Korvann, so close to where his family held their land, had always nodded or greeted him with respect.

The blue-robed woman from the Water Order still waited at the bottom of the gangplank. That surprised Jev since Targyon and his escort were moving away from the docks, the colored robes of Order representatives all around him, including someone else in a blue robe.

This woman had dark brown hair pulled back in a braid and an olive-skinned face one might have called beautiful if it had appeared less haughty and aloof. She pinned Jev with a cool green-eyed gaze and stepped forward as he reached the end of the gangplank.

He gave her a nod, recognizing the large silver clasp at her shoulder, the emblem of an inquisitor. He should have guessed from the monk standing at her side. He wondered who on the ship she had been sent to question. A sailor? All the soldiers had been gone for years, so they couldn't be associated with any recent trouble in the city.

A chain around the woman's neck suggested a dragon tear hung beneath her robe. For her, the gem's power would likely manifest as the ability to read minds and tell truths from lies.

After his polite nod, Jev started to move past her, hoping her gaze wouldn't fix on Lornysh. It was very possible one of the Orders' law enforcers would opt to pick him up instead of letting him roam free in the city.

As Jev rehearsed the defense he would utter if the woman stopped Lornysh, she reached out a hand to stop *him*.

"Zyndar Jevlain Dharrow?" she asked, her voice as cool as her eyes.

"Yes?"

"You're under arrest."

CHAPTER 3

ZENIA WATCHED THE OFFICER INTENTLY, not sure whether he would run or come calmly with her. While he gaped at her, stunned at her announcement, she glanced again at the wolf-head emblem on his cloak. She almost believed she had made a mistake, even though she had already checked the emblem twice.

Was this hairy, scruffy man truly a zyndar? One of the kingdom's privileged landowners? And one from a very old, very powerful, and very rich family? He looked like a common soldier rather than some noble officer.

Dirt darkened his hands, a scar marked his cheek, and his black hair and beard were in need of cutting. Badly. He carried a short sword on one hip and a pistol on the other, the weapons far better cleaned and polished than he. Broad-shouldered and a head taller than she, he wore a faded gray and blue uniform under a chainmail tunic, his rolled-up jacket sleeves the only concession to the warm spring sun. The ropy muscles of his forearms promised strength, so Zenia hoped Rhi was ready for a fight.

Approaching him here with hundreds of his allies nearby had been chancy. Zenia had considered following him for a time and arresting him as he was on his way out of the city, but she was gambling that few men, even hardened soldiers, would get in the way of an inquisitor making an arrest. She also believed they would be so eager to step on home soil again that they would rush away without paying attention to what went on here.

And exactly that was happening. Though the man—Jevlain Dharrow—stood in front of the base of the gangplank, others simply hopped off behind him and jogged for the waterfront, shouts of beer and women and home rising above the voices of vendors hoping to hawk their wares to men who hadn't had a way to spend their pay for a long time.

"What did you say?" Dharrow finally managed to ask Zenia.

He didn't add mage, ma'am, or inquisitor, or any of the half dozen titles or honorifics that would have been appropriate—and expected. Of course not. He was zyndar. Zyndar considered themselves above everyone else, usually even other zyndar.

"You're under arrest." Zenia kept her chin up, staring into his eyes. "I have orders to bring you in for questioning at the Temple of the Blue Dragon."

Actually, she had orders to acquire a carved ivory artifact he'd stolen years ago, one that was magical and extremely valuable, the archmage had said. But Zenia could, through the power of her dragon tear, sense nearby magical items, and she could tell he didn't have such an item on him. That wasn't that surprising, and she was more pleased than disappointed. If he had hidden it somewhere, she would have to figure out its location, and the idea of pitting her wits against his appealed to her.

"As lovely as being tortured and interrogated by mages sounds," Dharrow said, "I'd rather pass. You have the wrong person. I haven't set foot on kingdom land in ten years. I can't possibly know anything useful to you unless the Water Order cares about the numbers and locations of elf encampments in Taziira."

"Do you deny being Zyndar Jevlain Dharrow?" Zenia bristled at his suggestion that she would lead some torture-based interrogation. No doubt, he imagined fingernails being pulled off and brands being applied to his chest. As if, with her magic, she needed to be so crude to acquire answers.

"No."

"Then you're the right person." She drew upon the power of the gem resting on her chest, channeling it into a compulsion command. "Come."

His eyes widened, and she sensed that he felt her using magic on him. Few people did, but if he'd encountered elves often, he might be accustomed to the touch of magic. Recognizing it, however, did not keep him from taking a step forward.

A hand gripped his shoulder, and he stopped.

"What's going on?" A tall man stepped off the gangplank behind Dharrow and stood at his side.

No, Zenia realized, her heart jumping. Not a man. An *elf.*

By the founders, he looked like a full-blood too. What was he doing *here*? In a human city? And why weren't police running over to apprehend him? For that matter, why weren't all the soldiers on and around the ship shooting at him? The ones not busy racing off to find bars and brothels.

Admittedly, that wasn't many of them.

"It seems I'm being arrested," Dharrow said. "For reasons that my arrestor doesn't feel compelled to explain."

"You're being arrested?" a second person asked, stepping up to his other side. This one was a dwarf with flaming red hair and a matching beard. His head didn't quite come up to Dharrow's shoulder. The stout being's appearance surprised Zenia almost as much as that of the elf. With the exception of the master gem crafters that were enticed to work in the major human cities, dwarves were scarce in the kingdom. "You're the one who offered to protect *us* from such fates, Jev."

"As I recall, I only offered you a bunk," Dharrow said.

"I assumed it was at your home, not in a jail. There was talk of castles. And trees." The dwarf glanced at the elf, but the elf's face might have been chiseled in stone. It was cold and impossible to read.

"That offer is still open," Dharrow said. "Whatever this is shouldn't take long. Though it would be nice if our good inquisitor told me *why* she wants to detain me." He met Zenia's eyes, his gaze fearless, the opposite of the eyes of the thief from that morning.

For a moment, Zenia thought he might not realize what she was, but he'd identified her as an inquisitor. He just wasn't afraid of her. Because he believed being a zyndar would protect him?

"Theft," Zenia said.

She hadn't intended to state his crime, figuring he would be more likely to come along if he believed he was only to be questioned on some tangential matter, but she wouldn't lie if asked for the truth. Nor would she be evasive. He had a right to know why he was being arrested.

"*Theft?*" Anger flashed in his brown eyes. And indignation. "Zyndar do not steal."

She didn't let his outburst bother her. She'd expected it. The Zyndar Code of Honor. They all liked to claim they followed it, but from what she'd observed—and experienced firsthand—it was something that appeared more often in children's tales than in real life.

"Theft," Zenia said firmly.

He loosened his jaw and reined in his anger. Sort of. His tone was sarcastic when he said, "Theft from ten years ago?"

"The Order has waited a long time to get its property back."

"What property? And why do you presume that I have it?" He stuck his hands in his trouser pockets and drew out the linings, showing he carried only a few coins and a lot of dirt in there. Not a bad acting job.

Without a deep probe, Zenia couldn't fully read his mind, but she felt his self-assurance and his belief that he could handle the situation. Handle *her*.

"A magical carved ivory artifact in the shape of an eye," Zenia said. "It's called the Eye of Truth, and it's of great value."

His forehead furrowed. More acting.

"Come with me," Zenia said, adding the compulsion again. "There is a picture of it in the temple. I will show it to you to jog your faulty memory."

Zenia didn't know why someone from a wealthy family would bother stealing, but such a powerful artifact could have worth that went beyond coin. There were rumors that some of the Dharrows of old had been sympathetic to the elves, lending them sanctuary when they passed through the area. If Jevlain shared that sympathy—and the elf warden standing at his side suggested the possibility—then it was possible he'd acquired the artifact because it could give the enemy some advantage. Perhaps he'd even given it to their people. He could have worked as a spy his entire time in the army.

A tingle of excitement went through Zenia as she imagined that possibility, imagined being the one to uncover ten years of heinous crimes this zyndar had perpetrated, the betrayals he might have been responsible for as he pretended to fight alongside kingdom soldiers. Didn't his odd choice of companions hint of mixed alliances?

But, no, she shouldn't make assumptions, even guesses, until evidence presented itself. It was dangerous to grow overfond of one's suspicions lest the truth be overlooked or mistaken for something else.

"Come," Zenia repeated, turning toward the head of the dock and expecting the power in the word to compel him to follow.

Once again, he started after her, but once again, his silver-haired friend gripped his shoulder.

"Stop," the elf said, and Zenia felt magic in *his* word.

Did he have a dragon tear? Maybe not, since elves had innate magic of their own, but if he did possess one, that could make him a powerful and dangerous enemy. Zenia would report his presence in the city when she returned to the temple.

She was half tempted to arrest him now. Rhi was watching all this with narrowed eyes, her bo held horizontally in front of her, her stance promising she was ready to fight.

"All right, stop it." Dharrow lifted his hands and stepped away from Zenia and also from the elf. "Nobody's playing magical tug-of-war with me." That anger and indignation sparked in his eyes again. He clenched his jaw, his hand twitching toward the pistol hanging from his belt.

He'd gotten used to solving his problems with violence, had he? Well, that wouldn't work for him here.

"She is attempting to manipulate you," the elf said coolly, doing more than twitching his hand toward his weapons. He gripped the leather-wrapped hilt of a sheathed sword.

"We can put a stop to that." The dwarf grinned, white teeth flashing from deep within that bush of a beard, and slapped the side of a hook against his open palm. It took Zenia a second to realize the hook was attached to the stump of an arm rather than being an independent weapon.

Rhi stepped up to Zenia's side, her bo between them and the men. Zenia wasn't weaponless, but she did not yet reach for the pistol holstered at her hip inside her robe. She met Dharrow's eyes. Zyndar or not, he would not likely attack an inquisitor. His odd comrades, unschooled in the ways of human cities, might, so she had to be ready. The elf, in particular, had a gaze like lake ice, and she could almost feel power radiating from him. Mage, her instincts cried, even if he wore the simple green garb of a warden.

"No." Dharrow spread his arms to create a barrier between his allies and Zenia. "I can offer you sanctuary on my family's land," he told them, "but if you commit a crime, even if it's on my behalf, I might not be able to protect you from the Orders."

Might not? Zenia almost snorted at the notion that he could, just because he was zyndar, have people acquitted of crimes. The days when the nobility had that kind of influence were over. The laws applied to everyone. Or they should. When she made it to the position of archmage, she would fight to ensure that idea of equality was turned into a fact.

Zenia kept her disdain off her face. It looked like he was going to cooperate, so it would be better not to goad him or his unstable companions into action. Even if a part of her wouldn't mind seeing Rhi punch that elf in the nose, she wouldn't wish for it. He was dangerous. She could tell. As well-trained as Rhi was, it was possible she wouldn't be a match for him. Further, Zenia would be foolish to believe she could best a veteran with ten years of combat experience. Her job was to beat criminals with her mind, not with her fists.

"If you'll come without magical coercion, I won't use my gem on you." Feeling magnanimous, Zenia extended her hand toward the head of the dock. "I'm ready to escort you now."

"The cook said those born in the season of air would be lucky today," Dharrow said. "Who knew he was so wise?"

Zenia ignored the words. Dharrow walked in the right direction as he groused. That was all that mattered.

"Stay out of trouble," he added over his shoulder to the dwarf and elf. "I'll catch up with you as soon as I can."

They didn't reply. They exchanged looks with each other.

Zenia couldn't read the elf, neither magically nor with mundane reasoning, but the dwarf wore a surly expression. He didn't like what was going on, and he might do something about it.

"Trail behind," Zenia murmured to Rhi. "Watch those two."

"Why don't you tell me how to do a push-up while you're at it," Rhi said, already walking a half step back, her alert eyes alternately watching the way ahead *and* behind.

"Doesn't the Old Codex of the Monk warn its pupils not to be sarcastic to mages of the Orders?" Zenia asked.

"Nah, sarcasm isn't covered until the New Codex."

"I'm sure respect has been considered virtuous and proper since the founding of the temples."

"True, but you can be respectfully sarcastic. It's even encouraged. Otherwise, mages get uppity." Rhi slapped Zenia on the back, then fell silent, concentrating on her duty.

Zenia caught Dharrow looking at them, his eyebrows arched, and felt embarrassed for some reason, as if it wasn't professional to have someone witness them bantering. Maybe it wasn't, but she didn't like the feeling that he was judging her for it. Or dismissing her. She stared straight ahead, only watching him out of the corner of her eye to make sure he stuck to the correct path.

Soon, they would be back at the temple. She would enjoy questioning him and finding clues in what would doubtless be evasive answers. Before long, perhaps before the day's end, she would find the artifact and return it to the temple. Then nobody would question her worthiness of the position of archmage.

CHAPTER 4

J EV DIDN'T HAVE A GEM or any magic of his own to call upon, but he didn't need it to know Cutter and Lornysh were following them.

Oh, he didn't catch so much as a glimpse of them as the inquisitor and her monk assistant led him along the waterfront, around a corner, and onto one of the boulevards that headed toward the ridge where the Temple of the Blue Dragon stood. But he knew his comrades as well as the men in his company. They wouldn't amble into a bar for a beer while he was in trouble.

Jev did not yet know if he *was* in trouble—since he hadn't stolen anything, he shouldn't be—but they didn't know that.

He stole a few glances at his escort. Even though he planned to accompany them peaceably, he couldn't help but size them up as potential enemies. He had gotten in the habit of assessing the threat level of everyone he encountered, and he couldn't dismiss these two because they were women. The sea-blue gi that the monk wore meant she had completed at least six years of intense training and was a full-fledged member of the Order's elite fighting unit. And the inquisitor—neither she nor the monk had offered their names—would carry a weapon or two under that robe. A firearm, most likely. Inquisitors didn't typically receive a great deal of combat training, but the ones he'd known had always gone to the ranges to practice shooting.

"What's your name, Inquisitor?" Jev asked, alternating between watching the street and pedestrian traffic and her. The streets were largely as he'd remembered, especially in this older part of the city, but he spotted steam wagons and carriages with frames and engines that hadn't existed the last time he'd walked the city. They were almost as numerous as the horse-drawn conveyances clattering along the cobblestones. "You know mine, and if we're to spend time together with you pulling off my fingernails, it would be nice to know yours."

She gave him a flat, unfriendly look. It seemed to be her typical facial expression. Normally, he would have considered her attractive—of course, it had been so long since he'd experienced feminine company that he was starting to consider boulders attractive—but her frosty eyes would have kept him at arm's length even if she hadn't been arresting him.

"Zenia Cham," she said, her chin lifting. It did that a lot.

She watched him. Expectantly? She seemed to be waiting for a reaction. It wasn't a noble name—he knew all the zyndar surnames in the kingdom—and he didn't recognize it. But it wasn't as if he'd seen an issue of the *Korvann Chronicle* recently.

"And your sarcastic friend?" Jev waved toward the monk, who kept glancing behind them, watching the rooftops as well as the streets.

"Her name is hers to share if she wishes," Zenia said.

"I don't suppose you'd like to tell me more about this artifact I supposedly stole when I was... I guess I was twenty-three the last time I was here."

It seemed an eternity ago. Back when his father had ordered him to go off and fight for the king, as it was the family's duty to supply a son for the war effort, Jev hadn't guessed he would be gone for more than a year or two. So much of his life lost for something he'd never believed in. The cost for the kingdom had been ridiculous. And the cost for him? He'd lost countless friends over the years, but, as much as he hated to admit it, it was Naysha's loss that still stung most.

She had been attractive without being frosty. And far superior to a boulder.

"Archmage Sazshen will tell you more. I've only been ordered to retrieve it. Your fingernails need not be in danger if you'll tell me its location."

"Uh huh."

Jev had been captured and tortured four years earlier, after being appointed the leader of Gryphon Company. It had been by a human scout from another kingdom, one happy to fawn at those elves' feet. The man had enjoyed cutting on him, on his own kind. Whatever it took to please his pointy-eared employer. A cold snake of an elf who'd watched the whole thing with his face utterly impassive. Jev had been lucky to escape and survive the ordeal. Even though the elf had healed him at the end of each session, so he would last longer, Jev still had a lot of scars. Sometimes, he wondered if Naysha would even recognize him, should their paths cross again one day.

"Would you do it yourself?" he asked.

"What?"

"My fingernail removal." Jev wouldn't normally think a woman would have a stomach for torturing a man—physically, anyway, as they seemed to prefer emotional torment if they had a vindictive streak—but this Zenia had those frosty edges. She might like it. He definitely sensed that she was one of those people who held some bitterness toward the nobility, though she'd risen to a respected rank in society, so he didn't know why.

"I have no need to employ such crude methods." Zenia sounded offended. "You will answer my questions and tell me what you know."

He grimaced, remembering the magical compulsion she'd laid on him earlier. Even now, she might be using a tendril of power on him to keep him toddling along like an obedient retriever.

"Well, that won't take long. I don't know much."

"Clearly, the rumors that zyndar children receive an excellent education from private tutors are false."

"Clearly." Jev decided it wasn't worth getting upset over insults. After all he'd endured, they were a petty annoyance at most. Maybe if he didn't respond in kind, she would thaw a few degrees. He had never been questioned by an inquisitor and didn't know how much of their interrogation magic was rumor and how much was truth, but he hated having any of the dark arts plied on him. "We mostly just got lessons on how to be appropriately haughty in the presence of commoners."

She gave him another frosty look. So much for a thaw.

They turned down a narrow street framed by millennia-old whitewashed stone buildings.

"Look out," the monk barked.

She lunged forward, grabbed Zenia's arm, and pulled her to one side of the street. But not quickly enough. Few humans could match the speed of a full-blooded elf.

"No," Jev barked, trying to step forward and stop Lornysh before he hurt either of the women—where had he *come* from? A rooftop?—but the end of a bo slammed into his chest before he reached the fight.

The monk.

Jev stumbled back. His chainmail blunted the attack, but he would still have a bruise tomorrow. The monk reared back to thrust the weapon again—trying to drive him away from Zenia so she could jump in to help against Lornysh.

Jev whipped his forearm across in time to block the second blow. His instincts cried out for him to follow the block with an attack, to leap in before she could bring the bo to bear again, but he made himself lift his arms, a gesture of surrender. He didn't want to fight an inquisitor of one of the Orders, damn it. Even his title wouldn't protect him from retribution if he hurt one of them.

A sickening crunch sounded as the monk whirled from Jev and sprang toward her comrade's side. Once again, she was a hair too late. Lornysh slammed the inquisitor against the wall with strength one expected from dwarves—and steam hammers—instead of slender-armed elves. The woman's head struck stone, and she crumpled to the cobblestones.

"Stop, Lorn," Jev ordered, waving to get his attention. He also issued the order in the elven language, in case it would more likely get through to him.

Neither worked. The monk roared and sprang at Lornysh, and he defended himself with that deadly agility his kind were known for. He hadn't drawn a weapon. He didn't need to. With arms and legs that blurred with the speed of his movements, he knocked the bo out of the hands of the monk, then gripped her arm and slammed her into the wall, the same as he had Zenia. Bone crunched audibly, and she cried out.

When Lornysh drew back a fist to rain more blows down upon them, Jev jumped in and grabbed his arm. Lornysh's gaze jerked toward him, his pale eyes wild instead of their usual icy calm, as if he were living in some other moment, in some past battle.

Lornysh tried to jerk away, and Jev felt his strength, but Jev had strength of his own. He gripped that arm, using his wide stance for leverage, and didn't let go, afraid Lornysh might continue if he did. For a moment, Jev thought Lornysh might turn on *him*—might not see him as a friend in whatever past hell he was reliving—but those eyes slowly calmed, awareness returning to them.

Jev, who rarely dared touch Lornysh outside of sparring practice, released him and stepped back. He looked down at the women, both of them crumpled on the street against the wall, neither moving.

"*Founders*," he whispered with distress and rubbed the back of his neck. What now?

"This might be why your people lost the war," Cutter drawled, walking in from whatever doorway he'd been hiding in farther up the street, waiting to spring the second half of the ambush. Unnecessarily. He waved dismissively at the two women, at how easily they had fallen to Lornysh.

Jev knelt beside the women to make sure they were still breathing. They were, but both were unconscious, and an alarming amount of blood streamed from Zenia's temple.

"By the founders, Lorn," Jev said, "these are officers from the Water Order. Law enforcers, if religious law instead of city law. There's not much of a difference around here. You can't just knock them out. There'll be repercussions."

"Your laws mean nothing to me."

Jev rose to his feet, glowering at the blood on his hand. "While you're walking in our lands, they had better mean something. You can't take on the whole kingdom army or Korvann police force."

"That one intended to imprison you." Lornysh pointed to Zenia.

"To question me about… something. Whatever it is, it's nothing I had anything to do with, so I would have been released."

"That's not what *she* believed," Lornysh said with so much certainty that Jev suspected he had a magical way of knowing. "She believed you were guilty—she'd already made up her mind—and that she could wheedle some artifact's location from you. And that you would spend the rest of your days moldering in their temple dungeon."

Jev wanted to say that what she *believed* didn't matter because it wasn't the truth, but he paused. As an Order inquisitor, she had the power to act as judge over him, to proclaim him guilty. Her mind magic should have allowed her to see the truth in his thoughts, especially if he cooperated, but… hadn't he sensed that she had something against him from the start? Maybe her beliefs wouldn't have allowed her to see the truth.

"Better to be free," Cutter said. "Leave them here, and you can go investigate on your own. Find out what's going on, why you're being blamed."

"Yes," Lornysh said. "Find evidence to show that you are innocent. Or better yet, find their missing artifact, and return it to them if that is wise."

"You wouldn't be able to do that if you were stuck in a dungeon, Jev, and we wouldn't know where to start looking. This is your land. I'd be lucky if I could find my beard with my own hands here."

Jev rubbed the back of his neck again. It bolstered him that his comrades assumed he was innocent without truly having a way to know, but he wasn't sure this was a wise course of action. Still, they were right that he wouldn't be able to figure out what was going on if he ended up incarcerated in the bowels of a temple. He grimaced at the idea of being stuck there until his father heard and came to bail him out. Assuming the mages would even allow that. Would they? His father had power, but the sway of the zyndar wasn't what it once had been. Even in his youth, that had been true. And who knew how much had changed back here in the last ten years?

"Also," Lornysh said, "you should take us somewhere where we can bathe. Especially Cutter."

"You don't smell any better than I do, elf," Cutter said.

"I bathe in the ocean when I get a chance. I'm positive I'm less aromatic than you."

"You just smell like seaweed and fish piss instead of good wholesome dirt."

"Dirt is not what you smell like."

Cutter growled.

Though he was more concerned about the injured women at their feet than anyone's cleanliness, Jev bestirred himself to ask, "Will we find it easier to prove my innocence if we're clean?"

"Undoubtedly," Lornysh said, sounding like he meant it.

"All right," Jev said, "but we're not leaving a monk or inquisitor bleeding in an alley. Help me carry them to the hospital."

He gathered the inquisitor in his arms, leaving the stockier and more muscled monk to Lornysh. He deserved the heavier load. Cutter picked up the monk's fallen bo.

"This isn't how I imagined my first encounter in years with a woman going," Jev said, worried by the blood on the side of Zenia's face.

He thought about taking the women to the hospital run by the Water Order but foresaw all manner of problems if he showed up there when he was a wanted man. Especially with an unconscious inquisitor in his arms.

Jev set a brisk pace toward a kingdom-run hospital he knew of that was only a half mile away.

"Years?" Cutter asked, walking beside him, keeping up even with his shorter legs. "There were camp followers. And those human gypsy women who risk elven ire by strolling around and exploring their continent."

"Zyndar officers aren't supposed to sleep with camp followers and random gypsies."

"Oh? Did anyone tell Captain Thash that? Or Lieutenant Herringbone? Or Captain—"

"*They* weren't heading Gryphon Company and in charge of gathering intelligence." Jev glanced back to make sure Lornysh was following with the monk. He was. Good. "They wouldn't have spewed crucial information to the enemy if they'd been drugged by some spy masquerading as a camp follower."

"In other words, you're horny and would already be looking for a woman if we hadn't been detained."

Jev felt his expression growing wistful, though not for the reasons Cutter suggested. The only woman he'd thought he would sleep with for the rest of his life had married someone else.

The narrow street opened up into a wide boulevard, and the hospital came into sight, and Jev's shoulders loosened in relief. He just hoped the Water Order hadn't also told the city watch that he was to be arrested.

"Elf!"

Jev tensed anew at the cry from across the street. He had expected it, but he'd vainly hoped they might drop off the women and escape the city before someone noticed Lornysh. Unfortunately, the bright afternoon sun didn't leave many shadows for Lornysh—or his ears—to hide in.

More cries arose as men and women pointed fingers in their direction. Jev glanced at Lornysh, but as usual, his face gave away little. He strode at Jev's side toward the hospital.

"Get the watch!" someone cried. "Hurry!"

"Doesn't look like they're inclined to like you, Lorn," Cutter remarked.

"Dwarf!" someone else yelled, the alarmed cry holding the same fervor as the previous ones.

"Huh?" Cutter asked. "They can't object to my people, can they? We cut their gems."

Jev strode along the sidewalk opposite the yelling people, his focus on the hospital. If he could just make it inside…

"Perhaps they agree that you smell worse than dirt," Lornysh said.

A crowd grew on the far sidewalk, people peering at them between the vendors' wagons lining the street. Others trailed behind Jev's little group, pointing and whispering. Weapons weren't typical in the capital, since only zyndar, mages, watchmen, and soldiers were legally allowed to carry them within the city limits, and Jev suspected that was the only reason nobody had come forward to oppose them. His team *was* armed. Well-armed.

A boy of ten or twelve sprinted down an alley, yelling for the watch.

As Jev and Lornysh strode up the steps to the hospital, the doors opened, and a pair of nurses in white robes stepped out. The man and woman peered toward the increasingly loud commotion in the street. Someone grabbed an eggplant from a produce vendor and hurled it toward Lornysh.

"It's supposed to be tomatoes," Jev said as Lornysh ducked, the purple produce sailing over his head.

It thudded against another vendor's wagon. The noise drew out the owner, who immediately started cursing at the crowd. Then he spotted the young man grabbing produce to hurl and turned his curses on him.

"What?" Cutter asked.

"In the children's tales, it's always rotten tomatoes that get thrown. Occasionally, an overly lumpy potato sprouting eyes."

"Charming," Lornysh said.

"We have patients for you," Jev told the nurses, yelling over the crowd. He debated whether identifying himself would help, but he doubted the angry bystanders would quiet down enough for the nurses to hear him.

"Servants of the Water Order go to their own hospital," the male nurse said, though he came forward, frowning when Zenia groaned in Jev's arms. "If they're to be treated here, the director will demand payment up front."

"How much?" Jev pushed past them, not wanting to loiter on the landing when more vegetables were being hurled—despite the protesting vendor who was smacking the hands of anyone who grabbed something from his wagon without paying.

"Someone in a uniform is running this way," Cutter said.

Jev stepped into the cool, dark hallway and tilted his head for the others to follow him. He also looked for somewhere to set down the women, preferably before they woke up and attempted to arrest him again. Could he simply lay them on the marble floor tiles? He didn't see any stretchers.

"Twenty-five krons each for an initial appraisal," the man said, waving toward a lockbox on a stand where such deposits were made. "The final cost will be assessed after treatment. Or it's possible doctors from the Water Order hospital will be brought over to treat them."

"I'll cover it." Jev thought about telling them to send the bill to his father, but he had been receiving pay as an officer in the king's army, and it had been ages since he'd been anywhere he could spend it.

"Good, sir. Uh—" The male nurse's eyes caught on the wolf-head clasp. "Zyndar?"

"Dharrow, yes. Where shall I put her?"

Lornysh was already laying the monk on the floor as Cutter shut the doors behind them and dropped a thick wooden bar into place. A thump sounded a second later, followed by many more thumps. The female nurse stared at the door in concern. The stout olive wood ought to hold back the crowd, but Jev hoped for a back exit.

The man rang a bell. "We'll get stretchers out here, Zyndar. Forgive me for not recognizing you. Many apologies."

"Just take her, please," Jev said, pushing Zenia into his arms so he could retrieve the necessary payment.

"I, yes, Zyndar."

"Is that Zenia Cham?" the woman blurted.

"That's what she introduced herself as." Jev dug out his purse and fished out coins. He dumped what he judged to be enough into the payment box as the female nurse stared at the inquisitor in slack-jawed astonishment.

Jev had a feeling his elven friend had clubbed someone more important than he'd realized. More famous, at the least.

More thumps battered the door, followed by an authoritative shout, the words muffled by the stout wood. Jev was glad, since he guessed the watchman—or men—that Cutter had seen had made it up the stairs by now.

"Did you save her from street hoodlums?" the woman asked.

"Something like that." Jev kept himself from glancing at Lornysh, though Cutter snorted. "I'd rather not deal with the crowd. Mind if we go out the back?"

Jev pointed a thumb down the hallway. The woman was still staring at Zenia. The man seemed unaware that he held the unconscious inquisitor in his arms. His gaze had snagged on Lornysh—or maybe Lornysh's pointed ears.

"We'll see ourselves out," Jev said when neither responded. "Take care of the ladies, eh?"

"Of course, Zyndar," the woman said. "We wouldn't dare fail Inquisitor Cham or the Water Order."

"Good." Jev waved for Lornysh and Cutter to follow, then took off down the hall.

He kept himself from sprinting since zyndar were stately, respectable, and didn't run off with their tails between their legs, but he definitely set a fast pace.

They passed open bays full of beds, some occupied and some not, and corridors that led off to private rooms. The hallway opened into a central courtyard with a fountain where a few patients in nightclothes sat at tables and played dice and tile games. They looked up curiously as the trio strode through, and one accidentally dumped his tiles on the flagstones when he spotted Lornysh. Jev didn't pause to explain.

They ran into the back half of the building, down another hallway, and to a door that led to the street behind the hospital. Jev hoped nothing but a few trash bins waited out there.

Sunlight blasted them as he shoved open the door and strode out. His stomach sank.

Four men in watchmen's gray and white uniforms waited, sun glinting off the barrels of the rifles pointed at the doorway.

Though his instincts screamed for Jev to spring to the side and get out of their sights, he reminded himself that this was his city, not some elven encampment a thousand miles to the north.

"Gentlemen," he said, stepping forward and spreading his arms so they could see he didn't hold a weapon—and so they would focus on him rather than Cutter and Lornysh behind him. "I am Jevlain Dharrow, zyndar and captain in the kingdom army, leader of Gryphon Company, in charge of intelligence-gathering during the war. These are friends who worked with our people in the war." He tilted his head to indicate Lornysh and Cutter as he introduced them. He was careful to keep his arms spread wide to partially block them from the rifles.

"Dharrow?" the sergeant in the lead asked, his rifle tip lowering.

"Dharrow," Jev said firmly, hoping that little had changed in the last ten years and that his family was still held in high regard for its history of serving the king during peace and war times.

The sergeant looked at the cloak clasp. Jev didn't know whether to be amused or not that everyone was skeptical when it came to identifying him. He'd left home young enough that he hadn't truly expected anyone to remember his face, but he hadn't expected doubt. He was unkempt and dirty and in the same uniform as the rest of the soldiers arriving, but people hadn't had much trouble picking him out as zyndar when he'd been younger. Had the city changed that much? Or had he?

"You're related to Heber Dharrow?" the sergeant asked.

"My father."

The rest of the rifles shifted so they weren't pointed at Jev's chest. Shouts came from the direction of the hospital courtyard, and Jev feared that trouble was about to catch up to them from behind.

"It's important that I report in to him now that I'm home from the war," Jev added. Something he would do as soon as he figured out this artifact situation. "May we pass? I will personally vouch for the character of my companions."

"It's not their *character* that'll have the citizens worried, Zyndar," the sergeant said. "This isn't a good time to be a, uhm, foreigner in Korvann."

"A non-human, you mean?"

"A non-human foreigner. We have a wagon, Zyndar. Will you come with us? We'll escort you to your father's land."

Jev didn't want an escort. And he hadn't planned on going home right *now*.

The shouts in the building behind him escalated.

Jev forced a regal smile and nodded. "That would be appreciated," he made himself say.

"Good. This way, Zyndar. And, uh, your friends." The sergeant headed toward a steam wagon parked at the end of the street, the metal and wood sides painted in the colors of the watch. Soft puffs of black smoke wafted from its stack.

Not feeling that he had a choice, Jev trailed the man. The other watchmen waited for Lornysh and Cutter to pass, then strode along on their heels, their weapons still in hand.

Jev told himself this was a good development. Since the wagon was covered, he, Lornysh, and Cutter could make it out of the city without being waylaid again, and he *had* planned to visit his father and his home. Eventually. Unfortunately, with the watch escorting them, Jev wouldn't have a chance to sneak Lornysh out to one of the groves without mentioning him to his father.

Not his largest problem right now, he reminded himself.

"Why couldn't you just do that at the dock?" Cutter asked as they climbed into the covered wagon and sat on one of the wood benches. "Get us a free ride and an escort?"

"I thought you'd want to get some exercise after being cooped up on the ship for the crossing," Jev said.

"Exercise? Is that what you call battling women in robes, being chased by crowds, and having vegetables lobbed at our heads?"

"Fruit," Lornysh said.

"What?"

"Eggplants have seeds and are thus considered fruits."

"So are elves," Cutter said, "but we don't call them that to their faces."

"Wise," Lornysh said.

Two watchmen climbed in to ride in the back with them, and Jev's comrades fell silent. He watched the corner of the hospital building as the wagon rumbled into motion with a hiss of releasing steam. He thought of how the nurse had recognized Zenia, and he was positive he hadn't seen the last of her.

CHAPTER 5

SUN SLANTING THROUGH A WINDOW onto her bed made Zenia open her eyes. She squinted and turned her head, promptly aware of a dull ache from her temple. As her eyes focused on a blue gi in front of her, she grew aware of her surroundings—a hospital bay full of beds with Rhi standing next to hers, one sleeve rolled up to reveal a bandage wrapping her arm.

"What happened?" Zenia croaked.

"An elf beat us up."

Zenia grimaced. Unfortunately, she remembered that part well. The elf's unexpected power and preternatural speed. More than that, he'd had mental defenses that she hadn't been able to get through. Though their fight had been depressingly brief, she'd had time to try a couple of mind attacks. He'd shrugged them off as if they had no more power to disturb him than raindrops.

"*Then* what happened?"

Rhi shrugged but cut the movement short and winced, touching her shoulder.

"I woke up in the bed next to you there." Rhi pointed at wrinkled sheets. "A nurse informed me that Zyndar Dharrow and his unlikely friends brought us here and paid for our treatment. And then a very furry doctor spoke into my mind, and I got distracted."

"Furry?"

"A unicorn."

"Oh." Zenia had heard of the hospital in town where a black-and-gold unicorn from Izstara used his magic to heal patients and teach doctors. That meant they were less than eight blocks from the temple where she had been taking Dharrow. But she had failed, and now he walked free.

She groaned, imagining how disappointed Archmage Sazshen would be when her star inquisitor came home empty-handed.

"It wasn't that bad," Rhi said, mistaking the reason for the groan. "He said I would live and that I can use my shoulder a little bit now but that it will require three days to fully regenerate. I think he treated you too. Your face was a lot bloodier when I first woke up. The nurse sponging away the blood was cute. You should thank him for his efforts by taking him out to dinner."

Zenia groaned again, this time for a different reason. She'd gotten used to her monk colleague trying to set her up with men, but this wasn't the time for it.

"I'm not looking for men, especially when I'm on a mission," Zenia said. "You'll have to thank him for me."

"You know that the Codices of the Monk dictate that I be chaste, unwed, and fully devoted to the Order, heart, soul, and loins."

"I know that you and your loins frequently practice chastity with company."

Rhi smiled. "I'm positive I don't know what you're talking about. If I bring a pretty man to my room to entertain me by reading plays until the wee hours of the morning, there's nothing wrong with that."

"I've heard from your neighbors that the readings get noisy."

"Since they're plays, the various parts have to be acted out."

"Vigorously, no doubt."

Rhi grinned.

Zenia pushed herself gingerly up on one elbow, fearing the pain at her temple would intensify, but the dull ache remained at a constant level, one she could deal with. Good. She had a mission to complete. She had no intention of returning to the temple until she recaptured her man.

"I'm surprised the zyndar paid for our treatment," Rhi said. "Though his pointy-eared demon of a friend was the one responsible for our injuries, so maybe it's fair."

"I'm certain he was hoping to win leniency from the Order." Zenia pushed herself into a sitting position and looked for her robe. Someone had removed it, leaving her in her linen chemise. She grimaced when she spotted it hanging from the bed knob, damp and wrinkled. Had someone attempted to wash out her blood? Apparently, unicorn magic wasn't used for laundering.

"Will it work?"

"Winning our leniency? No."

"Are we going after them again?" Rhi looked to where her bo stood propped against the stone wall. Her words came out neutrally, without any of her typical enthusiasm for a mission.

"Don't want to face the elf again?"

Rhi took a deep breath and let it out. "If that's what we have to do, I'm with you, of course. But I do recommend taking reinforcements. This zyndar didn't seem to realize your fearsome reputation was supposed to cow him into coming along quietly."

"He came along. It was the elf who was problematic."

"Yes, he *definitely* wasn't cowed."

"Don't worry. I'm not foolish enough to try the same tactic more than once. We'll assume they're going to continue to travel together, and we'll requisition some help. The watch will be willing to supply some men to assist an inquisitor."

Rhi raised her eyebrows. "You don't think going to the temple for another mage and three or four more monks would be better? The watch has low standards."

Zenia smiled faintly, well aware of the nonviolent feud the watch and the monks of the four Orders seemed determined to continue for all eternity. She'd long suspected politicians from the kingdom and the Orders fomented that hostility, so one group could be convinced to fight the other if someone tried to claim more than their share of the pie of power.

"I think a squad of watchmen will be sufficient," Zenia said, not wanting to explain her desire to avoid the temple and Archmage Sazshen until she could stride up the stairs with Dharrow in shackles.

"If you say so. Any idea where the zyndar and his friends will run off to hide?"

Zenia stared down at the floor. She could use her gem magic to track criminals she'd met in person if they weren't out of her range, but she always preferred to use her mind. Though she was grateful with all her heart to the Order for awarding her a dragon tear, it was so much more satisfying when she captured men with nothing but her wits.

"Most criminals wouldn't be foolish enough to run back to their families, since the watch would look for them there first, but Jevlain Dharrow has been away for ten years. I think he'll go home. His father is still alive and, I believe, acting as zyndar prime for the estate. Jevlain may think the man has the power to help him out of this situation. I think he'll also be arrogant enough to believe we won't cross onto his family's property to collect him."

Long ago, a zyndar's land had been considered almost a country unto itself with extradition papers signed by the king required to retrieve someone who'd been granted sanctuary there. Those days were gone. The king's justice crossed all borders in the land, and no property was truly private anymore.

"But we will, right?" Rhi asked.

"I've never been one to bow to zyndar arrogance."

"I'm glad to hear it. But just so you know, I'm going to let you go first."

"Why don't we let the watchmen go first?"

"The New Codex says it's cowardly to hide behind lesser warriors."

"But hiding behind inquisitors is acceptable?"

"I believe it's encouraged."

"I really must read these Codices someday. To see how accurate your interpretation is."

"As a noncombatant, you'll surely find them dry and boring."

"You wouldn't be trying to discourage my perusal, would you?"

"Not at all." Rhi smiled benignly and reached for her bo.

"Inquisitor Cham?" a nurse asked, scurrying forward while ducking his head and wringing his hands. "I'm so sorry you were injured. Our director, the unicorn Oligonite, healed you himself. Your skull was cracked and your brain swollen. It must have been terribly uncomfortable, but all the pain should fade away by the end of the day. Our director is the best. Can I get you anything? The fees have already been covered, but even if they hadn't, we would not be comfortable charging you."

"I'm fine," Zenia said as the man continued to wring his hands and avoid her eyes.

Was he nervous because of her job and her reputation? Or because of some crime he had committed?

She knew from experience that even those who hadn't committed crimes sometimes felt guilty around inquisitors, perhaps for some long-past indiscretion that they regretted, or simply because they feared they could be dragged off to a dungeon by mistake.

As if Zenia made mistakes.

She drew upon the power of her dragon tear and funneled the magic toward his skull, gently probing to see why he was worried. Guilty thoughts floated at the surface of his mind. Thoughts of sneaking bandages, poultices, and medicinal substances home from the hospital so that his wife could use them on their six children and also the three nieces that they'd cared for since his sister had passed. He wouldn't have taken the items, but the nurses weren't paid much…

Zenia rubbed her head, withdrawing her mental touch.

"I'm fine," she added again. "You said our healing was already paid for?"

"By Zyndar Dharrow, yes."

"I see. Thank you."

"Please let me know if you need anything," the nurse said, backing away as he spoke. He almost tripped over his feet as he turned to leave the bay.

"It's going to be quite the feat to find a nice man willing to go to dinner with you," Rhi said.

"That's not my priority right now," Zenia said.

"From what I've noticed, it never is. Sometimes, I wonder if I should try to find you a nice woman, but I've never caught you ogling me, so I assume that's not where your interests lie."

"Maybe you're not ogle-worthy."

"I assure you, I'm terribly appealing when I'm out of this gi."

"Uh huh."

Zenia swung her feet to the cool stone floor so she could put on the damp robe and hunt for her shoes. It was time to retrieve a wayward thieving zyndar. Without thinking about the fact that he'd paid for her healing. She was positive he'd sought to win her favor so she would look the other way. That would *not* happen.

As the wagon rolled closer to Dharrow lands, the densely packed houses and commercial dwellings of the city giving way to small farms and horse pastures, Jev alternated between listening to the watchmen talk to each other and contemplating how he'd ended up wanted by the Water Order.

Zenia's absurdly brief description of the missing artifact wasn't that helpful. What had she called it? The Eye of Truth?

He'd never encountered an eye carved out of ivory. He had handled all manner of dragon tears and lesser gems over the years, and his soldiers had occasionally found tools and artifacts, ivory and otherwise, among the elven camps they had managed to overrun, but he'd never pocketed any of them for himself. Per his orders, he had boxed up any loot they recovered and sent it back to the king's castle for Abdor's people to analyze. It had always bothered him to take such loot, even if the items might be used to humankind's advantage, and he never would have considered pocketing interesting pieces. He'd always hoped the loot would be returned when the war ended, perhaps as part of a treaty. He doubted that had happened. In the end, there hadn't even been a treaty. The king had died, and his people had withdrawn. He didn't think anyone had even told the Taziir.

"You think we'll still have jobs after the coronation?" one of the watchmen asked the other.

The two guards sat on benches across from each other, placed so they could ensure Jev, Cutter, and Lornysh didn't jump out the open back of the wagon. As if the men could have stopped Lornysh if he was inclined to leave.

"Why wouldn't we?"

"They say the new king was a soldier and will favor soldiers. Give the men who just came back our jobs."

The watchmen looked over at Jev, eyeing his soldier's uniform. As if he might even now be contemplating his application to the watch. Or captain of the watch, he supposed. One of his distant ancestors had held that job at a time when only zyndar had been considered capable of such a critical position. The captain commanded hundreds of men and had to ensure that the underworld guilds never grew too powerful or became a threat to the average citizen. Jev had no idea whether a zyndar or common man held the spot now.

"What do you know of the new king?" Jev asked, having forgotten about Targyon's predicament while dealing with his own.

"They say he's just a boy."

"I heard he's bookish. Might be he's more likely to give librarians our jobs instead of soldiers."

"As if librarians can be watchmen. You can't use a book to bring in a criminal."

"You can if it's a big book. And you thump him over the head enough times with it."

Jev sighed and lifted his gaze toward the canvas top of the wagon. He doubted these two intellects knew anything worth knowing. Once he had cleared his name, he would go to the Alderoth Castle and check on Targyon in person.

"How much farther to your castle?" Lornysh asked quietly from his side. He had chosen a position as far from the watchmen as possible.

Jev glanced toward the countryside out the back. They were traveling past the Groshon family's estate now.

"About three miles until we reach Dhar-din Village and turn off the highway. It's another mile up a side road to Dharrow Castle. It won't take long in this." Jev waved to indicate the vehicle with its steam-powered engine, though neither it nor the boiler and smokestack were visible from inside.

"Would it be simpler on you if I disappeared?"

"*Now* you ask that?" Cutter asked from the bench opposite them, not bothering to keep his voice down.

The watchmen glanced at him.

"I invited you to stay on my land for as long as you wish," Jev said quietly, ignoring their guards, "and that invitation stands. You've spent years working with the army. You deserve a peaceful place to rest in our kingdom. Even if the common man doesn't know that yet." His father didn't know it yet either, but he would soon. Jev held back a frown.

To think, a few months ago, the only thing he'd dreaded about coming home was having to discuss the details of his brother's death with the old man.

"He didn't answer the question," Cutter observed.

"I noticed that," Lornysh said dryly.

"It would have been simpler if you'd been wearing a hood when you walked off the ship," Jev said, "but at this point, I'd appreciate it if you stuck around. I'm not sure what's going on, but I may need an ally or two."

Especially if his father denied him access to the only home he'd ever known, which might happen, given his father's feelings about elves. And if Grandmother Visha was there, she would be even worse. She would offer freshly baked cakes and cookies to Jev while screaming obscenities at Lornysh, seeing nothing odd about doing both at the same time.

"Hm," Lornysh said.

The steam wagon turned off the main road, and Jev's stomach flip-flopped in his belly. He watched the cottages, shops, and smithies they rolled past, the buildings leased from the Dharrow family by commoners who traded their labor and a portion of their crops or wares for reduced rent and protection from invaders. Jev thought he recognized a few familiar faces, but he didn't call out or try to draw attention.

As they left the village, Jev did his best to muster his courage, reminding himself that he'd fought countless times and commanded two different companies during his years in the army. It wasn't right for his knees to go weak at the idea of standing up to his father. Sometimes, he wished he had a little more of the flippancy and irreverence his brother had been known for. Vastiun had never cared if Father was angry or disappointed with him. It hadn't bothered him at all, especially as they'd gotten older. Jev wasn't sure why he'd always cared so much, tried so hard to do what was honorable and expected of him, to be the appropriate eldest son. To please a man who'd never been pleased by anything, or so it seemed. During Father's tirades, Vastiun had simply rattled his luck charms and run off into town to do as he pleased. He'd—

Jev straightened and gripped the edges of the bench. "By all four dragon founders, could *that* be it?" he whispered.

Only Lornysh, with his fine elven hearing, looked at him.

Jev didn't explain. He was already lost in the past, remembering the night his brother had died, the spearhead lodged in his guts, his cries of pain and Jev's shouts for someone to find a healer. But the healer had come too late. Vastiun had died in his arms, having never fully explained why he'd joined the army so many years into the war and requested to be sent to Taziira. He'd mentioned something about a girl back home, but he'd been oddly elusive when Jev had asked him for details.

"What is it?" Lornysh asked.

"You never knew my brother," Jev murmured, almost wishing Lornysh or Cutter had been there that night, so he would have someone else with him who could verify the memories of his death. Or rather, his memories of the next morning when they had burned Vastiun's body in a pyre, refusing to bury it in enemy territory. Before that, Jev had removed his brother's weapons and also the rings and luck charms he'd always worn on his wrists. Vastiun had started collecting them as a boy, and his wrists had been so loaded with them by the time of his death that he'd rattled when he walked.

Had there been an ivory one? Jev thought he remembered something like that. Not eye-shaped, as he had been imagining from Zenia's description, but the shape of a tree trunk with an eye looking out from a hole in the side. Could it be what the Water Order was looking for? One of Vastiun's luck charms?

It seemed a stretch, but Jev couldn't think of anything else he'd come across that might fit the description. But why would Vastiun have stolen some artifact from one of the Orders? It was true that Vastiun had worried less about upholding the Code and obeying their father than Jev, but he had still been a good man. A *moral* man. Sometimes, he'd mouthed off to Father and anyone else who told him what to do, but he'd never broken the law in any serious way.

"He died the year before I joined your company, as I recall," Lornysh said, a prompt perhaps.

Jev sat back against the frame of the wagon, the wood hard against his spine. Should he explain here? No, not with the watchmen within earshot.

"Yes. I'll tell you what I'm thinking about later." Jev made a point of not looking at the watchmen. They had turned away, but they had also stopped talking. He didn't need magic to know they were listening. "After I talk to my father."

A conversation he had been dreading but that might solve this problem. After removing Vastiun's valuable and precious belongings from his body and his pack, Jev had mailed them home with his latest intelligence reports. He'd addressed the package to his father, certain the army would send it along to Dharrow Castle. Those charms might be hanging from a peg in his brother's room right now.

The wagon came to a stop, the pond just visible beside the road. The nervous sensation returned to Jev's stomach. They had arrived.

The watchmen hopped out, not stopping Jev when he followed. He was aware of Cutter and Lornysh climbing down behind him and their escorts fingering their weapons uneasily, but Jev didn't wait for permission to leave the wagon. He strode toward the massive stone structure that had housed Dharrows for almost a thousand years.

The drawbridge was down, as it always was, water from the pond siphoned away to create a moat around the castle. A few trees swayed in the breeze wafting up from the sea a couple of miles below, but as Jev had told Lornysh, the land was mostly cleared around the castle and the pond. Cows munched grass on a slope on the far side.

Not only had little changed since Jev walked away ten years earlier, but he was fairly certain the cows had been in the same spot. He might have found comfort in returning to the home he remembered, if not for the tense relationship he'd always had with his father. He distinctly remembered being relieved when his father had informed him he would be going off to war. Even if Jev had never believed in the war, it had been an excuse—an order—to leave, and he'd been ready for that.

As he crossed the drawbridge, Jev thought of his mother for the first time in ages. He hadn't seen her since he'd been ten and had no idea if she was still alive or, if she was, where she was. Things had been less tense between him and his father when she'd still been around, but he'd long since stopped feeling nostalgia about those times—or wishing she would return.

"Is that Jev Dharrow?" a voice cried from the courtyard ahead. Laughter rang out over the gurgle of the wyvern fountain in the center. "Dear cousin, your own father won't recognize you. You look like an ape."

"Because of the beard or just in general?" Jev paused, turning as Wyleria rushed toward him, holding up her skirts so they didn't drag on the flagstone walkway.

"Can it be some of both?" She grinned at him, and he experienced a strange moment where she seemed the fifteen-year-old girl she'd been when he left instead of the twenty-five-year-old woman she was now. "You've gotten old," she added. "You were just an apeling before."

"That's not a word."

"Unless they trained you to be a scribe in the army, I don't believe you'd know." Her grin widened as she reached him, and she abandoned her skirts to wrap her arms around him.

Though he ached to find and question his father, Jev returned the hug, warmed by her enthusiastic welcome. He hadn't expected his cousins to be around. Father had feuded with Mother's sister for years after Mother disappeared, and for a long time, Jev's cousins hadn't been welcome anywhere on the land. Only Grandmother Visha had stayed from Mother's side of the family, either because Father had no qualm with her or because she'd been made guardian of the Dharrow family's heirloom dragon tears and it had been deemed undesirable to have her living elsewhere.

"Actually, they trained me to be a linguist," Jev said. "I speak six languages, and apeling isn't a word in any of them."

"I suppose I should believe you. Vastiun was the one who always fibbed to me, not you." She stepped back, her grin fading.

"He did do that," Jev agreed quietly. "You look good, Wyleria. Are you and your mother living here now?"

"Yes. There were riots in the city earlier in the year. Uncle Heber, in his gruffest and surliest manner, insisted we come stay."

"Ah. Is he around?" Jev hated to rush his reunion with his cousin, but it was possible Zenia had already been healed and was on her way out here. She had definitely seemed the determined sort.

"He should be here soon. I saw you get out of the wagon and sent one of the servants off on horseback to fetch him. He's been cutting wood and repairing one of the barns out back." Wyleria arched her dark eyebrows, a hint of bemusement in her eyes.

Jev merely nodded, not surprised in the least. The castle had a handful of servants, not the dozens that some zyndar families claimed, but Father did most of the work around the place himself. He was happy enough to let someone else cook and clean, but if something needed to be repaired or improved, he sprang to the task, claiming the nobility had gone soft, with so few zyndar doing anything except eating and shitting—he had a number of favorite expressions evoking that sentiment.

"By the way, Jev…" Wyleria poked him in the side. "Care to explain why a city watch wagon brought you home? You didn't get drunk and start busting up furniture in a pub as soon as you got off that ship, did you?" Her grin returned at this image.

"There hasn't been time. I had been dreaming of getting drunk and sunburned on a beach, but…" Jev heard hoofbeats and trailed off.

"Most people don't dream of sunburns."

"I was a long time in those frigid northern forests." Jev turned as his father rode in on a great brown stallion, trailed by a servant Jev didn't know, the man riding a gray mare.

Wiry and lean, Father never looked that intimidating at a distance, but up close, he had a presence that always made him seem tall and powerful, not a man to be angered. His short hair had gone from dark gray to white, but he still appeared hale, his gray eyes keen and bright above his trimmed beard. He dismounted with easy grace and handed the reins to the servant.

Jev snorted when he realized he'd come to a rigid attention stance, his heels together, his back straight, and his chin up, but he didn't break it. Maybe it was appropriate. He'd always felt like a private reporting to a general when facing his father, and as odd as it seemed after ten years of being an officer himself, his feelings hadn't changed. Maybe it had to do with the fact that his father *had* been a general, battling the desert nomads to the south when Chief Sirak had united them, determined to take the kingdom's sea ports and lush agricultural valleys.

"Good to see you, boy." Father stepped forward and lifted his hands.

For a startled moment, Jev thought the old man might hug him. But Father gripped his arms briefly, then let his hands fall. Formality was the order of the day, as it always had been.

"And you, Father." Jev bowed slightly.

"It's regretful that the campaign was unsuccessful."

Father shook his head, and Jev braced himself, expecting him to talk about how successful his campaigns had been and how soldiers had been better trained and more disciplined in his day. As if those scruffy desert nomads had been anywhere the equal of the Taziir elves.

"But it's good that you've returned alive," Father said.

Jev let out a breath he hadn't realized he'd been holding. It wasn't exactly an effusive display of warmth and affection, but it was better than he had expected.

"Thank you, Father. It's good to be back." Jev was tempted to ask about Naysha and whether she and her husband were doing well, but his father wouldn't be the best source of information.

Besides, Jev would have preferred gossip to straightforward information, a sullen part of him wanting to hear about how they argued and fought often and were on the verge of breaking up. But that was too petty to put into words. He should want her to be happy. He just couldn't help but feel… He wasn't even sure. Bitter, yes. But if she had left her husband, would he want her back? Ten years after they'd parted?

Jev shook his head. This wasn't what he had come home to discuss with his father.

"You'll stay?" Father asked. "Come to dinner? Your grandmother heard your ship would land today, and she's been driving the cook crazy by taking over the ovens for all manner of baked goods. Some of the villagers and I are working on fixing a fence in the south thousand, and I could use some help in the morning. Big storm this past winter, and there are still repairs to be done."

"I would be happy to help," Jev said, though cutting wood and fixing a fence sounded tediously mundane after serving as an intelligence officer on the front, "but I do have a matter I need to resolve with the Water Order before I'm entirely free to do as I wish." Even though he was innocent, he hated bringing this up, hated the idea that his father might believe he had done something dishonorable. "You saw the watchmen out front, sir?"

"Yes." Father's tone chilled.

Was he annoyed that they had presumed to come onto Dharrow land? Or that Jev was in trouble? Or had Father perhaps seen Lornysh?

"I'm being accused of stealing an artifact. I never did, of course." Jev spoke quickly, the words almost tumbling over each other as he sought to explain before his father made any assumptions. "I thought it was all some error, that I'd been mistaken for someone else, but then I remembered the charms Vastiun wore and wondered if it was possible he'd somehow acquired something magical, perhaps by accident." The last thing Jev wanted to do was malign his dead brother or insinuate anything, especially to their father. "The Water Order, or at least an inquisitor from within the temple's ranks, seems to believe I have it or know something about it. Her name is Zenia Cham, and she, ah, may be up to the castle later."

"An inquisitor?" Father spat onto the flagstones. "If she dares come up here, I'll show her the moat."

"She's already irked with me, so that might not be a good idea."

"In my father's day, no watchman, inquisitor, or other servant of the Orders would dare question a zyndar. Zyndar honor was considered above reproach. It should still be considered above reproach." Father spat again.

Jev, knowing his father had been questioned after Mother's disappearance, suspected that anger was directed toward his own memories rather than indicative of any affront on Jev's behalf.

"Yes, sir," Jev said neutrally. "But the world is what it is now, right? I want to clear my name, and I would be happy to return this artifact to the Order if I can find it."

He wondered if that was the only way *to* clear his name. If he had allowed Zenia to question him while using her magic, might that have absolved him of any taint of guilt? Maybe, maybe not. She hadn't shown any respect for his rank in society and had even seemed irked by it—or by him—so she may have chosen not to see the truth so she could take pleasure in arresting a zyndar for punishment. He also didn't know if she truly would have used mere magic to augment her interrogation or if physical means of persuasion would have been employed.

"Describe it," Father said.

Jev did so, making sure only to use Zenia's description, not one based on the charm—the artifact—he remembered shipping back along with Vastiun's other belongings. It was unfortunate that he couldn't detect magical items himself. If he could, he would have known back then if any of those charms had been extraordinary. But he couldn't tell the difference between a true dragon tear and a knockoff being sold by an unscrupulous vendor.

"You don't know how large it is?" Father asked. "Is it the size of one of Vastiun's charms or the size of a house? Why didn't you ask for more details?"

"If the Water Order thinks I can smuggle a house off the continent in my pocket, then they're attributing me with a lot of skills." Jev smiled.

Father frowned. He still had less appreciation for humor than one of those fences he liked to mend.

"As for the rest, the inquisitor wasn't forthcoming. She seemed to be under the impression that she should be questioning me and not the other way around."

"She." Father's lip curled.

Jev thought he might spit again, but he only ranted.

"When I was a boy, women weren't allowed to do anything except scrub the halls in the temples. To have some bitter vindictive bitch as an inquisitor is deplorable." Father shook his head.

Jev thought he was generalizing until he continued on.

"I've heard of that Cham woman. She's taken down a lot of heinous criminals but also a lot of men and women from the nobility. She's known to take special pleasure in that. You better watch out."

"I'm hoping if I can find the artifact and hand it to her, I won't have to."

Assuming she didn't hold a grudge. Jev hoped that she would forgive him—or, more importantly, forgive Lornysh—for that attack.

"Do you know what made Vastiun decide to join the army years into the war?" Jev added. "He was vague about it when he showed up, but I got the impression it was about a woman or some conflict at home."

Father's eyes narrowed. "He was fooling around, doing nothing with his life. I told him to grow up and be a man."

Which had driven Vastiun to join the army and get himself killed? Jev stared bleakly at his father, hoping for more of an explanation. Hoping they hadn't truly had some fight that had prompted Vastiun to leave in a huff.

But Father had nothing more to say on the subject.

After waiting several long seconds, Jev asked, "Do you remember anything made from ivory among Vastiun's belongings? I think at least one of his charms was, but I was distraught and frustrated by his death at the time, and I wasn't paying that much attention to what I boxed up to mail off."

"You've always had a tendency to let your emotions get in the way of rational thoughts," Father said, an observation he'd made many times over the years.

"Yes," Jev said, not wanting to revive the old argument by pointing out that there was nothing wrong with being emotional about the death of one's only brother. "His belongings?"

"I never looked through them. I remember the news of his death arriving, and…"

Father frowned around the courtyard, his gaze growing distant in memory. It *had* been almost four years.

A green and silver banner flying the family wolf emblem hung on one of the walls, a breeze slipping in to stir it.

"I don't believe I ever saw his belongings," Father finally said, "though I do remember hearing that a package came while I was out working. I believe Butler Corvel would have received it. It's probably in Vastiun's room. Nobody has touched his belongings since he left. I'm not even sure if the maid dusts in there."

"I'll check with Corvel."

"He no longer works here."

Jev blinked in surprise. "He retired?"

Corvel had worked at the castle since before he had been born, so it was hard to imagine him gone. The quirky and eccentric man had always had time for young Jev, Vastiun, and his cousins, so they had all considered him a favorite among the staff.

"Without giving notice, yes." Father's jaw firmed in disapproval.

That struck Jev as odd. After spending so many years working for the family, why would Corvel take off without a word? He'd been a little distant with everyone after Jev's mother disappeared, but he'd still seemed happy to serve here.

"Shortly after your brother's death, I believe," Father added. "I haven't seen or heard of him since then, so I don't know where he ended up."

An uneasy sensation crawled up Jev's spine, reminding him of the time he'd led a scouting party through the Death Morrow Swamp deep in elven territory. He'd known danger lurked all about them then. Did it also lurk now?

"Check his room. What you seek is likely there. I'll see you at dinner." Father nodded once, then strode out of the courtyard.

Jev realized he hadn't mentioned the sanctuary he'd promised Cutter and Lornysh.

Later. He had a room to search.

CHAPTER 6

J EV GRIPPED HIS CHIN AS he gazed down at his brother's desk. His brother's empty desk.

A curtain stirred, and he barely registered it until someone stepped away from one of the tall windows. Jev jumped, reaching for his sword.

"It's me," Lornysh said.

"You grew tired of waiting by the watchmen's wagon?" Jev thought about pointing out that the castle had dozens, if not hundreds, of doors throughout, but he knew full well why his friend had avoided coming straight in.

"I slipped away when they weren't paying attention. They left to go meet with another wagon carrying more watchmen onto your land."

"Oh?"

"I jogged down to a bluff overlooking the turnoff and saw people get out of each to discuss something. How to apprehend you, perhaps. The blue-robed women came up with the new wagon."

Jev scowled. He had expected Zenia to come after him, but he'd hoped he would have more time. He had spent the last half hour poking around his brother's room, opening drawers and wardrobes and even looking between the mattress and bed frame and into the secret niche in the wall stones where Vastiun had kept his boyhood treasures. Logically, Jev had known Corvel wouldn't have stored Vastiun's belongings in any of those places, but he hadn't known where else to search. He had expected the package he'd mailed to be left unopened on the bed or desk.

"Where's Cutter?" Jev didn't want his other friend to be arrested simply because he'd been with Lornysh when he'd jumped the two Order women.

"Last I saw, taking a nap in the back of the wagon we came up in."

"He's concerned about the company, I see."

"I haven't noticed that dwarves are overly concerned about the doings of humans in general."

"Elves usually aren't either." Jev raised his eyebrows.

"Your people's incursions into elven lands have *made* them concerned." Irritation flashed in his pale blue eyes.

Jev wondered for the hundredth or thousandth time why Lornysh had joined the kingdom army, but he'd asked the question before and never received an answer. Others in Gryphon Company and especially in Wyvern Company had accused him of being a double spy, but Jev had never believed it. He remembered how close to death Lornysh had been when Jev had stopped what had been more torture than interrogation by his men. They'd captured the elf walking solo through the woods and not believed he did not have ill intent. Jev knew Lornysh would have integrated into the army much more smoothly if he had truly wished to be there from the start.

Pushing away the memories, Jev took another lap around the room, peering up toward the ceiling, as if he might find the package dangling from the old candelabra.

He spotted a familiar box wrapped in canvas perched atop a bookcase and snorted. "There you are."

He had to jump to reach it, and he wondered why Corvel had chosen such an out-of-the way spot. Had he worried the maid would come in and disturb Vastiun's things?

"This is the package I mailed back after my brother died," Jev explained as he took it to the desk. The strings tying it were clumsily knotted, and he frowned, knowing that wasn't the way he'd prepared it for mailing. He'd spent a summer sailing on one of his uncle's merchant ships as a boy, and he'd learned how to tie various knots. This wasn't his work. "It looks like Corvel or someone else opened it to see what was inside."

"There's nothing magical in it. I can tell you that now."

Jev glanced at Lornysh as he untied the knots. "You're sure?"

"Positive. I can sense magic. You should remember that. You found the ability useful on more than one occasion."

"In finding people, yes, but I didn't know you could sniff out magic in boxes like a hound finding jerky in his master's pack."

One silver eyebrow twitched. "That isn't the precise simile I would use to describe my talents."

The knots gave way and the canvas fell open, revealing the box. Jev hadn't locked it, and it wasn't locked now. His stomach knotted with the anticipation of pain, knowing he would look again upon his brother's most treasured belongings, knowing he would dwell upon how Vastiun had been taken from the world far too soon.

As he opened the lid, shouts drifted up to their third-story window. The window Lornysh had left open when he came through it. Like many windows in the castle, it overlooked the main courtyard.

"Someone at your gate is challenging the watchmen's wagons and the inquisitor riding on a horse beside them," Lornysh said.

His hearing had always been superior to Jev's. Superior to that of any human.

Jev hated that he had to rush and tried to detach himself emotionally as he sorted quickly through the box's contents: gems, metal trinkets, and wooden carvings that had hung on leather bracers. There was also a necklace and scarf, along with the bone knife that Vastiun had inherited from their grandfather.

"No ivory," Jev murmured.

"Is that good or bad?"

"If it had been here, I could have handed it over to the inquisitor."

"If it never was, then it's likely she was mistaken and neither you nor your brother ever had it in your possession."

Jev sighed. "That's the problem. I remember there being an ivory charm. Or what I *assumed* was a charm." He closed his eyes, bringing the carving up in his memory as clearly as he could. He held up his thumb and forefinger to give an approximation of the size. "It was about that big, the tusk made to look like a tree trunk with a hole in it. The single eye peeked out of the hole. The charm—artifact?—was yellowed and seemed old."

"I don't recognize the description, but it sounds like something my people might have made."

"It must have been made by the Water Order if they consider it theirs. And stolen."

"Humans don't make magical artifacts. You haven't the ability to do so."

"True. Well, perhaps the Water Order purchased it at some point. You don't have any idea what the artifact's power would be, do you?" Jev reminded himself he didn't know if the charm he remembered was indeed the artifact Zenia sought.

"I would only be guessing."

Jev was tempted to ask for his guesses, but they were short on time.

He closed the box. "Someone sorted through this during the time between when I mailed it and now, and the ivory item I remember is gone. That's... a lot of miles and a lot of years. It could have been taken out yesterday or four years ago, here or on Taziira, but Corvel's disappearance is odd. I'd like to talk to him. Maybe others of the staff know more than my father about where he went and where he is now. I—"

"Jevlain!" his father called in a booming voice that floated in through the window.

"Damn." Jev curled his fingers into a fist. He needed more time.

"They're all in the courtyard now. The women included." Lornysh had moved from the desk to the window and looked down to the flagstones and the fountain. "The women appear healed."

"How many watchmen are there?"

Should Jev contemplate running? If he was dragged off to a dungeon in the basement of the Water Order Temple, he wouldn't be able to get to the bottom of this. He suspected the answers he needed were here, in this castle, among those who had lived here when this package arrived and perhaps also who had lived here just before Vastiun went off to war.

"Eighteen between the two wagons," Lornysh said. "I don't see Cutter."

"Your sensitive ears can't hear him snoring in the back of one of the wagons?" Jev wrapped up the box and returned it to its position atop the dusty bookcase.

"If he were snoring, I would hear him. It's possible he slipped out when the wagons were traveling up and down the hill."

"Or he might still be back there." Jev had no trouble believing Lornysh could slip out of everything from a secured dungeon to chains and stocks in a public square, but Cutter wasn't known for his stealth.

"Possibly." Lornysh sounded skeptical.

His father bellowed his name again, and Jev stepped up to the window. He looked down into the courtyard and spotted Zenia right away. The inquisitor's cool gaze locked on him, as if she'd known exactly what room he was in. Maybe she had.

"I'm coming down," Jev called, though he still wasn't sure he should. He wished his father would have lied for him, said he wasn't here or that he didn't know where he was. But Jev wasn't surprised the old man hadn't. His father wore his honor closer than his undershirt and never did anything that might besmirch it.

"You will go willingly with her?" Lornysh asked as Jev headed for the door.

"Yes. Don't attack her again, please. Just…" Jev paused and met Lornysh's eyes, tempted to ask him to lurk around the castle and see if he could suss out information. Even if it wasn't his family or his world, he'd been an army scout for years, and he was even better at gathering intelligence than Jev. But this wasn't Lornysh's problem, not his fight. He'd done enough. He deserved to rest under the branches of a spring-flowering tree or head off to seek that culture he'd mentioned.

"What?"

Jev shook his head and smiled. "Stay out of trouble. And out of my father's sight for now. I'll try to arrange a more inviting welcome for you and introduce you to my family when I return, but for now, you have my leave to enjoy the trees and rest where you will. If anyone spots you and questions you, say you're there by my leave. I hope I'll be back very soon."

"Very well." Lornysh clasped his hands behind his back, as if he meant to stay in the room, but Jev knew that if someone were to come up in five minutes, he would be gone. "But do not fear to ask me for a favor if you want one. I owe you my life."

"A debt that you've repaid five times over by now."

"Hm, no more than four, I should think. You were crucial in assisting in the defeat of that tree golem."

"By screaming and running so it would focus on chasing me while you shot it full of arrows?" Jev asked.

"You were cursing, not screaming. And I believe you also shot a few of your bullets into it."

"It's good to know my actions appeared manly from the outside."

"Indeed."

"Anyway, you don't owe me anything." Jev lifted a hand as he opened the door, wanting his friend to know that he appreciated the offer even if he wouldn't take him up on it. "Find a place to rest and relax before you head off on your next adventure. Oh, and if things haven't changed in the last ten years, there's a stash of elven wine in the cellar. You're welcome to it."

Lornysh's ears visibly perked up. "Oh? Ryleshno'ronar? Or Synsesthilia?"

"The one I can pronounce," Jev said, though he had no idea. He remembered quite a few varietals down there.

"Synsesthilia, then."

"Yes, my mother acquired it. I think it's a few decades old."

Lornysh sniffed. "That wine isn't even drinkable until it's aged two hundred years."

"Stick it in your backpack for later then." Jev smiled, well aware of elven longevity. Sometimes, he wondered if his people's tendency to loathe the elves had more to do with the greater gifts the founders had given them rather than their haughty disdain for humanity. "Just avoid my grandmother if you see her. She would pelt you with stale baked goods. She and my father are both... I'm actually not sure what the full story is, but they've always made it clear they don't like your kind."

"Few humans do."

"Judging by the number of half elves I've seen in my life, I know that's not true."

Lornysh curled a lip in distaste. Apparently, he didn't have his eye on any human women.

Jev left before his father could bellow his name again. As he headed for the stairs and down them, he passed a couple of servants he remembered, and they gave him friendly pats on the back. Mildrey the cook gave him a hug that left him covered in flour. What did it say about his family that the hired help greeted him with far more warmth than his own father?

When he reached the first level, the door to the courtyard coming into sight, his cousin Wyleria strode out of a side passage. She lifted a hand to stop him.

"Jev, before you go, I need to tell you something."

He glanced toward the courtyard, wondering how long the watchmen would wait before coming in to forcefully retrieve him. Though worried, he nodded for Wyleria to speak.

"I heard you and your father talking about Vastiun."

"Yes?" Jev leaned forward and rested a hand on her forearm. Could she be the very source of information he needed?

"I know I shouldn't have eavesdropped, but... I *was* there first." She sniffed.

Jev nodded, not concerned at all about eavesdropping. "What about Vastiun?"

"We weren't living here when he left, so I don't know if he had a blowup with your father, but Mother and I suspected... Well, he'd been running around with an elf woman. *Dating* her if his words were to be believed."

"Elf? Or half elf?" He remembered Vastiun alluding to a woman. Pointed ears hadn't been mentioned.

Wyleria hesitated. "I don't know. I saw her in the distance once. She was so graceful and beautiful, I would have believed her a full-blood. But I don't know what a full-blooded elf would have seen in him."

Jev thought of his offhand comment to Lornysh about the existence of half elves. Pairings between the races certainly happened, but they had happened a lot more often in the past, before King Abdor turned all of Korvann against the Taziir. Jev hadn't even seen full-blooded elves around when he'd been growing up, nor had he heard of any interracial romances. It was hard to imagine an elf wandering into the kingdom to date Vastiun while a war between their peoples was going on.

"What happened?" he asked.

"I don't know, but many people saw them together over a space of a couple of weeks. There was some speculation that her relatives might have come looking for Vastiun, to physically convince him to leave her alone, but I don't think anyone ever saw them. We were just trying to figure out why he left so abruptly. We had dinner with him and the rest of the family here one night, and the next day, he joined the army and caught a ship sailing to Taziir without saying goodbye to anyone."

"Hm, I don't suppose you ever saw Vastiun with a carved ivory charm?"

"Sorry, no. I just thought you should know that it was likely his love life that got him into trouble and had him scurrying for another continent, not anything your father said. We—my sisters and I—speculated that he got her pregnant and that her brothers wanted to kill him."

"I..." Jev rubbed his head, having no idea what to say. What if he had some half-elf nephew out there that he didn't know about?

"Jevlain," his father's booming voice came down the corridor.

"Thanks, Wyleria." Jev released her arm and nodded, then strode out to meet Zenia, though inquisitors weren't at the top of his mind now. He was perplexed about everything going on and had no idea how to start solving a mystery that was more than four years old.

"And here I thought I'd just get some cool beer and get drunk on a beach somewhere," he mumbled as he walked out into the courtyard.

When Zyndar Jevlain Dharrow walked out into the courtyard, he looked the same as he had earlier in the day. Still scruffy, still dirty, his beard and hair still in need of a barber. Whatever he'd been doing in the hours since his elf buddy jumped Zenia and Rhi, it hadn't been bathing.

Zenia watched him as he walked across the flagstones toward her, Rhi, and the six watchmen they had brought into the courtyard. The castle's guards had come out of the woodwork like termites when she'd tried to lead the watchmen's two steam wagons inside, so they remained on the other side of the moat. She had envisioned a fight breaking out during which it would have been useful to have metal vehicles inside the castle to hide in and behind. Maybe the guards had envisioned that scenario too.

Fortunately, Jevlain's father, Zyndar Prime Heber Dharrow, hadn't rushed out wearing armor and waving weapons. The rangy white-haired man had simply asked what they wanted, then called for his son. He hadn't appeared surprised by Zenia's appearance, so she assumed his son had warned him.

Heber stood to the side now, forearms crossed over his chest. He wore patched and dirt-encrusted workman's clothing, and Zenia had been surprised when he'd introduced himself. There was no sign of the silks and velvets so many of the zyndar favored.

"Jev," a woman blurted, making Jevlain pause before he reached Zenia.

A plump, white-haired woman rushed down a set of stone stairs leading from a garden balcony overflowing with vining flowers and potted shrubs. She carried a wicker basket and hustled along remarkably quickly considering she looked to be in her eighties.

"Were you going to leave without coming to see your grammy?" she demanded. "I baked for you. We were preparing a special dinner." She waved toward an open doorway.

The scents of cooking food had been wafting out of it since Zenia arrived, a simmering seafood stew, baking bread, and roasting eggplant. It did smell appealing.

Jevlain winced. "I'm sorry, Grandmother."

He bent to hug her as she approached, a movement made clumsy by the basket in her arms. As soon as they broke the hug, she thrust it at him.

"You can't leave again without snacks. You must be famished after ten years away from home."

"We occasionally ate in Taziira."

"Bird food, I'm sure. Worse, *elf* food. Look how skinny you are. You must stay for dinner so I can fatten you up. And I'll catch you up on all the news. The Dangledorts are getting married, you know. Second cousins marrying. It's scandalous. So is the size of the wart I've developed. Do you want to see it? I've got something growing under my toenail too. I keep telling your father to bring a healer to attend me, but I can see I'll have to take a horse into town myself. My butt gets terribly sore, though, when I have to sit in a saddle for more than an hour."

Zenia blinked slowly a few times at the randomness of the "news." As the woman rattled on, Zenia decided she must have lost a few of the spokes in her wagon wheels over the years.

Jevlain patted his grandmother on the back and glanced at Zenia, his expression surprisingly apologetic, as if to say he hadn't intended to delay her further.

Zenia folded her arms over her chest.

Next to her, Rhi fingered her bo.

"We're not going to beat up any eighty-year-old grandmothers while we're here," Zenia whispered to her, though perhaps a little tap to her hip to prod her out of the way would be in order.

"Actually, I was thinking of hooking that basket by the handle and claiming it for the temple," Rhi said. "That looks like banana bread."

"I see something green. Everything's probably wrapped in gort."

"Gort is fine if it's sautéed and doused with cinnamon and honey."

"That sounds awful."

"It's delicious, I assure you. All vegetables are tastier when smothered in honey."

"You're an odd monk. Doesn't one of the Codices command monks to eat healthful foods?"

"The New Codex, yes, and I eat lots of healthful foods. I had a huge steaming pile of gort and fish this morning."

"Smothered in honey?"

"It was a *glaze*, and it was only on the fish. There's nothing in the Codices about honey. Unless one counts the maxim that it's easier to steal honey from bees once you've blown smoke into their hive."

Heber Dharrow came over and helped Jevlain extricate himself from his grandmother's attention, drawing her aside so his son could continue his walk toward Zenia.

Rhi let out a wistful sigh. Because Heber had claimed the basket and it wouldn't be coming with them?

"I'm sorry, Inquisitor Cham," Jevlain said, bowing when he stopped in front of her. "I hadn't meant for our earlier conversation to be interrupted, but I see that you're diligent in performing your duty and have located me again. Would you care to stay for dinner? My grandmother would be delighted."

Rhi cast a hopeful look at Zenia.

"No," Zenia said without looking at her.

"Then I won't feel bad that I didn't bathe and shave," Jevlain said.

"We don't require it for questioning sessions."

"So happy to hear that my armpit odor won't upset your interrogation."

"We're professionals." Zenia closed her mouth, irritated that she'd allowed herself to be drawn into bantering with him. She traded jokes with Rhi, but Rhi was her friend and colleague. This man was a suspect and perhaps a criminal. Maybe even worse if he spent time with elves. "Where is your elf colleague?"

Rhi gripped her bo at this reminder, and she looked around the courtyard anew, eyeing the doors and windows.

"Elf?" Jevlain asked mildly, arching his eyebrows.

As if he didn't know.

"*What* elf?" Heber left the grandmother's side and stepped forward, his hands balling into fists. His gaze skewered Jevlain.

Zenia almost would have called the expression hostile, and that surprised her. *Her* father was an ass she'd only spoken with once, but she'd assumed relatives who actually lived together would have better relationships.

"Elf?" the watch sergeant Zenia and her team had met out front asked. "We captured an elf and a dwarf with Zyndar Dharrow." He pointed to Jevlain.

Heber's eyes grew even harsher as he glared at his son.

"Captured, Sergeant?" Jevlain asked, not looking at his father. "I must object to your verb choice. We came willingly with you. In fact, you called it an escort."

"What were you doing with an elf?" Heber asked his son. "It had better be a prisoner you took to be your manservant."

"I'll show you, ma'am," the sergeant told Zenia and hurried toward the drawbridge and the wagons parked outside.

Zenia didn't follow him. She didn't want to take her eyes off Jevlain. Just because he'd come out at his father's beckoning didn't mean he intended to come with her peacefully. His elf buddy might be waiting outside the castle walls to spring another ambush. Her temple throbbed at the memory of the last one.

"Go check," Zenia told Rhi when the watch sergeant paused in the gateway and looked back at them.

"And leave you without a bodyguard?" Rhi protested. "You're in hostile territory."

Jevlain raised his brows again. "I didn't know a discussion of armpit odor signified impending hostilities."

"Funny," Zenia said flatly.

He bowed.

Heber crossed his arms over his chest again, his eyes closed to slits as he watched the proceedings. He was glaring at just about everyone, but he especially looked like he wanted to drag his son aside for questioning. The grandmother had stopped speaking, but she held a concerned hand over her mouth as she listened.

"Rhi." Zenia tilted her head toward the watch sergeant.

She didn't like to order Rhi around, but Rhi *was* assigned to work for her.

"Fine, but if his armpits assail you, don't blame me." Rhi stalked out of the courtyard.

Jevlain lifted his arm and turned his nose. The watchmen shifted, hands twitching toward weapons. Jevlain only sniffed and lowered his arm.

"I do believe that she and her bo would be powerless to halt such an assailing," Jevlain said.

Zenia didn't know what to make of his humor—people didn't *joke* with inquisitors—but she found it suspicious. Maybe he wanted her off guard so she wouldn't be ready when the elf attacked.

Rhi walked back in. "They're gone."

"The elf and the dwarf the watch supposedly captured?" Zenia turned her flat stare on a corporal—the sergeant hadn't come back in.

The corporal spread his arms and gave her an I-don't-know-anything-about-it look.

"Oh, I believe they were there at one point," Rhi said. "There are two watchmen tied up in the back of the wagon."

Jevlain regarded the revelation blandly.

His father continued to watch his son, looking like he wanted to question him. Or throttle him.

Jevlain glanced at him but only for a second. "Shall we go, Inquisitor? I'm ready for your questions. I'm hoping you'll be able to use your magic—or toenail-removing tools—to see that I'm innocent of your accusations."

"If you're innocent of the theft, then you have nothing to fear."

Judging by Jevlain's wry twist of the lips, he didn't believe that.

Heber grumbled under his breath, then turned and stalked away. Zenia didn't catch all the words, but she thought it was something about how zyndar hadn't been accused of crimes in his day.

Well, his day was over.

"Hand your weapons to one of the watchmen, Zyndar," Zenia said.

Jevlain's eyebrows disappeared under his shaggy bangs. "What?"

Zenia pointed exaggeratedly at the sword and pistol on his hip—he'd left his rifle and pack somewhere since she'd seen him last—then pointed at the corporal. She had made the mistake of letting him keep his weapons before. Even though he hadn't been the one to attack her, she had no doubt he'd conspired with the elf and commanded him to do so. And since she expected to see that elf again… she wouldn't make it easy for Jevlain to join in against her and her team.

"You're under arrest," she said to the consternated expression on his face. "Prisoners don't get to retain their weapons."

"I thought I was just being brought in for questioning."

"Hand over your weapons." This time, Zenia drew upon her gem and added magical compulsion to the words.

His fingers twitched toward them but stopped. His jaw clenched.

"Corporal," Zenia said. "Remove Zyndar Dharrow's weapons."

"Uh." The watchman hesitated, looking back and forth between her and the steely-eyed Jevlain. His last glance toward her took in her long blue robe. "Yes, ma'am."

He walked warily toward Jevlain, and Zenia felt smug satisfaction that the corporal had decided he would rather not irk her than a zyndar. She did her best to keep the emotion off her face, since inquisitors were supposed to be too wise and mature to feel smug.

Rhi watched Jevlain as the corporal stopped next to him. Would her prisoner object?

Jevlain looked like he wanted to. A hint of that arrogant zyndar indignation came through the dirt and beard growth on his face. But he lifted his arms so the corporal could remove his weapons belt.

The corporal wobbled slightly and wrinkled his nose. If those armpits were bad enough to affect a sturdy watchman, Zenia decided she wouldn't put her nostrils anywhere near them.

As soon as the corporal backed away and Jevlain lowered his arms, Zenia said, "This way," and strode out of the courtyard. She glanced back to make sure Jevlain did not dawdle.

He didn't. He strode beside her, matching her pace.

His quick willingness to depart made her believe his elf friend was indeed waiting somewhere to spring a trap.

When he turned toward the back of one of the wagons, Zenia raised her hand. "Sit up front on the bench with the driver. I'll ride beside you. So we can talk."

She nodded toward the two horses that she and Rhi had ridden out to the castle. She hadn't wanted to be stuck on one of the steam wagons if she needed to chase someone into the hills. The vehicles could match a horse's speed on a flat and groomed road, but they couldn't tear off into pastures and forests.

"So we can talk or so you can watch me?" Jevlain asked as Rhi mounted her horse.

"Given that people riding in the backs of those wagons have a propensity for being tied up, I'd think you would be glad to ride out here in the open air." Zenia nodded toward the sky. The sun was setting, painting the sea orange below them, and she hoped they could make it back to the temple before darkness fell.

"I would have been willing to take the risk, but if you want to start our talk now, I'm willing. Perhaps you can find me innocent, and I can return to the castle tonight." Jevlain sent a pensive look over his shoulder at the towering structure.

Zenia was surprised he was eager to return to his father's frostiness.

"We'll see," she said, though she had no intention of trying to use her interrogation magic on him on the road. It took concentration, and with the dwarf and elf unaccounted for, she dared not let her attention stray for long.

As she mounted up and the two steam wagons rolled away from the castle, Zenia looked at the pond, the pastures, and the countryside that stretched away for miles, seeking places where one might set an ambush. Copses of trees dotted the land behind the castle, but the wagons wouldn't head in that direction. There weren't any dense forests along the road back, either, unless one counted the mangroves that lined the Jade River. The road did pass within a half mile of them later on, so she would be vigilant. It would be twilight by then, and elves reputedly had excellent night vision.

As the caravan descended toward the highway, Zenia watched Jevlain as often as she did the surrounding land. Though she didn't want to risk being distracted, she occasionally drew on a trickle of magic to try to get a feel for his thoughts, to see if he expected his friends to jump her and the watchmen.

He seemed more resigned than anticipatory. She mulled on that. Was it possible he didn't have anything planned? He likely could have escaped through some secret passage under the castle if he'd wanted to avoid her.

"Why did you run to your family grounds, Zyndar?" she asked. "You must have known it would be the first place I would look for you."

Earlier, she'd assumed he would go to get help from his father, but now that she'd seen the two men interacting—or not interacting—she doubted they had a strong relationship.

"You can call me Jev." He shifted on the hard metal bench he shared with the wagon driver. The stack puffed black smoke behind them.

She opened her mouth to tell him to answer her question but paused. She couldn't remember a zyndar ever telling her to use his first name. Was he attempting to win leniency with the offer? And maybe he'd meant to soften her attitude toward him with his humor. She couldn't imagine that a zyndar would otherwise invite familiarity from someone who'd grown up a lowly commoner.

"Answer my question, Zyndar Dharrow," she said firmly to let him know that no matter what he wanted, *she* was not interested in developing familiarity with him. She'd only started thinking of him by first name because it had been confusing when his father, who would also be addressed as Zyndar Dharrow, had been around.

Rhi, who was riding on her other side, shook her head as she listened. No doubt, she thought Zenia should trade witty banter with the man and then invite him over for the reading of plays.

"I was looking for something." Jevlain tilted his head and looked at her. "Your artifact, in fact."

"The artifact you claimed to know nothing about?"

"I still know nothing about it, but I thought… I'm not sure if I'm circling the right tree at all. Can you tell me more about why your Order thinks I have it? They don't truly think *I* stole it, do they?" Though he was speaking casually, his shoulders stiffened at that last question, and he sounded genuinely affronted. "Is it more that they think it may have come into my possession? Did it make its way overseas and to the Taziir continent where it might have ended up in my hands?"

He was asking reasonable questions, and Zenia was embarrassed to admit she didn't know the answers. Archmage Sazshen had said he took the artifact and would know where it was. Zenia hadn't had a reason to question her. It was normal for her to be assigned missions without in-depth explanations. She was typically expected to learn any extra information she needed along the way.

"I—"

"Is that smoke?" the driver next to Jevlain asked, half standing to peer into the twilight sky ahead.

"Yes," Jevlain said.

"I see it too," Rhi said as Zenia located the spot.

Ominous black plumes rose from one of the villages ahead and to the right of the highway, plumes far larger than those coming from the stacks of the steam wagons.

"There's not a smelter or anything there," Rhi added. "That looks like trouble."

"Conveniently timed trouble." Zenia frowned at Jevlain.

He pointed at the road ahead of them. A horse had appeared around a bend, its rider slapping its flanks with a crop to encourage greater speed. The beast was already galloping, heading straight toward the wagons.

"Rock golems!" the rider yelled, spotting the watchmen. "Two rock golems are smashing our village. We need help!"

"I knew it," Zenia snarled, her frown turning to an outright scowl. She was tempted to yank out the pistol holstered inside her robe and jam it to Jevlain's temple. "You've got the dwarf helping now too."

"Cutter?" Jevlain shook his head. "He can carve gems and bring out natural magic, yes, but I've never seen him summon stone creatures."

Zenia had to nudge her horse into a gallop to keep up, for the sergeant of the watch ordered his wagon drivers to pick up speed and race toward the village.

The rider from the village drew even with them, but he continued past instead of turning around to ride with the watchmen. He yelled again about the rock golems but didn't want to answer any questions. He threw terrified glances over his shoulder and kept going.

Jevlain turned on the bench to watch him, then frowned over at Zenia. "Why would he have run this way?"

"What?" she asked, not grasping Jev's question. She was too busy being suspicious of *him*. And watching their surroundings. The highway had turned toward the river, so they weren't that far now from the mangroves. The perfect hiding spot for ambushers.

Rhi stood up in her stirrups, also scouring the landscape with her eyes.

"If he wanted to warn people or get help for his village," Jevlain said, "he should have ridden toward the city."

The driver didn't pay attention to him. He was alternating steering and loading more coal into the firebox behind the bench. The vehicle threatened to outpace Zenia's horse, and she was tempted to tell Jevlain to jump off. She hadn't imagined him getting away by simply being on a watch wagon that was too fast for her to keep up with.

"I think it's a trap," Jevlain added, yelling to be heard over the clattering of the vehicle and hooves on the stone highway.

"Of *course* it's a trap," Zenia yelled. "Your friends set it."

Jevlain shook his head and opened his mouth. Before he could speak, a rifle fired from off to the side of the highway.

"Get down," Rhi barked, dropping low in her saddle.

Jevlain jerked, then tumbled off the wagon seat, right into the path of Zenia's horse. The mare reared up with a screech of alarm, almost throwing Zenia.

Jevlain had enough presence of mind to roll away from the hooves as the wagon kept going. The driver glanced back as Zenia struggled to quiet her mare, looking like he might slow the wagon. But the sergeant in charge yelled at his man and pointed to the smoking village, saying the residents needed their help.

Zenia had always thought golems and trolls and other monsters were something explorers encountered on distant adventures in far-off lands. They certainly didn't appear *here*, scant miles from the capital city in one of the most populated kingdoms in the world.

But even as she tried to calm her horse and keep an eye on Jevlain, she saw exactly what the rider had promised. Giant rock golems. Two of them.

CHAPTER 7

FIERY PAIN SEARED JEV'S SHOULDER. He rolled off the side of the road to avoid the hooves of Zenia's horse, then rose into a low crouch beside a shrub. Should he run to the village to help with the massive rock golems smashing fences and buildings? Or toward the mangroves along the river to hide from whoever had *shot* him? He didn't know what was happening, but he recognized an ambush when he saw it. The alarming part was that someone apparently wanted him dead. Thank the deepening twilight that had given his attacker poor aim.

"Rhi!" Zenia barked.

Hooves thundered as the monk urged her horse toward the mangroves. Had she seen the shooter? Jev didn't know if Zenia had. She was glaring at *him*.

"Get off the horse," Jev yelled up at her. "You're an easy target."

Zenia glanced toward the mangroves. "Nobody in the kingdom would shoot an inquisitor."

Unless things had changed a lot in the last ten years, half the kingdom would happily shoot an inquisitor. Assuming there was a way to do it without getting caught.

Despite her certain words, her brow furrowed with concern. Her cohort had already disappeared into the trees.

Shouts of alarm and pain came from the village. Jev stepped in that direction, but he had no weapons, no way of hurting golems. At least he could punch a human shooter in the face. Despite the pain in his shoulder, he could still move his arm. He thought the bullet had only grazed him.

Movement from within the shadows of the mangroves caught his eye. "Look out," he barked, fearing another shot.

He dropped to his stomach. His shoulder protested, and he gasped with pain. A gun fired, and he heard the bullet whiz over his head.

Broken hells, whoever was shooting was definitely after him. He crawled on his belly into the deeper brush to the side of the road, lamenting that it wasn't higher. And denser. A nice boulder field would have been appealing.

"That's my prisoner," Zenia shouted into the mangroves.

To Jev's surprise, she thumped her heels to her horse's flanks and charged in the direction of the shooter. She stayed low on her mount's back and withdrew something from within her robes. A pistol?

Jev rose to a crouch, staying as low as he could and running toward the trees. He hated having people risking themselves to protect him, but she had ordered his weapons removed. The last he'd seen, they had been tossed into the back of one of the watch wagons.

A shot fired. Zenia roared. With pain? Or indignation?

Her horse tried to shy from its route, but she yelled and urged it forward again, then fired into the trees.

Halfway to the mangroves, Jev couldn't see if she had a target or was merely trying to scare the shooter into stopping. He hoped she wouldn't get herself killed on his behalf.

Jev sprinted the last hundred meters to the trees, not stopping until he was well inside the dense band that ran along the riverbanks and side streams for miles. The twilight was more like full nightfall under their sprawling canopy of branches.

Mud squished under his feet as he leaped over the high roots, making him aware of the noise he was making with his crazy run. He forced himself to slow down, then stop. He put his back to one of the trees and tried to listen to his surroundings over his own heavy breaths.

He'd gone into the trees well away from where the shooter had been, but there could be more people out here hunting innocent travelers. No, hunting *him*. How had he gotten into so much trouble when he'd been back on his native land for mere hours?

Stepping lightly and moving from tree to tree so he would always have cover, Jev headed in the direction the shooter had been.

A branch snapped off to his left, and he hesitated. Was that a second shooter? Or the first man running away?

A horse screeched up ahead. Jev quickened his pace, hoping the darkness would hide him and that he wouldn't stumble upon the very people trying to kill him.

A thunk sounded, like an axe striking wood. Jev squinted into the gloom, picking out moving shapes ahead of him. Two people? Three?

"That got him." It was the monk's voice. Rhi.

"Who *is* he?" Zenia asked.

She'd dismounted—or been thrown—from her horse, and now faced her assistant. A man writhed and groaned in the mud between them.

Jev started forward, opening his mouth to warn them he approached, but a faint snap of a twig came from the left again. Someone paralleling his path?

He picked out a large figure sneaking between the trees and heading toward the women. Whoever it was seemed focused on them and unaware of him. The figure stopped and lifted an arm.

Fearing the person had a gun and was taking aim, Jev ran toward the would-be shooter.

He slipped on a protruding root and must have made some noise. The figure spun toward him. Jev was close, and instead of dodging, he dropped a shoulder and bowled into the person. A man. Jev felt muscled mass through his foe's clothing. Fortunately, he had enough mass of his own to knock his target to the ground and land on top of him.

A thud sounded as something fell against a root. Hands reached up, grasping for Jev's throat. He smashed an elbow into his foe's face, and cartilage crunched. The man cried out. Jev struck again, this time slamming his elbow into the man's solar plexus.

The squish of a boot in mud came from behind him. Not from the direction where the women had been standing.

Expecting an attack from behind, Jev rolled to the side. Another man lunged in, but he tripped on his downed comrade.

As Jev scrambled away, his hand landed on something narrow and cool. The barrel of a rifle? He snatched it up, fingers grasping near the muzzle.

The man who'd tripped regained his feet and spun toward Jev. Jev swung the rifle like an axe, the butt smacking into the man's temple.

A hint of orange light appeared behind Jev's enemies, allowing him to see faces. Faces he didn't remotely recognize.

The man he'd smacked growled and whipped a pistol up. Jev swung the rifle again even as he leaped to the side. This time, the man ducked, but having to defend himself kept him from firing.

Jev lifted the rifle over his shoulder, intending to swing it again, but something slammed into his foe from behind, and the man tumbled forward. His face smacked into a tree trunk, and he crumpled at its base.

Rhi lowered her bo. She glared at the man she'd struck, then glared at the man curled on the ground, trying to catch his breath from Jev's blow to his chest. Finally, she glared at Jev and pointed at his rifle.

He thought she would demand that he drop it.

All she said was, "Some people like to use the end that bullets come out of."

"I have no idea who these people are and if I should be shooting them." Jev lowered the butt of the rifle to the ground.

"They were shooting at you."

"I am aware of that." Jev resisted the urge to prod his injured shoulder, though it throbbed with pain, and he could feel his sleeve sticking to the warm blood. "But I like to gather intelligence before I return fire."

Zenia stepped into view, still holding her pistol. The soft orange glow lighting the branches and trunks around them came from the dragon-tear gem she now wore outside of her robe.

"Do *you* have any idea who they are?" Jev asked.

He could no longer see nor hear the commotion coming from the village up the road, and he hoped that meant the watchmen had arrived and found a way to deal with the golems. Not that such creatures were easy to deal with, even with bullets and arrows.

"Not yet," Zenia said, "but I will."

The one who'd smacked face-first into the tree appeared to be unconscious, but she knelt beside the one struggling to recover his breath. Jev glanced toward the third one the two women had been dealing with, but if the man was conscious, he wasn't moving.

All three men were human and wore nondescript clothing. Jev hadn't heard anyone speak yet, so he couldn't verify that they'd come from within kingdom borders, but they looked like locals with the coarsely woven shirts and trousers favored by the working class in Korvann. Usually, only nobles and those who worked in the temples opted for silks and robes.

"Who are you?" Zenia asked.

"Remmy," the only man conscious muttered.

Jev couldn't tell if she was using magic when it wasn't directed at him, but he suspected she was. Getting answers was exactly what she would have been trained to use a dragon tear for.

"Why did you shoot at us?"

"Not you, Inquisitor." His eyes widened with fear as he looked up at her. "Wouldn't pick a fight with one of the Orders or you. Just... had to get something."

"What?"

"The Eye of Truth. Ivory. Old. She said the zyndar might have it. Big money if we could get it."

Jev leaned against the rifle for support. How was it that the entire world knew more about this artifact than he did? And why were so many people convinced he had it? Was the charm Vastiun had worn even the right item?

"She?" Zenia stared straight into the man's eyes. "Who sent you?"

"Iridium."

Jev frowned. Was that a name? It sounded vaguely familiar, but more like something from Targyon's books than a name. He'd been the only one to bring a dozen textbooks with him to the war, several on science, and he'd occasionally read to the men. Jev remembered Targyon saying he couldn't sleep at night unless he read a few pages and learned something first. Jev wondered if he was learning about being a king now. And if he would be bothered if Jev showed up at the castle and asked for asylum.

"From the Fifth Dragon guild." Rhi kicked a thick root that rose several feet from the mud. "Damn underworld criminals. Iridium is leading the guild now, isn't she?"

"Yes," Zenia said. "Since her lover and the former guild leader mysteriously disappeared."

"Mysteriously got a dagger stuck in his back before being dumped in the river, no doubt."

Zenia focused on the thug again. "What does Iridium want with the artifact?"

"Dunno." The thug prodded his broken nose and grimaced. "But she promised a big bonus and promotion to anyone who brought it in.

Enough to make it worth getting beat up a little. The thing is magic, they say. Elf magic. But I wasn't scared. Not of it and not of the zyndar." His brow creased as he looked up at Zenia. He didn't claim not to be scared of *her*.

"Did Iridium and your guild send the golems?" Zenia asked.

"Dunno. We were just told to wait for the zyndar to visit his castle and collect the ivory, that there'd be opportunities to take it from him on the way back to the city."

Zenia's eyes narrowed, and Jev shifted, wondering if the stories of inquisitors being able to read minds were true.

"Opportunities," Rhi muttered. "Right."

"Why did they assume I would have the artifact when I was clearly your prisoner?" Jev didn't think everything here added up. "If anything, you two should have had it."

Zenia didn't answer. She and the thug were still staring at each other, gazes locked and their bodies stiff, frozen in tableau.

"I'm guessing these boys weren't doing a whole lot of thinking," Rhi said. "Might be, they were afraid to shoot at Zenia and hoped that shooting you would somehow let them achieve their goal. Criminals never seem to mind taking out zyndar." Rhi grinned, leaned over, and thumped Jev on the shoulder. "I should thank you. Usually, *I'm* the target if someone wants to irk Zenia without actually touching her."

After dealing with the elves for so long, Jev had forgotten what it was like to be hated for the family he'd been born into and the entitlements he received. The Taziir had targeted him because he'd been an officer with a lot of knowledge. Now, he was just… he didn't even know anymore. A man who needed to find this artifact and get it far, far away from his person, so he could go get drunk on the beach and figure out the rest of his life.

"It doesn't sound like it's safe to stand next to her," he remarked since Rhi was still smirking at him and seemed to expect a reply.

"Not safe to stand next to either of you right now," Rhi said.

Jev reached up and laid a hand over his wounded shoulder. "Not if shooting zyndar has become a popular kingdom pastime lately."

"I was thinking of the miasma of odors wafting off you. Might knock me out if I take too big a whiff. If you get a chance tonight to stumble into the river—" Rhi waved deeper into the mangroves toward the distant sound of running water, "—you might want to take it."

"I would happily stumble into a soap-filled bathtub if you would let me go back to my father's castle."

"If the Fifth Dragon are after you, you might not want to bring that trouble home," Zenia said, rising to her feet.

The thug's eyes were closed now. Jev blinked. Could she use her magic to knock men out? He knew he hadn't injured the man badly enough to account for him losing consciousness.

"We taking these in?" Rhi pointed to the downed men.

"I would prefer to. Trying to kill a zyndar is highly illegal." Zenia's mouth twisted, and something akin to bitterness flashed in her eyes.

Trying to kill *any* of the king's subjects was illegal, but it was admittedly *more* illegal to attempt to murder a nobleman or woman. The punishment was death instead of flogging and a fine.

"We'll leave them unless we can catch up to the watchmen and get them to bring a wagon back here," Zenia said. "Rhi, I want you to ride over and check on the village. My horse was spooked and took off as soon as I dismounted."

"I'm not leaving you alone with a prisoner in the woods," Rhi said.

"Be careful too. I saw in his mind—" Zenia pointed to the thug at her feet, "—that there are many Fifth Dragon people out here. Apparently, Iridium didn't assign an organized team to get the artifact, but rather she announced a free-for-all opportunity to everyone in her guild. The person who gets the artifact and brings it in first will receive her reward. No questions asked."

"All the more reason why I should stay at your side."

"If you can, bring some of the watchmen back with a wagon for our prisoners. I'll stay here and see if I can find something to tie them up with."

Rhi surprised Jev by giving him a frank look. "Do you like the way she ignores all my objections and just assumes I'll do what she says?"

"Will you?" he asked.

"Well, yes, but not without a lot of surly grousing and proclamations that she's making a big mistake."

"How is that different from other times I've given you a command?" Zenia asked.

Rhi groused—in a surly manner—and thumped the butt of her bo on a root.

"Someone has to stay and watch these men and our prisoner," Zenia said.

"Am I still a prisoner?" Jev shook the rifle, more to point out that he'd helped them than anything else, but he added, "I'm armed."

Rhi swept her bo out, startling him. He started to step back, but the end cracked against his hand. He jerked it away, but it was attached to the wounded shoulder, and fresh pain erupted at the sudden movement. He dropped the rifle.

"No, you're not." Rhi picked it up.

Jev could have stopped her—she deserved a return crack on the hand, at least—but Zenia snorted. Maybe that was even a short laugh. He decided it might be safer to have her believe him unthreatening and maybe a little inept, even if his pride bristled at the idea. Then she wouldn't watch him as closely.

"Let him keep it," Zenia said when Rhi turned to start off with the rifle in hand. "He could have hindered us, but he helped."

Rhi frowned, looking like she intended another round of surly grousing.

"Do you promise, Zyndar, not to use the weapon on us or attempt to escape?" Zenia asked.

Jev suspected she was only attempting to extract his word to make her friend happy, but it made him pause. He wouldn't have used the rifle on them, regardless, but the addition of the words *attempt to escape* bothered him. He had fully intended to return with her, both to gather more information and so he wouldn't bring down the wrath of the Water Order on his family, but that had been before he'd known an entire underworld guild was hunting for him. Not just that, they were willing to *kill* him, even though he didn't have what they were looking for.

He wanted to go back to the castle and question everyone about Corvel's disappearance. He was positive the path to the artifact, if Vastiun had ever truly had it, started back at home with their old butler, not anywhere in the city.

"I won't use the weapon on you," Jev said, choosing his words carefully, "and I won't attempt to escape until we've made it back to your temple and talked to your archmage." A person who likely had more information than Zenia, information that might help him search for that path.

Besides, he didn't have much choice.

"Good enough for me," Zenia said, surprising him by not objecting to his wording.

Rhi scowled. "You're not alarmed that it took him a long time to answer?"

"I would be alarmed if he'd answered right away and just said yes. He may actually mean to keep his word."

"*Actually*?" Jev rocked forward on the balls of his feet, affronted by her insinuation. "I *always* keep my word."

What had he done to make her doubt it? Was she blaming him for Lornysh's attack? Even if he *had* been responsible, it wasn't as if he'd given her his word back before it happened.

"We'll see, Zyndar," Zenia said, her eyes cool and challenging.

CHAPTER 8

ENIA LET THE GLOW OF her dragon tear fade, worried the light would act as a beacon. Her interrogation of the Fifth Dragon brute hadn't yielded the exact number of guild people outside the city hunting for the artifact, but he'd believed it was a lot. That made Zenia uneasy. She hadn't expected competition, competition that was willing—if not eager—to shoot the only person who might know where the artifact was located.

She looked toward that person. Full darkness had fallen, and without her light, she couldn't see much, but she sensed Jevlain hadn't moved. He was leaning against a tree trunk, his newly acquired rifle in hand as he gazed into the night, listening to the frogs croaking near the river and the cicadas whining in the branches.

He had helped her drag the three prisoners together, and they'd crafted makeshift bindings from torn strips of the men's clothing, using it to tie their ankles and wrists. A couple of her new prisoners were awake now, but they weren't making a fuss yet. They probably wanted her to believe them unconscious, so they could find a way to take advantage.

That wouldn't happen.

"What made you decide to become an inquisitor?" Jevlain asked, startling her.

Nobody ever asked her that. They just assumed… well, she supposed she didn't know what people assumed. That she'd sought power, perhaps. She didn't know anyone among the Orders who had chosen the career for that. Most people wanted to help whatever Order they belonged to and to ensure justice was fairly dispensed.

"Why do you ask?" she replied, not wanting to discuss her past with a prisoner, nor where the guild thugs could hear.

"Curiosity. And a desire to pass the time while we wait for your monk friend to come back."

"The time can pass just fine in silence."

Zenia wondered if she'd made a mistake in not simply marching him out to the highway with Rhi and heading straight back to town. They would have risked being shot at again, yes, but getting him back to the temple *was* her priority. The reason she'd been sent out this morning. If she brought these other three back, they would likely disappear from the dungeon via some bribe or extradition agreement the temple had with the Fifth Dragon. It was unfortunate and unacceptable in Zenia's eyes, but the guilds had a lot of power, men, and even some magic, so the Orders didn't court trouble with them. Sometimes, her colleagues looked the other way. That grated on Zenia, even if the watch was known to do the same thing.

Choose your battles, Sazshen had once told her. *And choose them carefully for when the end result matters the most.*

"Are you this affable and cozy with all your prisoners?" Jevlain asked.

"You were expecting coziness from an inquisitor?"

"I suppose not, but I was open to being surprised."

Zenia shook her head and didn't answer. She thought he might fall silent, but he seemed to decide that her disinterest in talking about her career meant that he should talk about *his*.

"I didn't choose to be a soldier. You probably know that the eldest able sons were all supposed to recruit men from their lands and go off to fight in the war. The king—the old king—issued a decree. Some of the zyndar families protested, paid bribes, or found lawyers to argue why their children shouldn't be drafted, but not my father. He was eager to get rid of me. Oh, not because I was trouble or offended him, at least not so far as I know, but because he believed in serving the king loyally and without question. I also think... Well, he hates the Taziir. He always has. There are some rumors around the castle that my mother left him to go off with an elf. I don't think that's true—I suspect people were just trying to make sense of her disappearance and his subsequent vocal hatred of elves. But I remember her from when I was a kid, and how they were together as a couple. He was as distant with her as he always was with me and my brother. It was an arranged marriage, you see. Damn, I wonder if he'll start trying to arrange something for me now that I'm back?"

He lapsed into silence, perhaps taken aback by that last thought.

"Are you telling me all this in the hope that I'll start to like you and be more lenient toward you during your interrogation?" Zenia asked.

A lot of prisoners were simply surly and despondent with her, saying nothing as she took them in to the temple, but she'd definitely met others who attempted the amiable route, trying to humanize themselves to her. She didn't know why they bothered. It wasn't as if she would go against the Order or the archmage to free them. She'd taken vows long ago, and the Order had given her everything she had today. She owed the organization and the people much.

"Sure," Jevlain said. "Is it working?"

"No."

"So, there's no hope of leniency, and I should start clipping my nails now so your fingernail gripper won't have much luck taking hold to pull them off?"

"Do you have nail clippers with you?"

"No. I suppose I'd have to try to grind them down on something raspy and blunt. One of these fellow's heads, perhaps."

She snorted, then immediately regretted it. Whatever he was scheming, she shouldn't respond to it—to *him*—in any way.

Zenia clamped her mouth shut and resolved not to speak again. It wasn't hard. As the minutes trickled past, she started to worry, and that occupied her thoughts. They hadn't run far into the mangroves, so it shouldn't have taken Rhi long to ride to the village, check on its status, and return, especially on horseback.

"Come with me, Dharrow." Zenia leaned over and groped in the air until she located his arm. She gripped his sleeve and tugged him away from the tree.

Had he wanted to be difficult, he could have resisted her pull—he had the size and mass to resist most people's pull, and he could have likely slipped away into the night by now if he'd wished. Earlier, she'd seen him deal with those two thugs without taking so much as a fist to the chin himself, so she would have known not to underestimate him even if she knew nothing of his military career. But she believed him when he'd given his word not to attempt to escape, so she wasn't worried about it now. As huffy as he got when she questioned his word, it had to mean something to him.

"Are we going off for a tryst?" Jevlain shifted to avoid stepping on one of the prisoners they were necessarily leaving tied on the ground.

"Do you think that's likely?"

"Not after all the jokes your monk friend made about my travel-inspired aroma."

"Good. Delusional men are difficult to work with." She lowered her voice, leading him in the direction of the highway. At least, she *hoped* she was heading in the right direction. They were too far from the sea to use its roar as a guide, nor could she hear the running of the wide Jade River any longer.

She wished she hadn't lost her horse since they had better night vision than humans. But the gunshots had alarmed the old girl, and she'd taken off at the first opportunity. It was just as well. Zenia wouldn't have wanted to ride double with Jevlain, and she would have felt strange riding while he walked. There was probably some rule against making zyndar prisoners travel on foot.

"You're worried about your friend?" Jevlain asked quietly. "Rhi?"

"Yes." Zenia wasn't sure why it surprised her that he had taken note of her name. Because so few zyndar bothered to learn the names of commoners?

She also wasn't sure she liked having him identify Rhi as *her friend* instead of her monk or bodyguard. It suggested he knew they were closer than that, that he'd been paying attention when they'd bantered. That probably wouldn't matter, but she had dealt with criminals in countless capacities, including blackmail attempts. They had few qualms about using a friendship against an inquisitor or other law enforcer.

Not that she was positive Jevlain *was* a criminal. Archmage Sazshen had implied that, but Zenia was starting to believe Jevlain was as in the dark as she when it came to the artifact.

Unfortunately, that didn't help anything. It would have been easier all around if he *had* been able to pick it up at Dharrow Castle. But when she wore her dragon tear, Zenia could sense magic on others, and she knew he wasn't carrying any powerful artifacts. If he had been, she would have had him stripped and searched before loading him onto that wagon. She wondered if the rest of him was as grimy as his hands and face. Rhi, she was certain, wouldn't mind checking, despite all her comments about his so-called travel-inspired aroma.

"She should have easily made it back by now," Jevlain said from right behind her.

Zenia jumped. Even though she'd stopped and wouldn't have expected him to be anywhere else, it startled her to hear his voice so close. If he proved her wrong and *didn't* keep his word... Well, she would be a fool to make it easy for him to club her in the back of the head.

"Yes," she said and took several quick paces to put some space between them.

She almost ran into a tree. Four founders, it was dark in these mangroves. Fortunately, she spotted a break in them ahead, the grassy land between the forest and the highway.

"Did you learn anything about the golems when you interrogated that man?" Jevlain asked.

"He didn't expect them specifically, but he was told there would be opportunities for him and his guildmates to jump you."

"I thought that was a trap right away. Hm."

Yes, he had, hadn't he? Zenia felt a twinge of irritation that it had taken her a few seconds longer to figure out that something strange was happening. Oh, she'd known the appearance of rock golems wasn't a random occurrence, but she had believed Jevlain's allies responsible, not someone else.

"Would this Fifth Dragon guild have dwarven allies?" Jevlain asked as they reached the edge of the trees. "I don't know of another race with the power to conjure rock golems. The elves have a sort of tree golem, though they call it something else on their continent, but the one time I encountered rock golems, I knew our whole company was in trouble. The dwarves and the elves living in that valley put aside their centuries-old racial animosity toward each other to fight what they considered a greater common enemy. Us."

"You're the only one I know of around here with a dwarven ally."

"If that's true, our people have grown depressingly xenophobic."

"I think it's more that the dwarves feel xenophobic toward us."

"So long as the bearded female master gem cutter still works in town. I promised my friend an introduction."

Zenia peered toward the village. The fires had dwindled, but lanterns burned here and there on the highway. People out searching for someone? For *them*?

A few riders without lanterns rode along the highway too.

"Also, my ally doesn't make golems." Jevlain stepped up beside her, also looking up and down the highway. "He carves gems and crafts watch fobs."

"Watch fobs?"

"Not enough gems in the world to keep a dwarf's bills paid, I'm told. Cutter can engrave guns too. Intricate stuff. I bet he could make a scene of you capturing a criminal and carve it into the ivory handle of your pistol."

Zenia shifted her weight, wondering when he'd seen her pistol up close for long enough to know of the ivory grip. As chatty as he was, it would be easy to think of him as a blathering fool, but he was clearly observant. When he'd asked what prompted her to become an inquisitor, had he been seeking some thread on her that he could tug on if need be? She made a note not to speak too freely around him or underestimate him.

She stirred again, her shoulder accidentally brushing his. She almost snapped at him for being too close, but *she* had been the one wiggling around.

"People are hunting you," Zenia said, uncharacteristically frazzled. "Perhaps it would behoove you to speak less."

"Perhaps, but how dreary would it be for you if your prisoner never spoke?"

"My prisoners *usually* don't speak."

Typically, they were far too intimidated by her reputation and the reputation of Order inquisitors in general to chat with her. Maybe that was why she was frazzled. He wasn't acting as expected, and it was throwing her off.

"Not at all?"

"No."

"Does that mean you find me a delightful change from the norm?"

She almost snorted again, damn it. But she caught herself in time. She was *not* going to laugh at his jokes.

"No," she said firmly.

"Ah."

Two riders walked their horses down the highway in front of them. They wore dark clothing and hoods, not typical garments for the warm Kor climate, especially this time of year. They did not carry lanterns, but Zenia could tell they were looking back and forth, peering into the brush to one side and the grass and mangroves to the other. She also thought…

She gripped her dragon tear and focused on them. Yes, one of them had magic. A dragon tear of his own, likely.

Zenia patted the air, found Jevlain's hand in the dark, and pulled him behind one of the thick trees, stepping carefully so she didn't trip over the raised roots. Normally, she would have trusted the darkness of the forest behind them to render them invisible from the highway, but depending on what that man's profession was and how he'd been trained to use his dragon tear, he could have augmented night vision.

She half-expected Jevlain to make a joke about trysts and handholding, but he must have also sensed the danger they were in, for he stepped wordlessly behind the tree with her.

"If this guild has dwarven allies and dragon tears," Jevlain whispered, his mouth close to her ear, "then the underworld crime organizations are a lot more powerful and resource-rich than they were ten years ago."

His breath tickled her ear. For a moment, she found herself noticing the warmth of the back of the hand she still held, the callouses where her fingers brushed his palm.

Frowning, she let go and shook away the awareness.

"In recent years, the Fifth Dragon guild has become one of the two most powerful in the city," she replied, speaking as softly as he had, doubting she should be speaking at all. She couldn't see the riders around the tree, but she didn't hear the clip clop of hooves and feared they had stopped. "The other is the presumptuously named Future Order. There are many lesser guilds, but those two vie with each other for control over the underworld part of the city. They're both known to work outside of the city as well and have long reaches. It seems unlikely the rest of the races would care enough about humans to ally themselves with either guild, but they *are* criminal organizations. They could have stolen artifacts capable of summoning golems from dwarven communities."

Zenia fell silent. She still hadn't heard the horsemen ride off. Or was it possible they had slowed down and gone quietly enough that she hadn't heard the shoed hooves striking the stone highway?

"And this Eye of Truth artifact," Jevlain whispered, "what would a criminal guild want to use it for?"

She didn't know. She was almost glad she didn't know because she might have let an answer slip out before realizing his question hadn't been as casual as it sounded. He was gathering information, as much as he could. Maybe he hoped to find the artifact before she did and had no intention of returning it.

"Trade, power, influence." Zenia shrugged. "Who knows?"

He didn't ask any more questions. They stayed still behind the tree until Zenia started to again question her belief that the riders were still out there. Jevlain must have been questioning the same thing. He slowly leaned his head out from behind the trunk. Then he jerked it back.

"Hells," he breathed.

The clip clops she had been waiting to hear started up. Afraid the riders were charging off the highway toward them, she looked out.

The riders had taken off at a gallop, heading down the highway toward the city. In the opposite direction they had been going before. To tell someone they had located Jevlain? Or to set an ambush outside the city?

"I don't think it's going to be safe to go back on the highway," Jevlain said.

"I don't want to leave Rhi out here without figuring out what happened to her." Zenia squinted toward the village that had been under attack, but it was too dark to see anything. The earlier shouts had stopped, with the night lying quiet in that direction.

"She seems to be a competent woman who can take care of herself."

"True, but…" Zenia didn't want to admit that she was worried and also that she would feel guilty if she'd been the one to order Rhi to go her own way and then Rhi had landed in trouble. Unfortunately, inquisitors weren't supposed to prioritize friendship above their duties to the Order. Her primary duty was to return with Jevlain. Technically, the archmage just wanted the artifact, but he was the road to it. "You're right. She's probably fine. And like you said, I don't think the highway will be clear into the city. Not for us."

"We could go back to my family's castle," Jevlain said, the words coming out casually again, as if he made the offer for her sake and not his.

"We're going to the temple."

"I believe the answers we're both looking for may be at the castle. Someone may know what happened to the person who was the last one who likely handled this artifact."

"My job is to bring you to the temple, and that's what I intend to do. There are other ways into the city than the highway and the main gates."

"Only the river and the sea that I know of."

"What's the matter, Zyndar? You don't know how to swim?"

"I know how. And so do the crocodiles that make the river home. I assume ten years hasn't changed that."

"They're hunted down often. There aren't many within twenty miles of the city."

"It only takes one hungry crocodile to make for a bad night."

"You pick then, Zyndar. Crocodiles or assassins." Zenia peered down the highway again in the direction those two riders had gone.

Jevlain sighed. "Crocs. And it's Jev, remember?"

CHAPTER 9

AS JEV WADED INTO THE slow-moving Jade River, he reminded himself that he'd fought elven weapons masters one-on-one, stood his ground at the front lines on a battlefield, and ventured alone through enemy-infested wildernesses in a strange land where humans were hated. It was unseemly to worry about crocodiles. But he'd always found them alarming. One had wandered up the hill from the river when he'd been a boy and had eaten one of the pigs in the village, one that he'd named and ridden. He'd had nightmares after that, and there were always stories of one occasionally attacking fishermen out in wooden boats in the delta. It wasn't as if his fears were *entirely* unfounded...

Still, it was probably good that he was trying to make Zenia think him inept and unthreatening rather than manly and appealing. She'd sounded dismissive when he'd protested the swim. And now, as they alternated between walking and wading along the shore, inlets thrusting inland often to force them into the water, she led the way. Fearlessly. Even though he doubted her mind manipulation magic worked on predators.

He was surprised she hadn't wanted to go out on the highway and deal with the guild people, if only because she *could* affect people's minds. But she would need to be within speaking range for that. It wouldn't work if someone was shooting at them from the cover of the trees.

"Is that a log or a crocodile?" Zenia paused and pointed.

Even though the darkness wasn't as complete along the shoreline as in the depths of the mangroves, the moon wasn't out, and Jev had trouble seeing more than a dark lump thrusting out from the shore ahead of them.

"I can think of reasons to avoid it, either way," Jev said, tugging his foot to remove his boot from mud trying to claim it. It didn't seem to matter if they walked on shore or in the water. The mud had the inevitable ferocity of lava flowing downhill to incinerate a village. There was a reason the land along the river had never been cleared and built on, even though it was close to the city.

"You've had a lot of run-ins with logs that didn't come out favorably?"

"My shins have." Jev decided to take it as a good sign that she was speaking with him more now, even if she was poking fun at him. It reminded him of the occasionally barbed camaraderie he'd shared with the men in his company. She was a lot *prettier* than the men in his company, so it wasn't quite the same. He would rather date her than exchange barbs. Not that dates were likely to happen. He reminded himself that she was a renowned inquisitor and would be tickled if she found out he'd committed some heinous crime and could order him hanged.

"If it's a log, we could use it to float downriver. If we walk the whole way along the shore, it'll take until dawn to get there." She veered toward the dark lump, her pistol drawn. "Technically, we could float downriver on a crocodile, too, I suppose. If we killed it first."

"I had no idea inquisitors were so bloodthirsty." He sloshed out of the inlet, hurrying to catch up with her. If it *was* a crocodile, he ought to stride forward and deal with it instead of hiding behind her robe. "Or that it mattered if we waited until dawn to reach your temple."

"In the dark, it should be easier to get there without being identified or shot."

Jev reached the dark lump first and prodded it with the butt of the rifle. He'd been carrying it above his shoulder to ensure the bullets didn't get wet.

"Log," he said at the dull thuds. "Sounds like it's partially hollow."

"Good. Help me drag it into the river. If we both hang on, we don't have to worry about being separated."

"Yes, I'd hate it if a river current carried me out to sea and forced me to be forsworn."

"People fish in the delta on rafts. The current isn't terribly threatening most of the year."

Meaning she wouldn't believe it had been an accident if he were carried off by the current.

They dragged the log into the water, and Jev balanced the rifle atop it. As cold water reached all the way up to his shoulders, and a fresh flash of pain came from his bullet wound, he decided that dealing with the assassins would have been better than this. He also lamented that he'd told Lornysh to stay out of trouble instead of coming to assist him again. Jev could have sent him after these guild thugs like an attack hound loosed on coyotes.

He slung an arm over the log and let the slow current carry them away from the shore. "Will your archmage mind if you drip water all over the temple floor when you drag me in?"

"Not as long as I have my man." Zenia floated ahead of him, gripping a broken branch on the log and kicking to direct their conveyance to stay near the shore. "Though technically, she was a lot more interested in getting the artifact than you."

"I'll hope she doesn't plan to simply shoot me to get it."

"She would never do such a thing." Zenia managed a haughty sniff despite the water kissing her nostrils.

They kicked their way down the river for a couple of miles, doing their best to stay close to the shoreline and keep their heads low so nobody would see them. Twice, Jev glimpsed lanterns in the mangroves. Maybe this hadn't been a bad idea, after all. There had to be dozens of people out there searching. For him. Or for the artifact they thought he had.

Not for the first time, he wondered what, by the pointed teeth of all the founders, this Eye of Truth did. More than a dragon tear, he was certain. Dragon tears were rare, but not *that* rare. One could purchase them if one had enough money, and they were frequently given as dowries with arranged marriages among the zyndar.

What kind of artifact could be so desirable that the leaders of the Water Order Temple wanted it, as well as the leader of a powerful criminal guild? Whatever it was, he doubted he wanted either organization to have it. If he found it, and Zenia wasn't pointing a gun between his shoulder blades at the time, he would take it to Targyon and let him have it. It sounded like something that would make a nice coronation gift, and with access to all the books in Alderoth Castle, Targyon would be able to research it and figure out what it could do.

Jev smiled, imagining Targyon accepting the position of king simply so he could claim that library as his own. His stewards would be looking all over for him, needing him to sign documents and revise treaties with neighboring nations, and he would be at some back table with open books scattered all around him, oblivious to the passage of time.

The log came to a stop, pulling Jev from his musings.

"We've snagged on something." Zenia shifted and kicked, trying to knock the log loose from whatever had caught it.

"A crocodile?"

"I don't think so, though I did see one swimming upstream a minute ago."

"Comforting." Jev also kicked, trying to manipulate the back half of the log toward the shore.

The river was wide and shallow where they were, and his boots brushed the bottom, but he didn't find any submerged logs or boulders that might have caught their ride.

Zenia grunted with exertion or maybe annoyance. "It's some fishing net." She scooted closer to the front of the log. "What the—" Her splash drowned out the rest of her words as she tried to disentangle the log from the net.

The rumble of a steam engine reached Jev's ears, and his stomach sank to the bottom. "That's on the water. Behind us. A boat."

Ten years ago, paddle boats and small skiffs had made up the majority of the river traffic, but he wouldn't be surprised if more steam-powered craft plied the waters now. He also wouldn't be surprised if the location of this net wasn't an accident. Did it stretch across the entire waterway?

"Swim to shore," he ordered.

Zenia was still splashing about, trying to disentangle the log. Or maybe she'd been caught up in the net herself?

Jev pushed away from the log.

"Zenia?" Worried she wouldn't hear him over the splashing, Jev raised his voice. "Can you get free?"

The noise of the steamboat grew louder, its wheel splashing as paddles rotated in and out of the water.

Jev glanced back and spotted lanterns burning on the deck. With the current helping it along, the boat approached quickly.

Jev paddled backward toward the shore, keeping an eye on Zenia and on the boat. If they were tangled in the net when it arrived, they would be hauled in as easily as fish.

"I got caught, but I'm coming." Zenia shoved away from the log. "Go."

She turned and swam. The current carried Jev into the net, and he cursed. It did indeed seem to stretch all the way across the river. He tried to swim away from it while still angling toward the bank.

He wanted to dismiss the net as some new fishing tactic, but he knew nobody was out here fishing in the middle of the night. This had all been placed for him. For the artifact.

Realizing he would keep getting caught in the net if all he did was push himself back upstream, he gripped it. The rope was taut enough that he could pull himself along it, almost as if he were climbing a sideways ladder.

A gun fired from the boat.

Jev's heart jumped into his throat. These people were determined to kill him.

"This is getting old," Zenia growled.

Jev couldn't agree more.

Aware of the boat looming closer and closer, he took a breath and dunked his head, pulling himself along underwater. Another gun fired.

His legs streamed out behind him as he pulled himself along, so his elbow struck the bottom first when he reached the shore. He came up with a gasp, letting go of the net and scrambling to get his feet under him. He glanced back, hoping Zenia hadn't been hit by that shot. He didn't see her. Was she also staying underwater? Or had she been—

Her head came up, and she gasped for air less than three feet away. He grabbed her to help her out of the water. Now, he could make out several dark figures out on the deck of the steamboat, all with weapons in hand.

Gripping Zenia's arm, Jev rushed for the cover of the trees.

A lantern was unshuttered right ahead of them, yellow light spilling out.

"That's far enough," the man holding it said.

Two men with pistols stood next to him, the muzzles pointed at Jev.

Zenia stopped beside him, her sodden robe clinging to her. As with the other thugs, these men did not target her.

Jev calculated the distance to them and whether he might be able to dive behind a tree before they could shoot. It was doubtful.

"Search them," someone said from the side, and Jev realized there were two more people over there. Two dark-hooded people. The riders they'd seen earlier?

More men walked out of the trees, more lanterns being unveiled. Jev's shoulders slumped. He might have taken his chances against three men, but there were too many now.

One of the two men with pistols holstered his weapon and stalked forward. Even though the others were aiming at Jev, he went straight toward Zenia. There was just enough light to see the eager grin on his face. He lifted his hands, reaching for Zenia. No, for her breasts.

Her eyes blazed before he touched her. Jev took a step, intending to block the oaf's path, but Zenia lunged toward the man first, launching a palm strike at his face. Even though he looked like a lustful idiot, he had the presence of mind to throw up a block and deflect her attack. She dropped into a crouch with her fists raised, clearly ready to defend herself.

But one of the other men came forward. He circled his buddy and pointed his pistol at Zenia's face.

Her chin came up in defiance.

"Don't think we won't kill you because of your robe, Pretty," the man said. "People die and get thrown in the river all the time. Accidents happen. Nobody pays attention."

"Lower your weapon and back away from me," Zenia ordered, touching her dragon tear.

Both men stepped back, and the one aiming at her let his arm droop to his side. They wore befuddled expressions.

One of the dark-cloaked figures made an exasperated noise and strode toward Zenia. Jev was positive he was one of the riders and possessed a dragon tear of his own.

"Stay back," Zenia ordered.

But the man didn't falter.

Even though Zenia could defend herself, her doing so might get them both shot.

Jev stepped forward to intercept the cloaked figure, raising his hand. "We have nothing on us that you want, but I'm not opposed to working with your leader to find the item. Take us to her, and I'm sure she will reward you."

The cloaked figure paused to stare at him. Deep shadows in the hood hid the person's face, and Jev had no idea what he was dealing with. Some guild assassin? Something worse?

"You can tell I don't have anything magical on me," Jev said, guessing that was true. People with dragon tears could usually use them to detect magic elsewhere. "But the inquisitor and I have information. That's more valuable than a grope. Take us to your leader. We won't discuss what we know with minions."

"Minions?" one of the men protested.

The hooded figure said nothing, simply kept staring. Jev stared back. He'd dealt with enough elves and their terrifying magical creations not to be scared by anything his own city could throw at him.

"We'll take you to see Iridium," one of the men finally said. "But you'll wish you'd simply dealt with us."

"You *are* charming, but I'll take my chances."

"Remove her gem," the man told the cloaked figure with a gem of his own. "We don't want any surprises."

Zenia stirred, growling in her throat like a wolf.

The cloaked figure turned his stare on the order-giver, and Jev sensed that the man, or whatever was under that hood, didn't like being told what to do. However, he strode around Jev, nudging him aside with some magic that felt like a physical shove, and reached for Zenia's necklace.

She lifted her arms, as if she meant to punch him, but she froze mid-motion. The figure lifted a black-gloved hand and tore the dragon tear from her neck. She remained frozen with rage burning in her eyes.

The figure shifted her robe aside and withdrew her pistol, though it had gotten wet during their swim and wouldn't have fired anyway. Still, Zenia's eyes flared with even more indignation.

Jev wanted to step in on her behalf and clobber the thief, but the odds were too far in favor of him being shot. Judging by the night thus far, these people did not believe his life mattered.

The men surrounded Jev and Zenia and pointed them in the direction of the highway and the city. Jev supposed it was too much to hope that a watchman at the gate would stop their party and throw these louts in jail.

Zenia regained her ability to move and shook out her arms. Their escort didn't give her time to enjoy her freedom. Pistols prodded them in the back, leaving them no choice but to go with the men.

"Am I supposed to thank you?" Zenia growled, her fingers straying to the empty spot where her dragon tear had hung.

Jev shook his head, having no better reply to offer. His wet clothing chafed as they walked, and he hoped they would not have far to go. Weariness assailed him at the idea of dealing with some crime lord tonight. Or crime lady. Whatever this Iridium was. He was tired of this day and longed for a bed. He would even settle for a blanket spread deep within a Taziir forest right now.

"I don't suppose your elf friend is going to come to your aid again?" Zenia muttered as the highway came into view through the trees.

"I'm afraid not. That seemed to irritate you, so I told him to stop doing it."

"It would irritate me less if he was beating the piss out of *other* people."

"I'll let him know next time I see him."

Whenever that would be. Jev gazed wistfully up the highway in the direction of Dharrow Castle, but they were miles away from it now. Their escort turned them the opposite way, toward the city.

CHAPTER 10

I ASKED FOR ARTIFACTS, NOT PEOPLE," the raven-haired woman said, drumming her long black fingernails on the marble armrest of what could only be called a throne.

Its presence wasn't as out of place as one would have expected in the large subterranean room since all manner of pots, statues, paintings, and other items—stolen items—from past eras filled the space. A huge astrological painting behind the throne showed the four seasons, beautifully illustrated dragons of each color within each quadrant, along with their matching constellations. Zenia wondered if underworld guild leaders were as likely to pay attention to signs and portents as the average kingdom subject.

"They told us they don't have it, ma'am," said one of the men who had escorted Zenia and Jev into the capital and this underground warren via a secret passageway under the city wall.

There were multiple levels of tunnels, some as old as the city itself, and the scent of mildew and the sea permeated them, making Zenia suspect they had been flooded often in the past. Lanterns burned on the walls, and candelabras hung from the ceiling, hundreds of candles shedding their light. They didn't do that much to brighten the vast room, and Zenia had trouble guessing Iridium's age. Assuming this was she. She hadn't introduced herself, but a runner had gone ahead, and then she'd been waiting here on the throne when her people led Zenia and Jev in. She matched the description Zenia had previously heard of the woman.

"They *told* you?" Iridium's fingers halted their drumming. "Did you check?"

"Uhm, no, but your assassins…" The man trailed off and looked around, but the two black-clad figures had disappeared.

Zenia frowned. She hadn't noticed them leave. They'd been with the group most of the way, which was part of why she hadn't tried anything. Also, her weapon had been taken, and Jev had lost the rifle he'd acquired. Besides, he'd orchestrated this meeting, so he presumably wanted to talk to this woman.

"They would have known, right?" the man asked, his voice turning squeaky. He cleared it and glanced at his cohorts. For moral support?

"Hm," Iridium said.

Her gaze turned toward Jev and Zenia. She looked them up and down. Zenia, her robe cold and sodden as it clung to her body, felt like a bedraggled owl pellet abandoned on a barn floor.

"Zyndar Jevlain Dharrow, is it?" Iridium asked.

"Yes." He was scrutinizing her as much as she was him. "And you are?"

"Your captor." Iridium tilted her head. "Would your father pay to have you returned? And if so, how much?"

"It depends. How much longer am I likely to live if I imply he'd pay a handsome ransom?"

"At least six hours, I should think."

"A small eternity."

Iridium smirked and looked him up and down again. "Much can be done in a small eternity."

Zenia blinked. Was she implying sex? Jev was just as bedraggled as Zenia. More so with that shaggy hair and beard. The dip in the river had taken away the stink, but with leaves and grass sticking to his clothes, he didn't look overly desirable.

"Remove your clothes," Iridium told Jev, then waved a dismissive hand at Zenia. "Both of you."

"So your people can search them, or so you can ogle our nakedness?" Jev asked.

"That depends on how worthy your nakedness is of ogling." She waved at the men.

They pointed guns at both of them, though all their interest turned toward Zenia. She grimaced. Iridium might want to ogle Jev, but Zenia knew she'd have plenty of attention she didn't want.

She looked at him. How had she let herself get into this situation? What would Archmage Sazshen think?

She found Jev looking back at her, his expression apologetic.

"Sorry," he mouthed.

He held her gaze for a moment, but someone waved a gun, and he looked away. He unfastened and unbuckled his clothing, the same army uniform he'd been wearing all day.

A man behind Zenia cleared his throat to imply she should be doing the same thing. She thought about resisting, but these oafs might like it too much if they had to force her to remove her clothes. Besides, Jev was flirting with Iridium, or whatever one called it, and she seemed receptive to it. More than that, she'd been the instigator. Maybe something would come of it. If nothing else, they might learn why the guild wanted the same artifact that the Water Order wanted. And for that matter, Zenia wondered why the Order wanted it. As an inquisitor, she was supposed to dutifully complete her assignments without asking unnecessary questions, but she wished she'd asked a few.

Jev finished undressing first, dropping his wet boots to the floor with thuds. Zenia glanced over, more at the noise than at any interest in seeing him naked, but she immediately glanced back. *More* than glanced. The dirty, ripped uniform had hidden a beautifully muscled form. A few knots of scar tissue marred his flesh here and there, but they didn't detract from an athletic masculinity that Rhi would have drooled all over.

A chuckle came from the throne. "It seems the mighty inquisitor would like to spend a small eternity with you too, Zyndar."

Fiery lava scorched Zenia's cheeks. "I would not. I was just looking at… He's *injured.*" She pointed to the fresh gouge on his shoulder, though she'd been looking elsewhere and hadn't noticed it until that second.

Now that she saw the red gash, she remembered Jev being shot and falling off the wagon bench. A rush of guilt washed over her. In the chaos that had come after the shooting, she'd forgotten he had been hit. She had dragged him all over the countryside without even asking if he was all right. It looked like the bullet had only cut through the outside of his shoulder on the way past, but it still had to hurt.

"Indeed," Iridium said. "As a good disciple of the Air Order, I shall take it upon myself to see him healed." She drew a dragon tear on a thong out from under the lavish silks she wore.

At first, Zenia thought it was her own stolen gem, but a different image was carved into the front of this one. She was too far away to make out the finer details, but it looked like a dagger or sword. Fitting for some criminal mastermind. Or whatever she fancied herself. Iridium would have to be deadly in some manner or another to lead all these men, even if she had used her sexual wiles to get close and murder the old guild leader. She wouldn't have kept the position if she wasn't able.

"Fortunate for me," Jev said. "I do enjoy it when warrior women heal me."

Zenia doubted Iridium could wrap a bandage around a log, much less use her dragon tear to heal someone.

"That *is* fortunate for you then." Iridium waved at one of the men. "Search his clothes for the artifact." Her gaze shifted toward Zenia, and she flicked her fingers. "Finish undressing. You'll be searched too. And then, Jorgot, take her to a cell while I contemplate whether it's better for the world if she disappears or if she might have some value to us."

Zenia kept her face neutral as Iridium stroked her chin thoughtfully. She knew better than to show alarm. She reminded herself that she'd captured numerous criminals over the years, and she could figure out a way to escape if she was given some time. Admittedly, she usually solved cases from the comfort of her office in the temple, and when she did go out into the city to capture someone, she had a bodyguard along and watchmen that she could requisition at any time.

"Have you offended Brick of the Future Order at all?" Iridium asked. "I need something from him, and if you've had some of his people arrested, he may enjoy acquiring you. Have you heard of his torture chamber? I hear that it's lovely and that he particularly enjoys hosting women there." She smirked.

Zenia *had* heard of the Future Order leader's torture chamber and had to stifle the urge to shudder. This could be an opportunity. If Iridium wanted to trade her, she would keep Zenia alive, at least for now.

"It's a large guild, is it not?" Zenia asked. "I'm certain I've captured some of his minions."

Jev frowned at her, then told Iridium, "I'd think it would be useful to have an inquisitor indebted to you."

"Indebted?" Iridium asked.

Zenia almost asked the same question, but she caught the gist of Jev's comment right away. Unfortunately.

"If you were to spare her life and let her go, wouldn't she naturally be grateful?" Jev asked. "Perhaps she could become an inside resource in the Water Order Temple that you could tap for information and favors now and then."

Zenia gritted her teeth and clenched her fists. She knew Jev was trying to help her—and she wasn't unappreciative—but the very idea that she would trample all over her integrity and her vow to the temple to help some criminal overlord... He would never suggest *he* would do such a thing, she was certain.

"I don't think you know your traveling companion that well," Iridium said dryly, looking over at Zenia.

Zenia forced her fingers open, fearing she'd given away her feelings on the matter with her body language. Though it sounded like Iridium already knew her reputation.

"Inquisitor Zenia Cham is no friend to the underworld guilds," Iridium added. "Some of my colleagues have tried to bribe her and court her favor before, and most of them ended up in a dungeon somewhere, courtesy of her ferreting them out. She sticks her nose up in the air and pretends she's above all of us." Iridium examined her polished nails. "No doubt because some zyndar mounted her mother, she thinks she's not some common wench, but being a bastard doesn't make her any better than the rest of us. *My* parents both acknowledged me and loved me." She smiled viciously at Zenia.

"Which is why you came out so charming and well adjusted?" Jev cocked an eyebrow.

Zenia barely noticed it as she struggled to bring that neutrality back to her face. The turn this conversation had taken alarmed her, especially with Jev standing next to her to hear Iridium's words. Zenia didn't tell anyone who her father was—it wasn't as if he remembered her or had ever cared about her mother—and it horrified her that criminals knew all about her heritage. All about *her*.

"Precisely so," Iridium said, still smiling at Zenia.

Jev shrugged and stepped toward Iridium—trying to draw her attention to him? "I suppose I can't speak for her, but people with high morals occasionally change their stances when they're no longer in a comfortable place from which to practice them. Impending torture and death have a tendency to make people's morals and beliefs pliable."

"Yes, I've noticed that myself." Iridium tilted her head, regarding him with interest again. "You came back from the war recently, didn't you? I imagine you were in positions to see that yourself."

"I was," Jev said quietly, the words hard to read. "Let's talk, shall we? I have things I can offer you in exchange for our freedom."

"Do you?" Iridium looked him up and down, her gaze lingering on his penis.

"*Many* things. For instance, if you let Inquisitor Cham go, I would be willing to work with you to find this Eye of Truth. I have some ideas about where it may be located. Of course, you'd have to protect me as we went looking for it. The inquisitor has been trying to arrest me all day, and I'm sure she won't appreciate me working with you."

Zenia narrowed her eyes at him. Even though she doubted his vaunted zyndar honor would allow him to help a criminal find the artifact, she didn't like his negotiation tactics. She didn't want to be parted from him. He was *her* prisoner and her only lead on the artifact.

"If you knew where it was, you would have retrieved it already. I admit I'm surprised you didn't have it on you." Iridium waved to his pile of soggy clothing.

"Perhaps, knowing Inquisitor Cham was coming to look for me, I hid it somewhere in Dharrow Castle."

"If it's there, it should be easy enough to find."

"My father is unlikely to give you an invitation inside."

"No?" Iridium ran her fingernails across her chest, following the curve of one breast. "What makes you so sure?"

"He's focused and not easily distractible. And definitely not pliable."

"Nonetheless, I think I know enough to find this artifact without you."

"Why do you want it?" Zenia asked.

"I suppose I can think of other things to do with you though." Iridium ignored Zenia and gave Jev another scrutinizing look.

One of her men near the door sighed and rolled his eyes. She frowned at him. He straightened his face—and his back.

"There are other things I could offer." Jev pointed at her necklace. "I see you understand the value of dragon tears."

"Of course. Who doesn't?"

"My family has several of them."

"Does it?" Iridium tapped her fingernail to her chin, then slid off her throne. "How many?"

"Enough that I could barter one. I'll inherit them all eventually. In the meantime, my father wouldn't miss one."

"You're only offering one?" Iridium circled Jev, examining him from all sides.

Jev stood calmly, not trying to hide anything. "They're extremely valuable. Surely one dragon tear is a fair trade for a person's life."

Zenia didn't like being ignored, but she made herself keep her mouth shut. She might more easily escape later if Jev held the woman's attention and Zenia was tossed into a cell somewhere as an afterthought.

Still, Iridium's focus on Jev's naked form irritated her. She didn't know why, but the idea of this woman dragging him off for some sexual interrogation made Zenia want to punch her.

Iridium caught her glowering at them and smirked again. She flicked her finger at the two men closest to Zenia.

"Undress," one said, stepping close to prod her in the shoulder. "Unless you want me to do it for you."

Zenia had already unfastened her robe, so it was a simple matter to slip out of it and drop it on the floor. She tried not to see symbolism in discarding the garment that marked her as an inquisitor of the Water Order. As someone of import. This was temporary only. She would retrieve her clothing and her dragon tear.

As soon as she dropped her robe and chemise, the men gathered the items and poked through them, investigating the inner pockets. Another man went through Jev's clothes.

"I admit I'd be more interested in negotiating with you if you were more excited about the prospect," Iridium told Jev, glancing at his crotch again as she scraped one of her nails down his bare arm.

"Crowds don't get me excited," Jev said.

"But women do? It would be disappointing if that weren't the case."

"I like women just fine."

"Excellent. We'll check your excitement levels soon. After you shave and trim this, I think." Iridium flicked his shaggy locks with her free hand. "We'll spend some private time together just as soon as I send a couple of runners off with messages. One to the Future Order, I believe. I—"

"—in a meeting," came a raised voice from the corridor.

A thump sounded, followed by an angry snarl and another thump.

A stout bearded dwarf stomped through the doorway. He stalked inside, barely glancing at Zenia and Jev, then planted himself in front of Iridium.

Or was that... herself? The dwarf had a chest, and Zenia didn't think pectoral muscles accounted for the curvature.

With a start, she realized who this was. Arkura Grindmor, the city's master gem cutter. Why would *she* be visiting the leader of a criminal organization?

"Arkura," Iridium purred, neither looking surprised by the dwarf's appearance nor alarmed by the man who ran in after her, clutching a hand to his chest and grimacing. "What brings you to visit so late?"

"Sorry, Mistress Iridium," the man blurted. "She wouldn't wait. I..." The man frowned and held up the twisted barrel of a pistol that looked like it had spent an hour in a furnace. "She bent my gun."

"Her sexy beard wasn't enough to inspire you to keep it straight and erect?"

"Uh, what?"

Iridium waved dismissively at him. "Go back to your post."

"You know well what brings me to visit." Arkura propped her fists on her hips. "My diamond tools. You said one more favor, and you'd be able to negotiate for them with your rival. I'm this close to bringing down your entire damn den." She scowled and jerked her head toward the ceiling.

"I assure you I've been working to locate your tools. It's a delicate matter to dance with the other guild leaders. I need to make sure the person I think has them has them before I start negotiations."

"You said you had the power to find them and *take* them."

"Yes, of course I do. Once I'm positive where they are, then I'll use all my resources to retrieve them for you. I do appreciate the favors you've done for me thus far, and you have my gratitude."

"I don't want your gratitude. I want my tools back. My grammy gave those to me, handed down for generations. Blessed by the White Dragon Founder himself. They're more powerful than anything my people can make now."

"I think I know where those golems came from," Jev whispered to Zenia, his bare shoulder brushing hers.

Zenia nodded. She'd been thinking the same thing. She was surprised Arkura would admit the value of her lost items—or were they stolen items?—to some criminal overlord, but dwarves were known for being blunt and honest. And getting impatient with those who weren't.

How ever had she ended up coming to Iridium for help? Or had Iridium come to her and offered it? If so, how had she known the dwarf was in *need* of help? Zenia hadn't heard anything about the disappearance of the tools, and Master Grindmor was a notable person in the city. If she'd reported a theft, the newspapers would have mentioned it.

"Maybe she'd like to make a golem for *us*," Jev murmured.

Iridium frowned over at him, though she couldn't have heard the whisper. "Jorgot, take the zyndar to my room and stick our inquisitor in a well-guarded cell while I send a message to Brick and see if he's willing to pay for the honor of hosting her in his infamous abode."

A hand gripped Zenia's elbow from behind.

"Master Grindmor?" Jev stepped away from the guard reaching for him and turned the motion into a smooth bow toward the gem cutter. He smiled and spoke in dwarfish. Very rapid dwarfish. Zenia couldn't understand a lick of it, though she thought she caught the name of the future king in there, Targyon.

Arkura's bushy eyebrows rose, and Zenia hoped that whatever he was saying might turn her into an ally. But she soon said a few terse words, waved a skeptical hand at his naked form, then spat on the floor.

Jev rushed to speak further.

"Stop him from talking," Iridium ordered her men, her voice hard.

Jev, still speaking, tried to evade another grasp, but one man ran forward and jammed the butt of a pistol into his kidney. He stopped with a grunt of pain.

Zenia had the urge to kick his assailant in his own kidney, but someone grabbed her other arm. The men shoved her toward the doorway.

Jev did not speak again. He let his guards take him toward the exit.

As Zenia was pushed out into the corridor, she glimpsed Iridium placing a placating arm around the dwarf's shoulders and guiding her toward another door.

Eight armed men accompanied Zenia and Jev, prodding them down the passage with pistols and daggers. Had it been four instead of eight, Zenia might have attempted to escape, but the odds were too poor, and she wasn't desperate, not yet.

She arranged to walk shoulder to shoulder with Jev. "What did you say to her?" she whispered, trying to make the words too soft for the guards to hear.

He smiled lopsidedly. "I told her I had a friend who wanted to meet her and learn from her and would devote every day and every night to finding her tools. I also offered my family's resources and mentioned knowing Targyon. I said that if she was willing to use her magic to arrange for some rocks to strategically fall away to form a nice hole in a wall that I could escape through, I would do my best to help her."

"And she said?" Zenia feared she already knew the answer.

"That I looked like a naked fool who couldn't grow a beard to my balls if I had a hundred years."

Zenia raised her eyebrows.

"That's a heinous insult to a dwarf."

"Ah."

"I'm afraid my charm doesn't work as well on dwarves and elves as it does on humans."

"You have charm that works on humans?"

"Well, you keep brushing your naked shoulder against mine. You're clearly drawn to me."

"I'd knee you in the balls, but I'm too busy being appalled by the idea of your beard growing down to them."

One of the guards cleared his throat and gave them a shut-your-yaps glare as they rounded a corner and headed for an ornate carved-wood door. In the middle of it, an obsidian inlay with red marble insets formed the image of a black widow.

"I'm guessing that's your stop," Zenia said, not caring about the guard's glare.

"It looks homey." Jev lowered his voice to the faintest whisper. "I'll try to keep her distracted in the hope that you can slip out."

"Noble of you to sacrifice yourself," Zenia whispered back, not managing to bury the dryness that crept into her tone, "but I doubt you having sex with her is going to cause the guards to leave my cell door open." Dryness and... bitterness? Her own emotions surprised her. "I don't get why she wants to have sex with you, anyway."

"I'll try not to take offense at that. Besides, I'm still hoping she'll barter." He twitched a naked shoulder. "I'll see what I can manage. Just be ready to escape if you get an opportunity."

"I can't leave without my dragon tear. Or my prisoner."

Jev gave her an exasperated look. "You can come back with help if—"

One of the men behind them jostled him hard enough that Jev stumbled.

"No conspiring."

"What?" Jev asked. "Who said we were conspiring? Maybe I was confessing my love to her before we're irrevocably parted and sent off to vile ends."

"That's not allowed either," the guard said without apparent humor.

He opened the black-widow door, and he and three other guards escorted Jev inside. The other four turned Zenia back toward the intersection. She glanced back and caught Jev giving her a long look over his shoulder. Then the door thumped shut, leaving her alone with her guards, on the way to some dingy cell. Or to be traded to a torture-happy loon.

How had this assignment gone so wrong so quickly?

CHAPTER 11

THE STONE WALLS IN IRIDIUM'S room held no windows, as it was twenty or thirty feet below the surface of the city, Jev guessed, but lanterns burned on most flat surfaces. The scents of dragon-scale incense and dried oleander competed in the air, pungent and hinting of death, much like the macabre decorations. Ancient torture implements were mounted on the walls, skulls rested on shelves, and she had framed pages from books that showed surgeries in progress.

Jev supposed he should have been alarmed by it all, but the thought *trying too hard* floated through his mind. He also suspected this was a show room and not Iridium's true sleeping place. Either way, he didn't want to spend any more time there than necessary.

Iridium reminded him uncomfortably of the elven priestess who had forced him to spend several nights with her when he'd been captured by her people. She'd dressed in pretty dresses and smiled prettily at him, but her cruelty had gone far beyond physical torture implements.

Years had passed since then, but the memories still made him bitter and ashamed, both because he'd allowed himself to be caught and put in that situation and because he'd eventually spilled all the secrets he knew. That had been what she'd truly wanted, though he'd gathered later that she'd slept with him to irk some lover or husband.

"That's me. The means to make other men jealous," he muttered, eyeing notches carved into a bedpost. Men Iridium had slept with? Maybe she *did* use this room.

He peeked through a side door to a bathroom complete with a carved stone tub, a stone sink, and a stone washout. He almost gaped because everything looked to be plumbed. How had criminals living under the city managed to tie into the water and sewer systems? Less than half of the city—the legal and tax-paying portion—had been hooked up, at least when he'd lived here before.

More than the plumbing, the stonework was impressive, the work of a master. Had Iridium convinced Arkura to create this fancy bathroom for her? If so, those diamond tools the dwarf had mentioned had to be truly priceless to her.

Jev wished he'd had more time to talk to Arkura. He'd been too hasty, too desperate, in the throne room. He wasn't surprised she had dismissed him as a naked raving loon. Maybe it was a good thing Cutter wasn't there and hadn't heard him promising he'd go on a tool-finding crusade for Arkura... if she simply helped Jev get out of here. Of course, he was almost positive Cutter would happily do just that. He would jump at the chance to prove his worth to the master gem cutter.

A knock came, and the main door opened. Two guards leaned against the wall in the corridor, rifles resting in their arms. A filthy man in mismatched clothing stood in front of them, holding a silver butler's tray in his hands, a cloche resting in the center.

What rested under it? Another skull? A severed head? Some other garish message?

"A gift the boss *insists* you use." The man smirked.

Jev lifted it, bracing himself for more of the macabre. But a collection of shaving and bathing products were all that lay under it. Shampoos and soaps, small scissors, combs of various sizes, and a number of scented gels and rubs he wouldn't consider using under normal circumstances.

His father had always mocked the zyndar who came to visit smelling of strange colognes and oils, saying it was better to smell like a pig sty than a dandy who'd done no work in his life. Jev wouldn't say he preferred a sty aroma for himself, but he'd certainly grown accustomed to it during the last ten years. Early on in the Taziira campaign, he and his men had learned that tranquil pools and hot springs tended to be places where elves set ambushes.

Jev accepted the tray. "No razor?"

The man dug into a back pocket and held up a folding razor with a six-inch-long blade. "She said you could have it if you gave your word not to use it on her."

Jev looked bleakly at the blade. He was surprised Iridium would trust him to keep his word just because he was zyndar. Even if zyndar were supposed to hold their words and their honor closer than their lovers, he frequently encountered people who didn't believe that drivel from the old days.

"Well?" The man wiggled the razor.

"No," Jev decided.

He intended to escape and to do so in such a way that he could get Zenia out, too, and he didn't want to have that razor in his pocket and be unable to use it because of his word. He also didn't want to say anything to imply that he wouldn't try to escape. He would get out *without* being forsworn. Ideally, he would also get out without promising one of his family's priceless dragon tears. He'd only hoped to pique Iridium's interest with that offer, to get her talking.

"No?" The man arched his eyebrows. "Don't you zyndar all like to be smooth like a baby's bottom? I heard some of you even pluck other hair out. Shave your chests and pricks, all to prove you can spend your days grooming yourselves instead of doing honest labor."

"Some people have odd notions of what the zyndar are." Jev resisted the urge to press an offended hand to his chest and shudder at the idea of shaving anything there or anywhere lower. "And also of what honest labor is."

This oaf couldn't possibly believe *he* was doing honest labor, acting as a servant to some criminal overlord.

The man shrugged and pocketed the razor. "It's up to you. But Iridium likes pretty men. If you want to live, you might want to keep that in mind."

"You're not pretty, and she's keeping you around."

The man shrugged. "I came with the place."

He left, closing the door behind him. Mumbles in the corridor suggested the two guards remained.

Jev took the tray of grooming items into the bathroom and set it on the sink. He gazed down at the scissors and soaps while debating if he wanted to be defiant and wait for Iridium exactly as he was or if he should take the opportunity to wash off his grime and clean up.

He wouldn't mind looking and smelling less unkempt. It wasn't as if his bedraggled state had kept enemies from recognizing him. Besides, he hadn't planned to be defiant with Iridium. He wanted to negotiate a deal, something he'd done often with enemy representatives. Many times, he'd come out ahead in such negotiations. Even though he thought of Lornysh as a friend these days, their relationship had begun with a negotiation, with Jev convincing the elf that working with the very people who had been torturing him would be a good idea. It hadn't hurt that Lornysh had felt extremely bitter toward his own people at the time, or so he'd implied. All these years later, Jev could still only guess at the truth.

He picked up the scissors. He had to convince Iridium that he had something she wanted—and that it was worth keeping him and Zenia alive for it. That might be more easily done if he looked appealing.

In his youth, he'd been told he was handsome, but he didn't know if that remained true after years of war. He had far more scars than he'd had back then. Still, he believed he could present a respectable front if he wished, maybe making a woman conjure up bedroom fantasies when she perused him.

It wasn't Iridium that came to his mind at the thought. No, he pictured Zenia and that haughty look she so often wore. She'd even worn a degree of it when she'd asked in her most puzzled tone why Iridium would want to sleep with him. Given the circumstances, Jev admitted it was odd—or not without ulterior motives—but for some reason, it stung that Zenia didn't think he was someone with whom women would want to have sex.

He couldn't brush it off and say it was because she hadn't seen him naked because she *had.* Just as he'd seen *her* naked.

Heat rushed to his groin as he remembered the moment. He'd been careful not to look like he was looking, but he'd made sure he didn't miss any detail, that he had burned every curve into his mind so he would remember for later. To what end, he didn't know, except to inspire late-night fantasies. It wasn't as if she was interested in him, and even if she were, she was... not insufferable exactly, but her tongue was far too sharp, with her attitude toward zyndar too grating, for his tastes.

"Yeah, and that's why you're getting excited all alone in a lavatory," he grumbled, looking down.

He trimmed his beard in a small round mirror, did his best to make his hair hang in a straight line, then headed for the bathtub. He would make himself presentable for his discussion with Iridium, and maybe

Zenia would find him presentable too. Then she wouldn't be so startled when a woman showed an interest in him.

"Because *that's* what matters right now."

He forced thoughts of her aside and focused on what he intended to say to Iridium. Whenever she deigned to come see him.

Zenia watched the halls and doors they passed, hoping for inspiration, for something she might use in an escape. Not that her four-man escort was likely to let her stop and rummage through drawers for tools she could take into whatever cell they stuck her in.

Besides, if the meeting she'd witnessed with Arkura Grindmor was any indication, these people didn't know how to find tools.

No, that probably wasn't true. Iridium hadn't sounded truthful when she'd spoken to the dwarf. Even without her dragon tear, Zenia had sensed that. She wagered Iridium knew exactly where the tools were. Maybe she'd even been the one to steal them and had then created this ruse of a rival guild taking them to enlist Arkura's aid. In creating golems? No, it had sounded like the golems had been the latest in a series of favors.

What about that dragon tear Iridium had been wearing? Had it been newly carved? By the master gem cutter herself? Maybe that had been the *first* favor. Maybe the whole scheme had come about because the dwarf had refused Iridium at first, refused to cut a gem to help her kill people and commit crimes. Then her tools had mysteriously disappeared, and Iridium had offered to help find them...

If so, it had to have been cleverly done. Maybe someone from a rival guild truly had perpetrated the theft. Otherwise, Arkura would have been suspicious of Iridium. Dwarves were honest and blunt, yes, but that didn't mean they were dumb.

They—

A thud sounded behind Zenia, and she lifted her head. The guards had stuck her in a tiny, dark room, shutting the door behind her, and she'd been too busy thinking to notice she'd arrived.

She sighed. It wasn't the first time such had happened.

Hardly caring that she'd been left alone in the dark, Zenia dropped her chin onto her fist and continued to mull over the dwarf's problem, going over the words Iridium had spoken in the throne room and trying to find clues in them. Evidence. Right now, she only had conjecture, and as she well knew, it was dangerous to hare off on the basis of conjecture alone.

Not that she could hare anywhere at the moment. She ought to be mulling over her *own* problems. But she'd always had a hard time stepping away from puzzles before they were finished.

"I'll bet a hundred krons those tools are here," she murmured into her fist.

But where? Arkura was a powerful magical being—she wouldn't be able to increase the power of dragon tears if she weren't—so she ought to be able to sense magical objects nearby. She definitely ought to be able to sense her own magical tools since she would be intimately familiar with them.

Maybe Iridium had an agreement with another guild leader—this odious Brick, perhaps—and they were being stored in someone else's territory. But would Iridium truly trust some rival or even an ally with such valuable magical artifacts? More likely, she'd taken them far out into the wilderness and buried them.

"No, she probably wouldn't do that," Zenia muttered to herself. "First off, all the land within a hundred miles is owned by some zyndar family or another. Or the royal family. Bet she wouldn't have wanted to risk being caught burying something out there. Besides, she's a city rat, same as me. I wouldn't think to hide something in a rural area. Hells, I'd be afraid I wouldn't find it again. No, I'd hide it in the city. But if it's here, why wouldn't Arkura sense it? The city is large, but is it so large that a powerful dwarf's senses couldn't cover it?"

"Who's she talking to?" one of the guards left in the corridor asked, the door not muffling his voice much.

"Herself. Or a spider."

"It's weird either way, right?"

"Yup."

Zenia rolled her eyes and vowed to keep her musings silent as she tried to think of all she knew of magic and also of stories she'd heard.

Weren't there wrecks out in the Anchor Sea with magical loot in the holds, wrecks that even searchers with dragon tears hadn't managed to find because the water made it hard to detect them? She could have sworn she'd heard that piece of trivia multiple times in her life. Whether it was truth or rumor, she didn't know, but if water or sea water specifically had some element or density that made it hard to sense magic through…

Could Iridium have hidden the tools in one of the pumping stations near the river delta? Zenia had already smelled the proof that these tunnels connected to the water somewhere. Maybe the guild had direct access to one or more of the city's pumping stations.

Zenia nodded to herself. She might not have any proof yet, but if she were on this case, she would look there.

"Not that this helps me in my current situation," she muttered, frowning at the faint light seeping under the door.

If she crossed paths with the dwarf again, she would share her thoughts. But for now, she attempted to turn her mind to solving her own problems. How to get out of here and get Jev back to her temple. And find that damn artifact.

CHAPTER 12

W HEN THE DOOR OPENED AGAIN, Jev was lounging on the bed, his body scoured and scrubbed and his hair and beard trimmed. Since he still had no clothes, he had no pockets to hide anything in, not that he had anything to hide. He'd left the grooming materials, including the tiny scissors, in the bathroom. As far as weapons went, those scissors wouldn't be a danger to anything larger than a fingernail.

Two guards led the way into the room before Iridium stepped in behind them.

"Shall we search him, ma'am?" one asked.

"He's naked, stupid," the other said.

Jev watched them, his head propped on his elbow, and tried to look unthreatening. He didn't know if Iridium would send them away or have them stay in the room to watch. They were big, burly men with short swords, pistols, and truncheons hanging from their belts.

"He could be hiding things behind his back. Or under his balls."

The men stepped aside as Iridium nudged them out of her way.

"I'm honored you think my balls are so substantial that I can hide weapons under them," Jev said.

"*Small* weapons."

"Like pistols and daggers?"

"Take your positions, gentlemen," Iridium said, shooing them toward the door and stopping whatever reply had been forthcoming. She gave Jev a frank look—in the eyes this time. "Am I correct in assuming that you won't give your word not to attempt to harm me, escape, or do anything but assiduously attend my bedroom needs tonight?"

One of the men rolled his eyes behind her back, but neither said anything at the comment.

"That's correct," Jev said, surprised by the end of her question. Was sex truly what she wanted? It couldn't be *all* she wanted.

He wasn't arrogant enough to believe he had any particular appeal that she couldn't find elsewhere. He *was* his father's heir and had some power and land of his own already, but there were hundreds of zyndar living in and near the city. Granted, few were zyndar prime—or the heirs to the prime—but the options still numbered in the dozens.

"That's what I figured, but seeing you waiting in the ready position got my hopes up." She smirked and waved to the bedpost with the notches in it.

"Eager to add another notch?" Jev asked. "What is that, twenty-seven? And here I would have guessed you could have hundreds of interested parties attending your, ah, bedroom needs."

"Twenty-seven *zyndar* men. They're a little harder to bring down here than commoners." Iridium waved at the guards behind her without glancing back.

They had closed the door but stayed in the room, standing to either side of it. Glumly, Jev realized they were likely to remain there. Maybe they studied the ceiling while she had sex with her conquests. Or maybe they watched and that was their reward for loyal service. He hoped they weren't invited to join in. He also hoped he could finagle a way out of this before bedroom needs came up again.

"It's true that we don't usually frequent the subterranean lairs of villains," he said.

"Villains, really." Iridium sat on the base of the bed. "As if we're more villainous than the fat zyndar living off the labor of others."

"I'm not fat. As you can see. Were the other twenty-seven?"

"No, but that's because most of them were young pups. Tell me, Zyndar Dharrow, more about these dragon tears your family has stashed away."

Ah, so something he had mentioned had caught her interest. Good. That gave him a place to negotiate from.

"Are you looking for something in particular?" he asked. "You just acquired Inquisitor Cham's, and I see you have one of your own."

"Yes, it's very newly carved." Iridium slipped a hand into the top of her blouse, a blouse cut low enough to reveal the tops of her bosoms, and fished out a dragon tear with a dagger cut into the front. "Do you like it?"

"Carved by a certain dwarven gem cutter, I assume?"

"She's the only one in town that can do the work sufficiently."

"I hear her services cost a lot," Jev said.

"Less than you'd think." Iridium smiled, dropping the gem back into her blouse, then let her finger drift to the top button. "I might be willing to trade your inquisitor friend to you and let you go for three dragon tears."

"That's a hefty price. Would you also tell me what you want with this Eye of Truth artifact?"

"Is your freedom not worth a mere three dragon tears?" Iridium asked, ignoring his question. "And hers? I saw you admiring her ass."

Jev did his best not to react, but he felt warmth creep into his cheeks.

"You were pretending not to look. It was cute. In here..." Iridium unbuttoned her blouse as she spoke. "You can look all you like." Her eyes sharpened. "And I do hope you like."

Jev glanced at the guards. One was admiring the ceiling. One was watching, his interest even more disturbing than hers.

"I think I could be motivated to like it more if I knew why you wanted that artifact." He smiled and tried to sound smooth, but suggesting interest that he would never have felt dishonorable to him. Even if it was part of the negotiation game, and even if she saw through him.

"To sell it. Several wealthy and influential people have learned about it of late, and a great deal is being offered. With such funds, I could secure new alliances. Destroy old enemies."

Jev was debating whether he believed her when a shout came from the corridor.

He shifted, ready to leap from the bed if he got an opportunity. And maybe even if he didn't. But Iridium's eyes narrowed suspiciously, her gaze not straying from him.

A fist pounded on the door.

"Check it," Iridium said without looking back. She ran her hand over Jev's chest, nails scraping down to his abdomen. "Your muscles are quite lovely when you're tensed to spring." She smirked at him.

"Someone's drilling into the tunnel by our vault," someone blurted. "You can already see the tip of the drill head. It's huge. Some big steam-powered thing. We've got men running down to guard the spot, but what if it's armored? And there's a whole bunch of people behind it?"

"Uhm, boss?" one of the guards said.

Iridium finally tore her gaze from Jev—and his chest. She growled deep in her throat, glowering at the deliverer of the news. The man shrank back but didn't retreat entirely.

"What do you want us to do, milady?"

"I'll see to it." Iridium looked back at Jev. "Do stay there so we can finish this soon."

"I can't wait," he murmured.

She strode out of the room, not bothering to button her blouse. She snapped her fingers, and the two guards walked out behind her. The one who had been overly interested gave Jev a long look over his shoulder before the door closed.

He supposed it was too much to hope that one would run off and get himself flattened by whatever this drilling machine was. He couldn't imagine. Giant steam-powered tools weren't anything Lornysh would use. Cutter? Maybe, but how would either of them know where he was?

Maybe—

A thunderous cacophony sounded on the other side of the door, and the bed shuddered. Jev jumped to his feet, landing with his arms spread for balance. Rock dust flowed under the crack in the door, tickling his nostrils. A rockfall? Was that what was happening?

The door opened with a bang against the wall, and several head-sized chunks of rock tumbled inside. Even more dust hung in the air, obscuring his view, and he couldn't tell if the guards were still out there.

He looked around for a weapon in case he needed to defend himself, but the tiny hair scissors remained the only option.

The dust in the air stirred, and a short brawny figure strode into the room. "Foolish human, what're you doing just standing there? Do you not know a jail break when you see it?"

"Master Grindmor." Jev recovered enough to bow to her. "I am most pleased to see you."

A weak groan came from the corridor. One of the guards buried under rocks?

Arkura tossed Jev boots and a stack of clothing that included cotton coveralls and Zenia's wet blue robe. She must not have been able to find his clothing. Or maybe she'd deemed it too grimy to collect.

As Jev started to dress, she held up something on a chain.

"Is that Zenia's dragon tear?"

"If that's the name of the naked woman you were with, I reckon so." She tossed it to him. "Hurry up and get dressed, so I don't have to look at all that hairless human skin. We need to go. That woman'll figure out my diversions are diversions soon enough. She's a cunning vixen."

Jev decided not to mention that his hairiness was perfectly in line with the human norm—he remembered how furred Cutter's chest was. He yanked on the coarse cotton clothing and canvas boots. None of it fit well, but he wouldn't complain.

Not waiting for him, Arkura marched into the corridor. Jev rushed after her. The dust was settling, and he had no trouble seeing the oddly precise section of ceiling that had come down on the two guards. More groans emanated from below as Jev and his new guide clambered over the pile.

Without hesitating, Arkura led him through two intersections, then turned down a long hall with numerous doors placed close together. Cell doors? She stopped in front of the sixth one on the right, though there was nothing to distinguish it from any of the others.

"You were truthful with what you said, human?" Arkura splayed one hand on the door. "I've heard of your family. I believe you have the resources to help me. And I would like to meet another dwarf, assuming you spoke truthfully about that too."

"All of it was the truth," Jev said. "I'll help in any way I can, and I know Cutter will be eager to assist you. You've my word as a zyndar."

He knew that human social classes didn't mean much, if anything, to dwarves, but she had worked in the capital a long time, so she would be familiar with the zyndar and the culture around *being* zyndar.

"Good, because I'm tired of being swindled by thieves." Arkura shoved at the door with one hand. She either had immense strength or she applied some of her magic, for the lock snapped, and the door banged open.

Zenia stood inside and blinked at the sight of them. Or perhaps at the lantern light in the corridor. Her tiny cell was dark.

"We're being rescued," Jev told her, holding out her dragon tear and robe. "My charms worked after all."

"That's shocking but joyous news." Zenia grasped the gem first, fingers wrapping tightly around it. More sincerely, she whispered, "Thank you," to him and to Arkura.

"Save your thanks." The dwarf held up a hand. "I just want my tools, and your boyfriend promised to help me find them."

"My what?"

Jev wasn't heartened by the way Zenia looked like she would pitch over.

"I think that's me," he said.

"That's even more shocking news."

"And not joyous?"

"Uh."

"Let's go." Arkura pointed down the corridor. "There'll be guards swarming down here any second, but I can make a back door if we have time."

"What happened to the guards that were in front of my door?" Zenia jogged to follow her.

"I arranged a lot of diversions. Don't irk a master cutter." Arkura glared over her shoulder. A warning to both of them?

"I don't plan to, ma'am," Jev said, bringing up the rear.

"Have you by chance checked the city's pumping stations for your missing tools?" Zenia asked.

"What?" Arkura glanced back again. "Why would I?"

"Just a hunch I had. I'd be happy to explain."

"Do so, human. Do so."

CHAPTER 13

ENIA YAWNED AS SHE AND Jev walked into the square in front of the Water Order Temple, the dragon fountain spitting water into its pool. Though the sky lightened above the city, few people walked the streets yet. That didn't keep Zenia from glancing back often, worrying about spies or outright pursuers. By now, Iridium had to have realized that they were gone and that her dwarf ally was done doing her favors.

Arkura had shown them to an exit from the subterranean lair, then parted ways with them, saying she would check the pumping stations and also that she expected Jev and his dwarf friend to check in with her later. Zenia figured it was a long shot, but she would be delighted if Arkura found her tools in one of the buildings. And, if they were submerged, Zenia hoped they were waterproof.

As they drew near the broad temple steps, Zenia quickened her pace, eager to escape into the sheltered halls. One of the large doors already stood open, inviting in supplicants.

Jev did not quicken his pace, and his expression did not suggest eagerness, but he also did not turn away. He could have. He also could have left Zenia in that cell. She hadn't been the one to barter with Arkura. The dwarf never would have risked anything to help her.

Jev followed Zenia up the steps, not straying from what was, for him, a potential prison. Though she did not truly think it would come to that. He would tell her and Sazshen what he knew about the artifact, and they would use his clues to figure out where they could find it. Then, if he truly hadn't stolen it at some point, he ought to be released.

Though her thoughts were reasonable to her, Zenia couldn't help but feel twinges of guilt as he followed her across the landing, weariness—or defeat?—slumping his shoulders. He'd helped her with the thugs in the mangrove swamp, he'd gone along with her crazy plan to float down the river, and he'd helped her again in the Fifth Dragon lair. These were the actions of an ally, not an enemy.

"Zenia?" a familiar voice called as soon as she stepped into the grand entry hall.

"It's me, Archmage," she said.

Inside, a few candles burned around the base of the Altar of the Blue Dragon, but it was too early for more than a shred of light to enter through the large eastern windows.

Sazshen appeared out of the shadows, hurrying toward Zenia. "I worried when you didn't come back last night." She frowned at Jev. "He didn't have the artifact?"

"No. I had to bring him in for questioning."

"Does he know where it is?"

"He knows…" Zenia looked at Jev, not wanting to speak anything that wasn't true, and also finding herself reluctant to say anything that might incriminate him. "I'm not sure what exactly, but he knows more than he's told me."

Sazshen frowned. "Didn't you question him with your power?"

"Not yet. It's been an eventful night. And yesterday was eventful too."

"I heard you were treated at the hospital." Sazshen's frown deepened, and she stared accusingly at Jev.

He wasn't reacting to anything they said. He appeared too tired to care, but Zenia doubted that was the case.

"Yes. After being attacked by an elf. Oh, and Rhi and I were separated." Zenia barely resisted the urge to grab Sazshen's arm. "Has she made it back?"

"She did. Late last night. I had some of the story from her, but she had no idea where you'd ended up or how to find you. If she had, I'm sure she would have hurried back out to look. But, Zenia—" Sazshen held her hand up, palm out. "What do you mean you didn't question him? You've clearly spent some time with him, and he's the thief who stole the artifact."

"Is he?" Zenia realized that sounded like a challenge, or maybe even defiance, and hurried to add, "I mean, I've spoken with him enough to believe he didn't take it, but as I said, I do believe he knows more about where it is."

"Zenia," Sazshen said reprovingly, "a thief wouldn't *admit* that he took something."

"But he's zyndar, and he's…" Zenia groped for a way to explain that she'd come to believe Jev was trustworthy and honorable without sounding like she'd been suborned or tricked somehow. "Well, he's been gone for ten years. I don't see how he could have been the thief."

"Clearly, he ordered it stolen. *Zenia.*" There was that frown of reproof again. "This is not a man without resources and access to many, many minions."

"Who told you I stole this artifact?" Jev asked, speaking for the first time. "And how many years ago exactly did it disappear?"

"I will not reveal my resources to you, Zyndar," Sazshen said.

What about to me? Zenia wanted to ask, but she wouldn't question the archmage in front of anyone.

"As if you didn't know, it was stolen almost five years ago," Sazshen added.

"Stolen from your temple?" Jev asked.

"Stolen from a loyal member of the Water Order entrusted with it." Sazshen stood straighter. "You will not question *us*, Zyndar."

"No? It's easier for me to gather information if I do so." Some of Jev's casual irreverence slipped in, and Zenia had to hold back a smile.

Even though she thought she was successful in doing so, Sazshen frowned over at her again. Zenia, realizing Sazshen could possibly read her amusement even if she didn't smile, did her best to make her mind a blank.

"We will question him and find the location of the artifact," Sazshen said.

Zenia nodded. This was what she had assumed would happen, and she welcomed it. Jev could prove his innocence, if he was indeed innocent, and if he knew the location of the artifact, a magically augmented questioning session would reveal it. Even if he didn't know precisely where it was, she knew he had some ideas. He'd believed the answers might be back at his castle.

"But not this morning," Sazshen added. "You both look exhausted."

"Oh?" Jev rubbed his face. "I was hoping I looked dashing and alluring after my haircut and beard trim." He raised his eyebrows toward Zenia.

She frowned and shook her head at him, not wanting him to include her in any of his jokes, not with the archmage looking on. She already worried Sazshen suspected they had become closer than Zenia should have allowed.

"No?" Jev asked. "All that grooming effort for nothing. A shame."

"Take him to a cell in the dungeon," Sazshen said, unaffected by his one-sided banter. "I'll find a disciple to bring him food and water, and he can rest for a few hours. I expect you to do the same. You'll be more effective at questioning him after some sleep."

Zenia nodded, agreeing fully. She wouldn't be effective at anything right now.

"Zyndar Dharrow." Zenia extended her hand toward one of the doorways on the far side of the hall, one that led to the basement and the dungeon. "This way, please."

"Archmage," he said politely, nodding toward Sazshen before walking away with Zenia.

She was glad he didn't say anything to her as they crossed the hall. She already worried Sazshen would think them too familiar, that she should be taken off the case because she'd made friends with the suspect. Maybe that would be easier, but Zenia was reluctant to foist Jev off on someone else, both because she wanted to think nobody else in the temple was as competent at ferreting out truths as she and because… someone else, someone who hadn't spent a day and night with him, might not treat him fairly.

They passed a guard on the stairs leading down to the dungeon, and Zenia accepted the keyring from him.

A single occupant she didn't recognize snored on a bunk inside the first cell they passed. One of the other inquisitors may have been busy capturing criminals the day before. A little thread of nervous concern knotted in her gut as her subconscious involuntarily brought up the word: *competition*.

Archmage Sazshen hadn't mentioned other inquisitors being considered for her position when she retired, but there were five in the temple, in addition to Zenia. None had quite her reputation for finding ruthless and deadly criminals, but three of them had more years of service to the Water Order. And two had zyndar blood. One was even a distant relative to the Alderoths. Though the temple was fairer about offering common people opportunities than many organizations, Zenia would have to be blind to not see the bias toward the nobility.

Jev stopped in front of an empty cell. It was one of only two with a window high in the back wall.

He ticked one of the vertical iron bars. "It's rather different from an elven prison, in case you were curious. Theirs are less permanent, merely existing where they need them. No iron is involved in their construction. Somehow, they use their magic to convince trees to create cages with their branches. If you don't have an axe, a stout branch is a formidable obstacle to escape."

"I can imagine. Were you imprisoned by them often?"

"Never in the first five years I served, but three times in the last few, after I was transferred and made the captain of Gryphon Company. That was the army's intelligence-gathering and analyzing unit. I became a more desirable prisoner to them once I knew some of their secrets. Not to mention a lot of our own secrets." He turned and met her eyes. "Or maybe my allure simply grew stronger as I aged."

He smiled, but now that she had her dragon tear back, she could sense some of his emotions behind the smile. Though he joked on the surface, underneath, he was disturbed by memories of being imprisoned. *Haunted* by them.

And she, in locking him up, was bringing those disturbing memories to the front of his mind, memories he thought he'd forgotten.

"They have a tendency to appreciate age and wisdom over youth," Jev added. "Of course, they also tend to still be beautiful when they're two hundred years old. Going by what my father looks like now, I may not be that alluring when I'm two hundred. Or when I'm sixty. If you're thinking of falling in love with me, you should probably do it now."

The first morning sun slanted through the high window and lit up his face through the bars. Zenia opened the gate but paused before waving him in. He gazed at her, as if waiting for her to say something. She told herself she was doing the right thing, obeying the woman she'd worked directly under for the last ten years, the woman who'd hinted that Zenia could become her replacement as archmage over the whole temple. And yet... why did this feel like a betrayal?

"Are you contemplating my allure?" Jev asked.

"What?"

He smiled and shook his head. "Never mind."

"Oh." She caught on belatedly, and her cheeks warmed as she realized how close they were standing. She could have reached up and touched his jaw. Was his trimmed beard, now as freshly cleaned as the rest of him, coarse? Or soft? His dark hair appeared soft, and she had the urge to brush her fingers through it. "Your allure is fine."

"That didn't sound overly heartfelt, but I'll accept your faint praise, especially since the last time we discussed my allure, you had derogatory words for it."

"When was that?" Zenia thought of Rhi's comments about his body odor, but she didn't think she'd done more than nod in agreement.

"When you were puzzled that a woman would want to sleep with me."

"A woman? You mean Iridium?"

"Yes, she is a woman."

"I wasn't being derogatory. I was just confused, given the situation. Why would she find you so irresistible that she'd risk being in a vulnerable position with you?"

"I trust you've never felt so drawn to a man as to put yourself in a vulnerable position."

"Of course not. That would be ludicrous."

"Men are often ludicrous when it comes to women."

"I've noticed that during my career. I find it puzzling."

"I believe you." He sighed and stepped into the cell, his shoulder brushing hers as he eased past.

An unexpected tingle of awareness went through her at the touch. She stepped back, too tired to work through feelings and *tingles* right now.

She closed the gate and locked it. Jev clasped his hands behind his back and gazed at her. As weary as she was, she found herself reluctant to leave him here alone, to make him feel abandoned. But what would Archmage Sazshen say if she came down later and found Zenia napping in the next cell?

"I have to go," she said.

"Of course."

"If you're truly innocent, you have nothing to fear."

He smiled sadly and said nothing.

"Did you have sex with her?" Zenia blurted. She almost clapped her hand to her mouth, as if she could retract the words if she covered it quickly enough. She hadn't meant to ask that. What did she care?

"Iridium?"

"I'm just wondering if I need to worry whether you two made some kind of agreement that could threaten my quest to retrieve the artifact."

Jev arched a single eyebrow, and she felt certain he saw through her scrambled attempt at an explanation.

"Would it bother you if I had?" he asked.

"No," she said far too quickly. Damn it. Why hadn't she just waved goodnight and left him to rest?

"Ah, of course not."

"Except that she's a thorn in the Order's side, and if she were to add a zyndar ally to her stable, it could make her more powerful and harder to thwart."

There. That sounded plausible. Didn't it?

"I suspect she already has zyndar allies. Many of them."

She frowned. "What do you mean?"

"She had notches in her bedpost and informed me that each one represented a zyndar man she'd slept with. I don't know how many of them represented frequent dalliances with the same individual, but I suspect there is little that happens amongst the nobility that she doesn't know about. I regret that I didn't get a chance to ask her if she knew anything about the demise of the three princes. Perhaps if your people brought her in for questioning, you would learn much."

"I'll suggest it." Zenia waited for him to say more, to answer the question she'd originally asked. But he seemed to be avoiding answering her. She didn't know why it mattered, but it did, damn it. "So, she just wanted to add another notch to her bedpost?"

"I'd like to think she found me more interesting than some of the young fops she said she'd entertained, but perhaps I'm thinking too highly of myself."

Zenia wanted to press him and was tempted to draw upon the power of her dragon tear to do so, but she took a deep breath instead, telling herself to drop it. It was unseemly of her to care this much. Later, she would help Sazshen question him, they would learn where to find the artifact, and after that, she would likely never see him again.

"Sleep well, Zyndar Dharrow," she said and turned toward the stairs.

"Zenia?" He lifted a finger.

She paused, and he crooked it, inviting her closer to the bars. He glanced up the stairs, then leaned down, as if he meant to whisper something to her. The guard up there wasn't in sight, but he *was* within earshot.

Zenia didn't hesitate to step forward and turn her ear toward him. She wondered when she'd stopped worrying he would do something to her if she made herself vulnerable. Another prisoner might grab her neck and force her to drop the keys. But he'd had dozens of chances to escape, and he'd stuck with her, honoring his word. Even if he'd known this would be the result, being locked behind bars in a dungeon cell.

The thoughts kindled a warmth within her. Appreciation toward him? Gratitude? Pleasure at being surprised to find he was everything the zyndar of old had been reputed to be? But that was so rare to find these days? She wasn't sure. She only knew she was reluctant to leave him down here alone.

"I did not have sex with her," he murmured, his lips brushing her ear. At the gentle touch, the warmth changed into something far hotter, far more intense, and that earlier tingle returned in force. She realized with the subtlety of a gong being struck that she was attracted to him. When the hells had *that* happened? "I did not wish to, so I was relieved when Master Grindmor's diversion arrived in time."

"And you felt you had to whisper this so the guards wouldn't find out?" she asked, though she didn't lean away from the bars. A part of her that she didn't want to acknowledge hoped he would bring his lips to her ear again.

"No." He sounded amused. "I just had the urge to do this."

His lips brushed her ear again, and she froze. This time, they lingered, then opened to nibble on the lobe. A hot tingle of pleasure surged through her body, and her eyes flew open. He let go, and she turned to look him in the eyes.

That was a mistake. His face was only inches away. Maybe only an *inch* away.

And his eyes were warm and... amused, yes, but in a gentle way, an interested way. She had the desire to find out what his lips would feel like against her mouth. She leaned closer, or maybe he did, and parted her lips. They brushed his and—

"Inquisitor Cham," a cool voice said from the top of the stairs.

Zenia jumped back, horrified. It wasn't the guard.

"Yes, Archmage Sazshen." Zenia didn't make it a question. She didn't want to invite a lecture. Instead, she hustled for the stairs while avoiding the older woman's eyes. "The door's locked, and uhm, here's the key."

"So I see."

Zenia thrust it into her hand and rushed past. She felt cowardly for not meeting Sazshen's gaze, but she couldn't face the disappointment she knew she would see there.

What had she been thinking? Until his name was cleared, he was a *prisoner*. She *hadn't* been thinking, damn it. She'd been too busy contemplating tingles.

"Idiot," she muttered, almost running through the hall and toward the passage that led to her room.

* * *

Jev lay on the bunk in the back half of his cell, watching the sunbeam that slanted through the window creep from the far wall toward the floor as the morning passed. The tray that had been delivered with food and water remained largely untouched near the gate. He had been too tired to contemplate a meal, but he hadn't managed to do more than doze fitfully, waking from nightmares each time he drifted off. They alternated between being tortured for information he did not have and images of that archmage scowling down at him and Zenia.

He winced every time he thought of the way she'd jerked away from what had almost been a kiss, followed by her expression of utter horror. As if she'd realized she'd been about to kiss some mass murderer.

He didn't have a gem that allowed him to read minds, so he didn't know if she was more disturbed that they'd almost kissed or that they'd been caught almost kissing.

Jev hadn't meant for either to happen. When Zenia had asked him if he'd had sex with Iridium, he'd gotten the first inkling that she cared, that maybe she wouldn't like it if he slept with other women. And she hadn't rushed away after locking him in his cell. It had seemed like she hadn't wanted to leave him.

The kiss—the ear nibble—hadn't been premeditated, at least not for more than a minute, but he admitted it had been an experiment. To see if she would show any interest or not. She hadn't passionately thrown her arms around him—the bars would have made that difficult—but she hadn't pulled away. And he was positive that she had been the one to lean in for a kiss. At least he thought so. By that point, he hadn't been thinking about much except how appealing her lips were and how it would be nice to see her naked again someday, under less invasive circumstances.

A soft click came from the top of the stairs, followed by a faint creak. Footsteps sounded on the cement steps, and the guard said, "Archmage," in a polite tone.

Jev eyed the position of the sunbeam. It wasn't noon yet. Assuming the archmage would give her inquisitor at least five or six hours to sleep, Jev hadn't expected visitors until well into the afternoon.

The archmage—What was her name? Sazshen?—bypassed the other dungeon inmate and stopped in front of Jev's cell. She wore a blue robe similar to Zenia's, except braided gold thread lined the hems, and a thick gold chain, rather than a simple silver necklace, held her dragon tear.

Another woman stepped into view beside her. It wasn't Zenia.

Nerves thumped around in Jev's belly. Had she been taken off the case because of the almost-kiss? He hadn't intended to get her into trouble.

Still, maybe this was for the best. He wouldn't want Zenia to be a part of an interrogation, not when he was the *subject* of the interrogation. Though he didn't want to make assumptions, he thought it might distress her to interrogate him, no matter how benign she believed her methods were.

"Your meal did not agree with you, Zyndar Dharrow?" Sazshen asked.

Her assistant, a younger woman but still someone with silver threading through her black hair, clasped her hands behind her back and did not speak. She did, however, gaze with intense interest at Jev, and he thought she might be using magic on him, a gentle probing of his thoughts. Gentle for *now*.

"I haven't had time to eat it yet," Jev said. "I like to relax before I dine so I can truly savor the taste and appreciate the meal."

Sazshen looked down at the soggy pile of steamed gort and the hard biscuits on the plate, no sign of jam or butter to improve their flavor. She cocked her eyebrows.

"I hope you're not implying those biscuits aren't palatable," Jev said. "If so, I'll be terribly disappointed. Since this is one of the fanciest temples in the capital, I was expecting far better rations than I dined on during the war." He doubted anything would come out of it but figured it couldn't hurt to remind her that he'd been a soldier, a soldier who had loyally served the king for many, many years.

"I find your mouth wearying, and I've only just met you," Sazshen observed. "One wonders what spell you cast to alter Inquisitor Cham's perception of it."

"Well, she saw me naked."

If he'd hoped for a smirk or a snort with the comment, he didn't get it. Odd to think Zenia might be the least repressed inquisitor in the temple.

"Which unfortunately creates a conflict of interest," Sazshen said. "Admittedly not one I've had to accuse her of having often. She won't be punished, if it matters to you."

"Uh, I'm glad to hear that." The idea that she *might* have been punished—had this archmage contemplated that?—for having feelings toward him floored him. He wasn't a damn criminal. He was an army captain and a zyndar from a long line of men and women who had risked—and sometimes *given*—their lives for the kingdom. This situation was insufferable.

"I don't expect that it *does* matter to you. I assume you kissed her to win her leniency during the interrogation?"

Jev thought about pointing out that he'd only sucked on Zenia's earlobe—far too briefly—and that they hadn't *gotten* to the kiss, but he couldn't see the distinction mattering to the crone. "Assume what you want. You people seem to have decided I was guilty of a crime before I set foot on kingdom land."

He stared up at the ceiling. It was possible that being properly respectful and obsequious would get him further with the archmage, but after all he'd been through in his life, he couldn't bring himself to kiss her ass. Or her earlobe.

"With good reason," Sazshen said. "Tell us where the artifact is."

The back of his skull prickled, and the probe he'd only suspected earlier grew more unmistakable now. It started as an itch, but it quickly grew into a dull ache that throbbed in sync with the ache in his shoulder. It sure would be nice if someone would offer him a salve for that bullet wound.

"Doesn't it have a name?" Jev asked, though he already knew it. He hoped that in slipping in a few questions of his own, he might learn some information as they interrogated him. "Maybe people would have an easier time finding it for you if you called it by name and gave out a better description."

"You already know it's called the Eye of Truth, but if you truly need a description..." Sazshen flicked two fingers toward her assistant.

An image popped unbidden into Jev's mind. An ivory carving in the shape of a tree, a single eye looking out like an owl from a hole in the side. He had barely glanced at the carving years ago, but he recognized it and knew right away that his guess had been correct. This was one of the charms, or what Jev had taken for charms, that his brother had been wearing on a wrist bracelet when he died.

And where was it now? Jev still had no idea.

Really? a sarcastic voice spoke into his mind. Sazshen's.

He frowned over at the women, both of whom looked intently at him, their faces cool masks of concentration.

"If you can see my thoughts, you know it was my brother who acquired it somehow," Jev said. "I've only heard rumors and gossip about what he was doing before he shipped off to Taziira."

Sazshen looked over at her colleague. The woman looked back at her, and they shared nods, then focused again on Jev. He didn't find their mental intrusion as alarming as he would have in his youth, before he'd had countless experiences with elven magic, but he did find it disturbing. And he wasn't surprised when the ache at the back of his skull grew more intense.

We'll see, Sazshen spoke into his mind.

Jev tried to stare at the ceiling and appear indifferent to the pain. At first, he managed a stoic facade as they scoured his mind, their search of his thoughts feeling like fiery knives raking across his brain. He didn't know if they needed to cause pain to search, but they were doing so, perhaps believing he would be more likely to yield what he knew if they hurt him. Maybe there was some truth to that. Maybe a man in pain would have a harder time walling off his thoughts. Or maybe they just enjoyed this excuse to hurt him. He got a sense of self-righteous satisfaction from one of them, the belief that she was right in punishing him for all the sins he'd ever committed, all the blasphemous thoughts he'd ever had toward one of the dragon founders or those who served them.

Then the pain rose in intensity, and he could no longer contemplate their motives. He couldn't contemplate anything. It all grew to be too much, and he cried out in pain, grabbing his temples and praying this would all end soon.

CHAPTER 14

ZENIA WOKE WITH A START, her heart thundering in her chest. Her blankets lay rumpled around her, and sweat dampened her nightshirt. She felt like she'd been entrenched in the clutches of a nightmare, but she couldn't remember anything.

That morning, she'd closed her shutters on the bright sun, taken a sleeping draught the healer Mage Heryn had brought by, and hoped she wouldn't lie awake and dwell on Sazshen's disappointment. She hadn't. She'd dropped off into an exhausted slumber.

Feeling hungover and groggy, Zenia pushed herself to her feet. She stepped over the sheepskin rug to open the shutters and let in sunlight. The clock on the wall said it was a little after noon, and vendors in the temple square shouted, hawking their lunchtime offerings.

She wondered when Sazshen would come get her for the interrogation. Or *if* she would.

After seeing Zenia so close to Jev, Sazshen might doubt her reliability or willingness to interrogate him. Her dedication to duty. But Zenia *would* question him. She wouldn't let burgeoning feelings get in the way of her duty. If she was able to clear his name, they could pursue a relationship later. If he truly wanted that. Did he? Or had he had an ulterior motive for kissing her? Almost kissing her.

A stab of disappointment went through her that they hadn't gotten a chance to truly kiss. But perhaps this was best. He might have simply been trying to manipulate her. Suborn her somehow. Make her want to sneak down to the dungeon in the dark of night, let him go, and then turn her back so he could escape.

As if she could do that. But did she truly think he would ask? If she'd accepted him as honorable in other areas, could she truly believe he would try to manipulate her?

"I don't know," she muttered, donning her robe.

She plucked up her brush from the dresser and poured water into the washbasin. She *did* know it would be wise to wait until after Jev was cleared of doubt and this artifact had been recovered before contemplating anything romantic. It boggled her mind that she might even *want* to contemplate romance. She, the woman who men always considered too dedicated to her duty to approach, too frosty. Too intimidating.

Jev had never been intimidated by her. She smiled, suspecting there weren't many people who had ever intimidated him.

But could there truly be any future for them? She had always wanted to wait for marriage to have sex, to risk having children, and he was zyndar. What zyndar, especially one from such a renowned family, would marry a commoner?

A distant scream reached her ears, and she slammed her brush down. Had that come from within the temple or from outside somewhere? The thick stone walls muffled sound and made it hard to pinpoint origins.

The scream sounded again, a male scream. Her gut sank as certainty grasped her. Jev.

Zenia spun, yanked open the door, and sprinted down the corridor of sleeping quarters and through the great hall. As she ran, she realized Mage Heryn must have brought that draught by at Sazshen's request. To make sure Zenia slept through the morning and stayed out of the way.

Supplicants, devotees, and people there to pay for their official blessed fortunes all turned at her swift passage, gaping at her as she ran, her blue robe slapping at her ankles.

She ground her teeth in anger and worry and ignored them all, racing through another corridor and to the stairs. She almost mowed over the dungeon guard as she passed, but he wisely stepped back, pressing his shoulder blades to the wall.

When Zenia rounded the corridor to sprint for Jev's cell, she almost crashed into Sazshen and Inquisitor Marlyna.

"You started without me?" Zenia blurted, unable to keep it from sounding like an accusation.

She craned her neck to look past them, toward Jev's cell. And her gut sank again. She could only see his arm but could tell from its position that he lay on the floor on his back. And that he wasn't moving.

"We've completed the interrogation," Sazshen said unemotionally. "He—"

Zenia pushed between them and ran to Jev's cell. His eyes were closed, his arms and legs splayed, his face tilted toward the ceiling. Blood trickled from his nose and his left ear.

"What did you *do*?" she whispered.

They hadn't relocked the cell door, so Zenia thrust it open and went in, kneeling beside him. She touched his face and drew upon her gem's magic, though there was little she could do besides confirming he was alive but unconscious. For the first time ever, she wished she'd chosen a different career and studied the healer's profession, learned to use her dragon tear for helping people. Then she could have helped him.

"I deemed that you were too close to him," Sazshen said, "and might not perform an effective interrogation."

"I can *always* perform an effective interrogation." Zenia glowered at Sazshen, knowing she shouldn't argue with her senior—the most senior person in the temple and the most powerful member of the Order of the Blue Dragon in the capital, if not the kingdom. But she couldn't think about her career now, only her anger. Anger that Sazshen had replaced her with someone else and anger that they'd hurt Jev when it hadn't been necessary.

She didn't hurt people when she questioned them. Marlyna was known for having a heavy hand and dragging her long fingernails through people's minds. Sazshen knew that. Had she chosen Marlyna on purpose? Had Sazshen, for some reason, *wanted* Jev hurt? But why? As far as Zenia knew, Sazshen didn't have a grudge against the zyndar the way some did. The way *Zenia* did.

"I'm glad to know that," Sazshen said, calm in the face of Zenia's ire. "Since I would like to keep you on the assignment. He trusts you, as we learned, and that could be useful."

Zenia took a deep breath, struggling to gather her wits—and her own calmness. Nothing could be gained by yelling at Sazshen. And much could be lost.

"He doesn't know where it is, does he?" Zenia asked.

"No, but he had it at one point four years ago."

"Oh?" That surprised her.

"Apparently, he didn't know what it was or even that it was magical." Sazshen's lips thinned in skepticism, and she looked to Marlyna. For confirmation?

Marlyna nodded once.

"His brother had it and died wearing it. He never said anything about it, not even with his dying breath. Maybe the fool also didn't know what it was." Sazshen lifted her eyes toward the heavens. "Jevlain Dharrow sent it home with the rest of his brother's personal belongings, and that was the last he saw of it."

"So... the brother was the thief?" Zenia still didn't grasp what had happened, and that frustrated her. She wasn't used to feeling slow. "He stole it from the temple, then sailed off to join the war to avoid our wrath?"

Zenia had worked at the temple when all this would have been happening, and she had already been an inquisitor, a trusted devotee of the Water Order. She didn't remember any news of an artifact theft.

"From someone who was bringing it to the temple for our safekeeping, yes," Sazshen said.

"Who?"

"One of our trusted inquisitors. It's an elven artifact."

"Something that had to do with the war? Or would have affected it?" Zenia hated vague answers. If she'd been questioning a criminal, she would have used her gem's power to ensure the answers she received were specific and exactly what she wanted. But she couldn't use her magic on Sazshen, not without her knowing it. Further, Sazshen had the power to defend herself from magical prying.

"Something that would have affected it greatly, yes. Something that could have caused riots in the streets here at home. In the entire kingdom. We couldn't have allowed that, not with our forces split between Kor and Taziira. We needed to keep the artifact safe. That it was stolen was horrific, a terrible failing on our part. It's only the founders' luck that it hasn't been used in the past four years."

Sazshen shook her head, and even though Zenia didn't draw upon her magic, she sensed the archmage was telling the truth, even if she was still being irritatingly vague about it.

"And would it have value now?" Zenia asked. "The potential to cause riots?"

Sazshen's gaze sharpened. "It has great value. And the potential to change the course of history. We must have it back." Sazshen extended her hand toward Zenia, not looking at the unconscious Jev beside her. "I know you're frustrated and want better answers, Zenia. Because I know *you*. But some secrets must be kept to a select few, to those who have been chosen to protect all that we believe and hold dear. Some secrets are too dangerous for the general populace to know."

Zenia kept her face from scrunching up with skepticism—and being considered part of the "general populace." Barely.

"One day, I will share all of my secrets with my successor." Sazshen spread her palm toward Zenia. "With you, I hope."

Behind her, Marlyna stirred, but she did not say anything.

"But you must do one more task for me, Zenia. Get the artifact and bring it home. Where it'll be safe, and where its secrets won't cause riots. It is up to us to protect the kingdom from further trouble. From future follies."

Future follies? Did she speak of the potential for another war? Or reference the last one?

Zenia knew that only one of the elemental Orders had sided openly with the king in his decision to take forces to Taziira, but she hadn't heard Sazshen speak against the war or the old king. None of the archmages had. Because they hadn't dared? Zenia didn't know, but she did know that King Abdor had been rumored to command numerous assassins and that people who vocally opposed his rule had occasionally disappeared.

"How do I find it?" Zenia laid a hand on Jev's chest. He still hadn't stirred.

"Go with him, and I think he'll lead you to it. He believes he can piece together clues from questioning people within Dharrow Castle. And if he can't, I'm sure *you* can."

Dharrow Castle. Zenia stared bleakly at Sazshen. Jev had wanted to go back there the night before. No, he'd never wanted to leave. But Zenia had finagled him into coming to the temple. If he had stayed at his home, he might have already located the gem. Zenia could have walked up this morning, explained that it was stolen, and taken it from him.

All this pain and effort had been for naught. She gazed down at him, at the blood dried on his face.

"Find it and bring it back to the temple," Sazshen ordered. "He shouldn't have any need for it, and he understands that it's not his to keep."

Zenia kept her face toward Jev instead of looking at Sazshen, but frustration welled inside of her. Not only had all this pain been for naught, but if someone from the Water Order had simply walked up and explained everything to Jev when he stepped off his ship, he likely would have cooperated. All this secrecy and suspicion had only made everything worse.

"I understand," she forced herself to say as she looked up. "I'll go with him, and we'll find it."

"Then bring it back to me. The new king will be crowned tomorrow. We must have this artifact in our safekeeping so it can't be used to cause trouble during or after the ceremony. The kingdom is already in an upheaval over the deaths of Abdor and the princes. It can't take more upheaval right now."

Zenia thought it was interesting that Sazshen mentioned keeping the artifact safe during the coronation, not sharing it or information about it with the new king. Would he ever be informed? This Eye of Truth sounded like something he should know about if it could possibly affect all of Kor someday.

Sensing Sazshen wouldn't answer any more questions if she asked, Zenia nodded and said, "I'll find it."

"And bring it back," Sazshen repeated, her eyes narrowing.

"Yes, of course, Archmage," Zenia said, stung that her superior might doubt her after all these years. And doubt that she would do everything she could to ensure Sazshen had good reason to name Zenia as her successor.

Zenia wanted that position more than ever now. So there would be no more secrets that were inaccessible to her. She wanted all the knowledge and to understand everything going on in the city and the world around her.

"I'll bring it back."

Jev woke with a throbbing headache and squinted at the light coming through the window. It was too bright. Too irritating.

A hand touched his face, surprising him. He turned toward it, even though his eyes couldn't deal with the light yet, and he couldn't see the owner. Immediately, he sensed that it wasn't either of those two shrews who'd tortured him.

"Zenia?" he guessed.

"Yes." Her thumb brushed his cheek.

That was promising. He realized he was lying on the floor of his cell. That was less promising.

"You'll have a headache for a while, I'm afraid, as I can't do anything about mental pain, but I've applied a healing salve to your bullet wound. And, uhm, also to your eardrum and the membrane in the nostril that split open."

"Membrane?" Jev touched his nose.

He remembered a warm trickle of blood coming from his ear earlier, but he'd been in so much pain from whatever those women had done inside his skull, he'd barely noticed it. He didn't remember a nosebleed at all, but it didn't surprise him.

"Yes, up in your nose. I couldn't find anything to more easily slide the salve up there, so I used my finger. Sorry about that."

"You stuck your finger up my nose? Huh. You're a good woman."

She snorted. "Yes, I am."

Her humor didn't last long. She laid a hand on his chest. "I'm sorry they hurt you. That wasn't necessary. I was—I still am—angry that I wasn't allowed to handle it. I know it doesn't make any difference to you now, but *I* don't hurt people when I question them." She lowered her voice to a whisper. "I'm also angry that Archmage Sazshen had someone bring me a sleeping potion so I didn't know any of this was happening. I thought she was being considerate. She just wanted me out of the way because she thought I was *biased*."

"Are you?" Jev remembered the almost kiss and managed a roguish smile for her. Or maybe it was a wan smile. That light was still bright, and his eyes were watering.

"Perhaps a little."

"Does that mean you'll quit your job in an indignant huff and flee the harsh ways of your temple?"

"Actually, I'm trying to get a promotion."

He managed a short, hoarse laugh. But she wasn't laughing. He pried his eyes open, looking for humor on her face, only to see that she was utterly serious.

"If I were archmage, I could do much to effect change in the temple, and it's what I've worked for my whole life."

"Your whole life? You can't even be that old. Thirty?" He felt like a hypocrite after the words came out. He was only thirty-three. When had that started seeming *old*? After five or six years of fighting in Taziira, he supposed.

"I'm thirty-two. I became an inquisitor at twenty-two, the youngest ever in the history of the Water Order. I'd been apprenticed to another inquisitor—he has since retired—for more than five years before that. And for the five before that, I was in school here in the temple, being taught everything. I didn't know how to read and had no education at all before I was orphaned, before they took me in. I owe the temple a lot."

"I... see." Jev had been joking when he'd suggested she quit—sort of—but he wouldn't have made the joke if he'd known all that. He had no trouble grasping loyalty and why it was important. Raised on the Zyndar Code of Honor, he understood it perhaps more than most. He just wished she didn't feel it toward the people who had tortured him.

"Who was—is?—your father?" Jev asked, remembering Iridium's words about Zenia's heritage.

If her father was zyndar, why would she have been orphaned? Jev knew about bastard children that randy zyndar men had out of wedlock, and that such a child would be denied any inheritance and might not be acknowledged, but most men quietly gave the mother some money and saw to it the child could go to school and have opportunities.

Zenia leaned back, looking toward the high window. Deciding whether to answer? Maybe she didn't want him knowing that much about her, or feared he would use the knowledge against her somehow.

"Zyndar Veran Morningfar," she said quietly.

"Oh?" Jev knew the name. He was familiar with people from most of the zyndar families in the kingdom since his father had often sent him to social gatherings in the city and dinners at Alderoth Castle—his father hated such things and had been glad when Jev had turned sixteen, the age one was allowed to be named heir and sent off to represent the family. "He's zyndar prime and owner of all the Morningfar land, isn't he? It's a small estate, and the Morningfars aren't the oldest and most prosperous family, but he should have had enough money to send any offspring to school."

He extended a hand toward her and didn't say more, not wanting to presume to know the story just because Iridium had blabbed some details. Details that might be little more than false gossip.

"Yes." Zenia shifted her gaze to the stone floor. "He has money enough to feed and clothe his mistresses if he chose, I'm certain."

Jev wrinkled his nose at the thought of the gangly rat-faced Veran having hordes of mistresses. Jev had only spoken to him a few times but distinctly remembered him being condescending and haughty. He always had a foul-smelling cigar dangling from his mouth at gatherings, the smoke lingering around him and his chosen cronies like a curtain. If he was Zenia's father, it was amazing she was such a beautiful woman.

"It wasn't money for school I wanted. I wouldn't have asked for anything since I didn't know the man—my mother gave me his name but not much else. I certainly never got the impression they'd had some passionate affair. More that my mother had made a mistake. She told me never to ask him for anything, but that was before she took ill. Shrumphasis. You know it?"

She didn't look at his eyes when she asked. She seemed to be finding the stone floor tiles fascinating. It would take too much effort for Jev to roll over and contemplate their fascination for himself.

"Something that causes heart defects, right?"

"A bacterial infection that does, yes. A healer using magic can cure it, but it takes several treatments to fully eradicate the bacteria, and then hours of work to repair the heart. We went to the public hospital and signed up, but we didn't have any money. My mother had worked as a weaver when I was growing up, and she made enough to keep us fed and in a room we shared with another mother and daughter. But there was never extra money to save, and she... I'm sure she didn't expect such a disease to strike her down." Zenia's already soft voice grew softer as she whispered, "She wasn't that old."

"How old were *you*?" Jev couldn't help but compare her childhood to his. Sharing a *room* with another family? He and his brother had shared the second floor in the north wing of the castle. They'd had the services of a nanny, tutors, and a cook whenever they wished.

"Eleven. As I said, we went to the hospital and signed up for the charity program, but as you probably know, you have to wait months for treatment." Zenia looked at his face. "I guess you wouldn't know, actually."

She didn't sound bitter. Maybe because this had all happened twenty years ago, some of the edge had worn off. Or maybe not. Jev remembered the cool way she'd originally greeted him, the little comments that gave away her bitterness toward the zyndar, toward their wealth and special treatment in society. Maybe she just didn't feel bitter toward *him* anymore.

If so, that was an improvement.

"She got worse while we waited her turn for treatment," Zenia said. "I realized she wouldn't make it. I went to Morningfar's townhouse." Now, she curled her lip. Showing her distaste for someone who had multiple homes across the kingdom.

Jev decided not to mention that the Dharrows had a townhouse, too, even if his father never used it, preferring working the land with his tenants to hosting social gatherings in the city. The last Jev had heard, one of his cousins who taught at the university lived there.

"It took three tries before I could get past his henchmen to talk to him," Zenia said.

"His henchmen? Like his personal guard?" Jev also decided not to mention that Dharrow Castle employed a couple dozen such men to protect the family on trips off the property.

"I think one was his butler. They all seemed henchman-ish to an eleven-year-old girl. I finally managed to yell across the courtyard to him as two men were pulling me away. I told him who my mother was and that she needed help. I asked for a loan, not a handout. I guess he didn't think a dumb kid could ever pay back a loan, but *I* would have."

She lifted her chin in that now-familiar gesture Jev had been considering haughtiness. He decided it was determination.

"He walked over to look at me and waved for his henchmen to set me down. I thought he was willing to listen, that he might help. A woman had come out of the townhouse by then. His wife, maybe. I thought he might want to look good—be generous—in front of her. He bent and looked me square in the eye to say he didn't give charity to beggars. I tried to tell him he was my father and about my mother's illness and that I could take him to see her if he wanted, but he ordered his men to carry me out, and I distinctly remember him saying he'd have them flogged if they let me back in." Zenia shook her head. "I didn't want to try again after that because I didn't want other people to be hurt because of me. Besides, he'd recognized my mother's name when I gave it. I'm sure if it. I saw it in his eyes. He knew I wasn't some street urchin with no connection to him. He just didn't care."

Jev was fairly certain he'd heard something about Morningfar and his wife celebrating their fortieth anniversary right before he'd gone off to the war. Which meant he'd been married when Zenia had been born—and conceived. The old man probably hadn't wanted his wife to hear evidence that he'd been unfaithful, even if such was common among some zyndar, despite the Code of Honor forbidding it.

"He's an asshole," Jev said.

Even if he could understand why the man hadn't spoken to his offspring by another woman in front of his wife, he didn't condone it. If nothing else, Morningfar would have had the resources to find Zenia and her dying mother in the city later if he'd wished to do so.

Zenia smiled slightly. "I certainly thought so."

"Did you tell him?"

"I was too busy being hauled out of the courtyard, kicking and punching at the henchman carrying me over his shoulder like a side of beef. I may have called *him* an asshole."

"Misplaced anger, I fear."

"Yes. Perhaps if I chance across Morningfar someday, I'll belatedly let him know."

"I believe he's in his seventies now," Jev said.

"Is there an age cut-off for when insults can be delivered to a man?"

"Probably not. He might even wet himself if you showed up at his door in your robe, implying he's guilty of some crime."

Zenia's smile turned bleak. "I wish he were, but not supporting your mistress's children—or your mistress herself—isn't a crime."

"A shame." Jev wondered if that was something she would try to change if she became archmage of the temple.

Sometime during her sharing of her history, she'd stopped stroking his face. Lamentable, but he hitched himself up on one elbow. He needed to figure out what he was supposed to do next. He assumed his interrogators had gotten everything out of his mind and realized it wasn't much. Would they keep him locked up?

He pushed himself into a sitting position. The cell door was open behind Zenia.

"Does your father have any bastards?" Zenia asked.

"Uhm, technically, yes. He's had a couple of lovers since my mother disappeared, and he never married any of them. They were women from one of our villages. They probably bonded over fixing some fences together, then got randy."

Judging by Zenia's dark expression, she didn't want a humorous answer.

Jev cleared his throat. "He acknowledges the women and their children. The last I knew—before I left for Taziira—I had three half-sisters and no half-brothers, at least not yet. I have no idea what's been going on lately. My cousin Wyleria wrote me from time to time, but her preference is to gossip about *other* people's families, not her own. My father never wrote me. We're not that close."

"Ah."

He didn't know if he'd given her the answer she wanted. It was the truth, and that was all he could offer her, but she may have hoped his father was too honorable to have children out of wedlock.

"Do you?" Zenia looked in his eyes.

"Have bastards? I don't think so. I was engaged to be married before I left, but her children... aren't mine." Jev looked at the cell door again, wondering if he could convince Zenia they should wander out instead of discussing his past. "She wasn't my first lover, but there weren't that many before then. I'd pined for her since I was about fourteen, you see. She was two years older, and it took me a few years to convince her she pined for me too."

Alas, her pining had not survived distance and time. Damn, he didn't want to talk about this with Zenia. Or anyone.

"So, what's my status among your Order friends?" He pointed at the open door. "Did you forget to close that or am I being encouraged to wander off?"

She kept looking at him, not at the door, and he didn't need magic to sense that she wanted to ask for more details about his one-time fiancée.

"Actually," Zenia said, "you *are* being encouraged to wander off. And I'm being encouraged to follow you."

"Oh?" Jev asked, relieved she'd dropped the subject.

"Archmage Sazshen believes you don't know where the artifact is, but she also believes you'll find it if she lets you go. You'll want to clear your name and remove any doubt about your honor, and you can only do that by turning it in. So, you'll look for it promptly. And if I'm with you, I'll be there when you find it. Or maybe I can see something you don't and *help* you find it. I know you haven't seen me do anything brilliant yet, but I *am* good at solving puzzles."

"If Master Grindmor finds her diamond tools in a pumping station, I'll surely believe you."

She snorted. "That was just a guess."

"A thoughtful one, I imagine. All right, the artifact. Once I—or we—find it, you're to take it from me?"

Zenia didn't hesitate to nod. "I am. The archmage believes you won't object since it's not yours. It's only chance that it passed through your fingers at one time."

"No kidding. I wish she'd figured that out before she sent her henchmen after me."

"Her henchmen?" Zenia touched her chest—she was clad in a fresh blue inquisitor robe. "Me?"

"I suppose I should have said henchwomen, but I don't think that's a word. It definitely *should* be." Jev rolled himself to his feet, glad his shoulder only stung minutely, and offered Zenia a hand, hoping she knew he was joking.

"The archmage has arranged for Rhi to meet us out front soon with horses." Zenia accepted his hand and let him pull her to her feet. "I'll share your label with her, that you consider her a henchwoman."

"Do you think she'll object?"

"Perhaps not. She's proud of her deadliness. She would prefer it if more people shrank away from her than they did from me."

"Would *you* prefer it?" Jev wondered if she had deliberately cultivated that reputation or if it had simply evolved over the years due to her deeds.

"I wouldn't mind. Being considered powerful and threatening isn't quite the boon I once thought it would be." She regarded him curiously. "It surprised me that you were never uneasy in my presence. Even though I'd come to arrest you."

"I'm not easily scared anymore. I've seen... a lot." A lot that he didn't want to talk about any more than he wanted to talk about the woman who hadn't waited for him. "Let's head out, shall we?"

Zenia released his hand and stepped into the corridor. "Yes, we should hurry, so you can start questioning people tonight. The new king's coronation is tomorrow, and all the zyndar families will likely attend, as well as everyone else with the wherewithal to snag an invitation to the event. Three days of festivities and holidays are scheduled after it. It may be hard to find anyone to question then."

"Yes, I imagine so." In addition, he might receive an invitation to the event and be expected to come.

Jev would like to see Targyon crowned and give him a solid thump on the shoulder, but would Zenia object if he wandered off before finding the artifact? Even if she'd stuck a finger up his nose and almost kissed him, he couldn't forget that she worked for the woman who had tortured him.

CHAPTER 15

WHEN ZENIA SAW RHI STANDING at the back door of the temple with three horses, she rushed over and hugged her, forgetting to portray a professional image for Jev and anyone else around. Rhi grinned and hugged her back, the bottom of her bo clattering on the cobblestones.

"I was *wondering* how long it would take you to get back," Rhi said when they parted.

Jev stopped a few feet away, waiting while they had their reunion.

"We got back early this morning," Zenia said.

"Yes, I heard you were taking a nap."

Zenia faltered over what should have been a witty reply as she tried to decide if Rhi had somehow been in on that deception, if she'd known Sazshen had ordered that sleeping draught brought to her. Probably not. Rhi wore an affable easygoing grin. One free of guilt. She likely didn't know anything about the potion—or that Jev had been tortured.

Zenia glanced at him, and Rhi's gaze also drifted in his direction.

"You're looking a lot prettier today than you were yesterday, Zyndar." Rhi gave him a lazy wink.

"I thought I might convince the inquisitor to change her gaze from withering to appreciative if I cleaned up," Jev said.

"If you manage that, let me know. You'll be the first man she hasn't withered."

Jev's eyebrows rose, and Zenia blushed.

"We have a new mission," Zenia said, taking the reins of one horse from Rhi. "We have to head back up the highway to Dharrow Castle.

Is the road safe now? Have you heard? And what happened to you last night? We came to the edge of the mangroves to look, but I didn't see you anywhere. And there were people searching for us so we couldn't stay."

"A couple of thugs leaped out of the shadows, startling my horse before I got to the village. I was thrown, and the men attacked me. No explanation. I attacked them back. As one does." She patted her bo. "They had guns, but I knocked them out of their hands, and they couldn't find them again in the dark. I then convinced them to run away. Wish I'd questioned them. By the time I got to the village, the golems were gone, and so were all the inhabitants. While I was trying to figure out why someone had constructed an attack in the first place, I came across two of the watchmen we'd been working with. They were injured, one badly, and I worried he would die if I didn't take him straight to the hospital. It wasn't an easy decision to leave you behind, and I apologize for not coming back to tell you, but I judged that he didn't have much time. When I got to the hospital, the healer said that judgment was right. I hope he pulled through after all that. I'll go check tomorrow. Before the coronation. Did you hear all about that? We should get a couple of days off."

"Was she this chatty yesterday?" Jev asked.

"No, but this isn't atypical," Zenia said. "Yesterday, she was being aloof and intimidating to keep you in line."

"*She* was? Or you were?"

"We use some of the same tactics." Rhi thumped Zenia on the shoulder, then mounted her horse. "I'm ready when you two slowpokes are."

Zenia and Jev mounted their horses and let Rhi lead the way out of the city. The sun had dropped below the horizon, and the waning light reminded Zenia far too much of the circumstances of the night before. Now, she wished she hadn't spent as much time with her hand on Jev's chest, talking to him in his cell. It would have been better to reach his castle before nightfall. Or to wait until the following day to go, but Sazshen had made it clear she wanted this resolved quickly.

"I hope Iridium doesn't have all her thugs out looking for us again," Zenia said.

She knew Master Grindmor had wreaked some havoc as part of her diversion, but she didn't know how long it would take Iridium to recover. Or how vengeful she would feel afterward.

"As do I," Jev said. "I don't want trouble to follow me home. Our villages aren't walled, nor do the people usually keep weapons close at hand. Not these days. Back in the days when highwaymen, mercenaries, and all-out invasions from Tortlar and Ska were common, they didn't go out to the field without their bows, but… it's been a peaceful fifty years. Except for the wars we've started with others." His jaw set as he gazed straight ahead.

Zenia wondered if that meant he hadn't been an advocate of the war. If not, why had he served for so long? She knew the eldest sons had been expected to join the king's army, but she'd also heard of wealthy zyndar families paying a fee as an alternative and the crown finding that acceptable. Surely, his family had the money for that.

"We might be going back to the ways of highwaymen." Rhi pointed to the road ahead. A single rider waited atop a hill, a cloak pulled over his or her head.

Zenia groaned. They weren't even a mile out of the city yet.

She touched the pistol she'd acquired from the temple armory, a replacement for the one she'd lost. "That's not another one of Iridium's assassins, is it?"

In the fading light, she couldn't tell if the rider's cloak was black or another dark color.

"Nah," Jev said after a moment of consideration. "That's Lornysh."

"Your elf friend?" That didn't make Zenia relax, not at all. "How can you tell from this distance when he's got his cloak up?"

"By the haughty way he sits on that horse."

Zenia squinted at him, suspecting a joke.

Jev only kept a straight face for two seconds before breaking into a grin. "There's also a bow and quiver of arrows poking up over his shoulder. Most people—human people—prefer rifles and pistols these days."

"Ah."

"Elves don't like the noise of firearms. Interferes with their stealthy sneaking about in the forest." Jev nudged his horse into a trot and passed Rhi.

The cloaked figure did not lift a hand or acknowledge his approach. Zenia worried Jev might have been mistaken.

"We're not going to have to fight Points again, are we?" Rhi asked, riding up the slope beside Zenia.

"Points?"

"The elf. With the pointed ears. You haven't heard that term?"

"No, but I don't usually arrest elves. Even half elves have been seldom seen in the city since the war began."

"True."

When Jev reached the top of the hill, the rider pushed back his hood, and silver hair spilled to his shoulders.

"You decided on a cloak?" Jev was asking when Zenia rode up. "After roaming through the city and the countryside in your distinctive warden greens?"

"Your cousin gave it to me and suggested I wear it around your land in case people saw me."

"And you listened to her? I'm positive I made the same suggestion."

"Yes, but she's female."

"So, her suggestions are more worth listening to?"

"They're harder to say no to. Even though I attempted to refuse, she thrust the cloak, a blanket, fire starters, food, a canteen, and round, flat sweet wafers into my arms."

"Cookies," Jev suggested. "You've heard the men speak wistfully of them."

"Ah. Regardless, it seemed rude to completely reject the suggestions of someone outfitting me for camping, as she called it, on your property."

"What do elves call it?" Rhi asked.

The elf—what was his name? Lornysh?—turned his cool blue eyes toward her, and Zenia feared drawing his attention hadn't been wise. He'd been chatting easily enough with Jev, but memories of that swift— and depressingly one-sided—attack flashed through Zenia's mind.

"Living." Lornysh tilted his head toward Zenia and Rhi, then looked to Jev.

"Yes, introductions are in order, aren't they? Reintroductions. Inquisitor Zenia Cham." Jev pointed at her, then at Rhi. "And monk Rhi She-didn't-tell-me-her-last-name."

Rhi snorted. "Lin. Sexy, isn't it?"

"These are the women who arrested you yesterday," Lornysh said.

"Elves are known for being observant," Jev told Zenia.

"Are you still under arrest?" Lornysh ignored the aside and gazed coolly at the women.

Zenia found his chilly gaze uncomfortable and believed she would have even if they hadn't fought before.

"No," Jev said. "I've been questioned, and now I'm being followed."

"Then they are still enemies."

"Not entirely." Jev looked at Zenia, and she flushed as she remembered the ear nibble.

It was growing darker, so she wasn't sure if she truly saw the elf wrinkle his nose in distaste, but he oozed distaste regardless of nose activity.

"Have you seen Cutter?" Jev asked him. "Is he all right?"

"Briefly, this morning. He sensed someone had called upon rock golems and went out to investigate."

"Yes, that was Master Grindmor's work, I believe. I have a story to tell him."

"If the female dwarf he wishes to apprentice to is involved," Lornysh said, "I'm sure he'll be interested."

"He's always interested in my stories. They're scintillating."

The elf's eyebrows twitched.

"My charm works on elves too," Jev told Zenia.

"Clearly."

"I have something to show you on your family's land, Jev." Lornysh turned his horse away from the city and started it forward at a quick pace without waiting for a response.

"Did you do research about my problem even though I told you to relax and enjoy yourself?" Jev nudged his horse into a trot to catch up with him.

Zenia did not want to rush to keep up and be seen as an eavesdropper, but she also didn't want to miss the conversation. Even though she no longer mistrusted Jev, Sazshen would want her standing at his side if he received any information about the artifact.

"Last night, I listened in on several conversations among the people who live in your castle," Lornysh said.

"Did they know you were listening in?"

"No. Most of them were talking about the death of the king and the princes and whether Targyon was somehow responsible."

"Uh, he's been in Taziira with the rest of us for the last two years. Him somehow plotting his cousins' deaths is about as likely as me stealing an artifact from across an ocean." Jev glanced back at Zenia.

She thought about retorting, but the elf responded first.

"Yes, he never seemed ambitious and impatient in the way of many young humans," Lornysh said. "Regardless, people were discussing current events rather than butlers who disappeared years ago. I did interact with your cousin when she was piling provisions into my arms, and I asked her directly if she knew anything about the missing man or the package. She said she wasn't living there at the time but remembered your butler well and thought it was odd that he left without word. It was almost as if he'd gone missing in the same way your mother had. He had always been loyal to your family, and your cousin recalled a time when he'd discussed with your father that he hoped to be interred in your family's cemetery, in a small place reserved for honored servants. Apparently, your mother had promised this honor to him before she disappeared. She said your father hadn't seemed pleased by this, but he hadn't objected either."

Zenia wanted to know about Jev's mother—when had *she* gone missing? Had she literally disappeared from the castle one day? Without anyone having a clue where she went? Or had she run off with another man, and everyone was being polite by using *disappeared* as a euphemism? And was it possible her disappearance tied in with the greater mystery of this missing butler? And the missing artifact?

Zenia thought about asking Jev for more details about his mother, but it might be better to keep a few ideas to herself, especially with the hostile elf in earshot. And she admitted that her pride would like it if *she* were the one to solve the mystery and find the artifact.

"That was all she knew," Lornysh said. "I roamed your castle, including all the cellars, last night, looking for clues. Mostly, I learned that you have some interesting art and pottery from past eras and quirky tapestries that seem far more recent. Your accountant's books were particularly dry and not useful."

"I could have told you that," Jev said. "He manages all the family's holdings. His ledgers are basically lists of people paying rent and of repairs made to buildings."

The men fell silent as another group of riders, these heading toward the city, passed them on the highway. People traveling to the capital for the next day's coronation festivities?

"I thought that if the artifact had been sold or some bribe had been made," Lornysh said, "it might be listed in a ledger from the time."

"Ah. But there was nothing?"

"Nothing. This morning, I walked around the estate. That is when I found something that you might believe interesting."

Several moments passed with only the clip clop of the horses' hooves breaking the silence.

"Are you going to tell me what it is?" Jev asked.

"I'm going to show you."

"It's a surprise, is it?"

"I believe it would be best if I didn't taint your perceptions with my own thoughts. You should see it and contemplate it on your own."

Jev didn't respond, and the two men fell silent again.

Zenia let her horse drop back so she could ride beside Rhi, who sat with her bo across her thighs as she looked left and right into the deepening night. They passed the village that had been attacked, dark rubble marking buildings the golems had stomped into pieces. Zenia wondered if Grindmor knew how much damage they had caused or if the Fifth Dragon people had guided them after she called them into existence.

"You think we're actually going to find the artifact before the coronation?" Rhi asked quietly.

"I hope so, but I think that I will, with my Order-provided power as an inquisitor, talk to people around the castle while those two go look at whatever is outside."

"Do you want me to loom threateningly by your side while you do it? Or go keep an eye on them?"

Lornysh's head seemed to turn—it was hard to tell since he'd pulled up the cloak's hood again. Did he object to the idea?

"We'll see," was all Zenia said aloud, but she gave Rhi a firm nod.

***

Lornysh stopped his horse about two hundred meters from the castle, its dozens of wall and walkway lanterns spilling yellow puddles of light onto the moat and pond. He pointed to the left of the road, toward dark land where neither village nor stable nor outbuilding lay.

Jev raised his eyebrows, puzzled as to what his friend could have found out there besides cows or sheep.

"I will take you in that direction," Lornysh said.

"We'll need lights if we're going tramping around in the woods at night. We lowly humans can't see in the dark."

"I can light the way if the female does not." Lornysh pointed at Zenia's chest, presumably suggesting she could illuminate their surroundings with her dragon gem.

She wasn't wearing it openly, but she'd found another chain to attach it around her neck.

"The female?" Jev asked. "That's Zenia. I introduced you."

Zenia and Rhi had been riding several paces behind, but they caught up now, drawing to a stop.

"Is she not female?" Lornysh asked.

"Yes, but I hear inquisitors like to be called by names rather than gender labels."

"They are an uppity folk," Rhi said.

Jev expected Zenia to glare at her, even if it was a mock glare, but her thoughtful gaze was focused on the castle.

"Jev, I wish to speak with your kin," she said, shifting her gaze to him. "While you follow your... friend into the night. I'm more equipped to question people than he is, and you yourself said the answers would likely be among them, right?"

"They're more likely to know where Corvel went," Jev agreed. "But I'm not sure my father will let you roam around the castle. I assume Lornysh roamed sneakily rather than openly."

"*Let* me?" Zenia lifted her chin. "I assure you, he will not impede an investigation by an Order-ordained inquisitor. In fact, he may be the first person I will question."

"That should go well," Jev said dryly.

Her chin did not lower.

"I already asked him about Corvel," Jev said. "He didn't know anything."

"That he told you about, perhaps. I shall see what he knows." Zenia touched her chest where the dragon tear rested.

Jev grimaced. He *did* think Zenia could question his family more effectively than anyone with pointed ears, especially these days, but he worried his father wouldn't bow and scrape sufficiently for her inquisitor tastes. He might throw her into the moat if she tried her magic on him.

Still, what could he do to stop her? She had her mission and was driven by it. All he wanted was to find the damn artifact so he could foist it off on someone else and no longer have to worry about being attacked for it. Or about someone he cared about being attacked.

"You're welcome to try him if you wish," Jev said, "but honestly, I'd start with Mildrey, the cook. She knows the gossip on everyone on this estate, including what's going on with the villagers and their families. My grandmother Visha might know a few things too. She's lived here since my parents were married more than thirty years ago. You just have to convince her not to wander off onto whatever topic comes to mind. She's a bit…"

He rocked his hand, not sure how to explain his grandmother's mental state. All he knew was that she hadn't changed much in the years he'd been gone.

"I'll keep your suggestions in mind. Thank you."

Zenia maneuvered her horse past them and headed for the drawbridge. It amused him that she would go straight into a zyndar stronghold by herself without even asking for an introduction. True, she had been in the courtyard the day before, but it wasn't as if she had done anything then, with her two steam wagons full of watchmen at her back, to endear herself to the family.

"You are not going?" Lornysh asked Rhi, sounding like he *wanted* her to go.

"Someone has to keep an eye on you two boys," Rhi said.

"*Boys?*" Lornysh asked.

"He's never told me," Jev told Rhi, "but I suspect Lorn of being a few centuries old."

"Is that how long it takes for elves to acquire their haughtiness?" Rhi asked.

"Oh, I think they're born with that." Jev smiled at Lornysh to let him know it was a joke, though he doubted Lornysh would be offended either way. He and Cutter were always quick to poke fun at humans, after all.

"Being a nanny there must be a trying gig."

"I'm fairly certain my nanny made the same comment about working here." Jev waved toward the castle. Zenia had already reached the gate and was speaking to the guard on duty.

"Working here and watching you? I believe it." Rhi waved off the road in the direction Lornysh had pointed. "Shall we? I'm sure Zenia will miss my company, so I'd prefer to get this side trip over with as quickly as possible."

As Lornysh wordlessly led the way across the cleared field, Jev wondered if Rhi also worried Zenia would run into trouble with his father. He believed Zenia could handle him, just that it would prove trying. Probably for both of them.

Jev glanced back at the castle a few times as they rode away, not feeling entirely like it was his home. Not the way it once had been. It had changed. Or he had. He still didn't know what he would do when this ended and his father asked him to take up duties related to running the estate, duties he would be expected to handle by himself one day. Not one day soon, he hoped. He didn't relish the idea of running all their properties and businesses. His father could go on living forever if he wished.

A chill breeze blew in from the sea as they wound their way along oft-used trails. For a time, the stars and a half moon provided enough light for them to navigate, but then Lornysh left the trails and headed up a wooded hillside. The leaves blotted out the stars, but soon, a silver glow blossomed from a small magical sphere that floated in the air behind Lornysh.

Rhi muttered something under her breath.

They followed a gully that wound farther inland, the trees thick on its slopes, the terrain rugged enough that nobody had bothered to clear it over the centuries. Or maybe previous zyndar primes had simply wanted some trees to remain on the property for shade and windbreaks. And scenery.

Jev and Vastiun had played in this area as children and even camped out a few times during the summers, so the territory remained familiar, but the gully stretched farther than he remembered. Had he never traveled back this far? He thought he'd covered all of the family's thousands of acres numerous times in his life.

A creek trickled out of a side gully, and Lornysh dismounted. He murmured something to his horse, lifting his hand in a staying motion.

"The foliage will be too dense for the horses," he said, then started up the creek, finding rocks and logs on which to place his feet between dense ferns.

Jev shrugged at Rhi and followed the example, tying his horse's reins to a tree and promising to return soon so the creature wouldn't be stuck in place for long.

Lornysh had already disappeared, and Jev hurried to catch up. Fortunately, the rustle of clothing sounded, guiding him. As stealthy as Lornysh tended to be in the woods, branches and briar thorns that had never seen an axe scraped and caught at his cloak. Of course, they seemed to do a lot more when it came to Jev's and Rhi's clothing, and he struggled to push his way through while keeping from stepping into the creek.

"What led you up this particularly inhospitable gully?" Jev asked as they pushed on for several minutes. It had to have been something. Nobody would simply wade through all this in the name of random exploration.

"You'll see."

Jev was tempted to join Rhi in grumbling—and cursing—under his breath. Lornysh did have a tendency toward the taciturn, but he was being more vague than usual. Because he saw Rhi and Zenia as enemies? People whom he shouldn't speak openly in front of? Understandable, but—

A strange zing of energy ran all over Jev's skin, and he halted. "Uh, Lornysh? Was that you?"

"It was here before I came," Lornysh called softly back, though he wasn't visible through the brush. "Likely since before your family claimed this land."

"We've been here for almost a millennium."

"Yes."

From the sound of his voice, Lornysh had continued on. Jev followed, and the energy subsided. A gasp came from behind him as Rhi passed through the spot.

"What was that?" she asked. "Magic?"

Lornysh didn't reply.

"Either that," Jev said, "or there's a plant back here with a kick."

He remembered the stinging nettles and biting thorns from Taziira.

Their touches had tingled painfully but not in an otherworldly way. Not with strange magical energy.

The silver light grew brighter, and Jev expected to run into Lornysh's back any second, into that orb floating behind him. But the gully opened up, the brush growing less thick, and he saw that the light came from a structure up ahead. A stone pillar that looked like a mix between a tree trunk and a giant mushroom stem. Four symmetrically placed branches arched out from the top and glowed softly, shedding light on the clearing. A couple of curving stone benches rested to either side, the leaves of vining plants threatening to obscure them from sight.

Lornysh stood on the opposite side of the stream. He had let his own sphere of light fade.

"Is this... has this always been here?" Jev asked. "Doing *that*?"

It seemed impossible that the foliage would have completely hidden that silver light at night, that nobody would have noticed this over the years.

"The stone activates when someone of elven blood comes near," Lornysh said.

Jev started to ask how he knew that, but a cheerful whistling from the back side of the structure surprised him. He leaned to the side and spotted a familiar figure crouching behind it, making a rubbing of carvings on the pillar.

"Cutter?" Jev asked.

"Yup, that's me."

"I didn't expect to find you here."

Judging by Lornysh's unsurprised expression, he had.

"Or for *here* to exist," Jev added, walking toward the structure.

He didn't know what it was—he'd never seen anything like it on his family's land or anywhere else—but he assumed it wouldn't sling some magical attack at him, not when Cutter was poking and prodding at it like an archeologist. Or a dwarven treasure hunter.

"I wanted to go looking for you today when I found out you weren't back from the city," Cutter said, "but I also wanted to look at this relic when Lornysh told me about it. These warring desires pounded at me like a pickax on stone. Until Lorn said he'd go find you and bring you back."

Rustling came from behind Jev as Rhi pushed her way out of the foliage and stopped to stare at the structure. The relic? That didn't seem the right word for something so large.

"Body's back there still," Cutter added, jerking a thumb over his shoulder. "Lorn said not to disturb it until you had a look. Not that I make a point of rummaging through bones."

"Just stones," Lornysh murmured.

"Stones are far more interesting than bones."

"*Body?*" Jev walked in the indicated direction.

"We thought it might be your missing butler."

Lornysh frowned at Cutter. "I was going to let him make his own conclusions."

"He can still conclude all he wants."

Jev stopped when the remains of a skeleton came into view. A human skeleton. The bones had been gnawed on and pulled apart, with the skull several feet away from the scattered ribs, but he'd seen enough human bones to recognize them. A few shreds of clothing had survived the years—how many years?—along with a single boot, the leather as gnawed as the bones.

He walked around the remains, careful not to disturb anything. "I have no idea what Corvel would have been wearing or how to identify this… person from what's here. Nor can I guess what would have led Corvel to this place."

"The presence of magic led me." Lornysh extended a hand toward the glowing structure.

"Yes, but you can sense magic. Corvel was human, and as you've pointed out many times, we humans are as sensitive to magic as moss-covered boulders."

"True, but if someone had told him where to look, he could have found the place."

"But who would have?" Jev scraped his fingers through his beard, momentarily startled by how little of it remained after his trim the night before. "I didn't know about this place, and I grew up here."

"What is this thing?" Rhi stopped under the structure.

"A meeting stone," Lornysh said. "If you touch it, it will rejuvenate you. Early elven explorers left them in places where fresh water could be found, using magic to turn them into a beacon that magical beings could sense."

"The interesting part," Cutter said in a tone that implied none of what Lornysh had said was interesting, "is that there are dwarf carvings on here as well as elven ones. Must have been a dwarf adventurer on that party."

"What do they say?" Rhi asked.

"Oh, I've no idea," Cutter said. "I'm copying them down to show Master Grindmor in the city. Some of those from the older generations can still read Trade Dwarf. Assuming the person who promised to introduce me to the master carver doesn't get arrested."

"I actually met her last night," Jev said.

Cutter lurched to his feet. "What? Without me?"

"You should have allowed yourself to be arrested, then captured by criminals with me. You could have met her too."

Cutter stamped around, looking like he genuinely regretted not coming along for the adventure.

Jev held up his hand. "Don't worry. I told her about you. She actually has a problem, unless she's resolving it as we speak, and I told her you'd like to help her."

Cutter pressed his hands to his chest. "I'd mine a thousand veins for a chance to assist her. I must prove my worthiness so she'll one day be willing to teach me."

"Almost precisely what I told her."

Cutter tried to get more details from him, but Jev said he would explain more later, then knelt by the skull. By Corvel's skull?

Unless Jev found more clues, he couldn't assume that. He couldn't even guess how long ago this man had died. Four years ago? Forty? Not four hundred, he didn't think. The bones weren't yellowed yet.

Jev turned over the skull, revealing a hole in the back.

"Now there's a clue," he murmured, lifting it to peer inside, expecting an arrowhead to fall out. Had some elf been waiting at this meeting stone to guard it? But why would Corvel have come if he expected an enemy?

Something small and dark fell through one of the eye holes and clinked against a boulder. Not an arrowhead. A bullet. A wyvern-cutter from an old percussion-cap rifle. He'd loaded bullets exactly like this for the firearm he'd learned to hunt with as a boy. The rifle had been old then, and that had been over twenty years ago.

"You think this was Corvel? That this happened only a few years ago?" Jev held it up for Lornysh to see.

"Judging by the weathering to the bones, yes. I know it's an older bullet than what your army uses now, but I'm sure many of your villagers around here have older rifles hanging over their hearths."

"True. And I'm positive you can still buy wyvern-cutters from gunsmiths today."

The silver light from above gleamed on the bullet, and Jev imagined he could still see the fallen man's blood on it. He still didn't know if this had been Corvel, but he felt a sense of loss at the idea. The old butler had been a mainstay in his boyhood, serving the family for as long as Jev could remember. He'd been stately and proper, but he hadn't been above sharing confidences with ten-year-old boys. And Corvel's eyes had twinkled as, with the barest tilt of his head, he gave away Vastiun's hiding spot after Vastiun made off with Jev's treasured raccoon-skin cap for the dozenth time.

Whoever had shot Corvel, or whoever the person ended up being, it had happened on Jev's family's land, and that filled him with indignation. And a need to get to the bottom of this, to avenge the person.

What if someone in his family had been *involved*? No, that couldn't be. But it could have been someone from one of the villages. Or someone who worked in the castle. Someone who had seen Corvel open that package? And had known it contained something valuable? And had followed him out here to kill Corvel and take the item? The Eye of Truth?

But why would Corvel have brought such an artifact out here to start with? Why hadn't he simply left it in Vastiun's room? How had he even known it was something valuable? Jev hadn't.

Jev sighed and stood up, all the questions in his head making it ache. He hadn't expected to walk out to a crime scene when he'd followed Lornysh off the road.

"No other clues?" Jev asked. "Nothing to identify this person for certain?"

It would have been handy to find a leather-bound diary that had fallen out of the man's pocket.

"No," Lornysh said, "but if you agree with my assessment that this man was killed in the last few years, it would coincide with the time period during which your brother's belongings were returned and the butler disappeared, right?"

"Yes."

"If he realized he had a magical artifact, he may have brought it here to contact someone."

Lornysh walked to the structure and pointed out a carving different from most. Jev recognized Taziir runes, even if he couldn't read the ancient dialect, and knew most of what adorned the pillar was writing. This, however, was a carving of a spread hand.

"Touch this, and an alert will be sent to all the meeting stones within roughly three hundred miles," Lornysh said. "If someone is monitoring them, they will know a request for communication has been made. Whether they will travel here depends on factors that I can't guess at in this circumstance. How important the people living near this stone are, most likely, and what relationships exist between them and those who monitor the other stones."

Jev realized he was staring at Lornysh with his jaw dangling open, and he made himself shut it. But the words raised so many questions—so many *more* questions—and he couldn't imagine answers that wouldn't stun him.

"There are meeting stones like this all over the kingdom that are *still* monitored by elves?" he asked.

He knew there were dwarven and elven ruins all over the continent, but he'd always heard, both from history tutors and elves themselves, that the Taziir hadn't found the warm southern Anchor Sea climate hospitable to them for long-term habitation, that they'd preferred their temperate northern forests. The elves were supposed to be long gone from this area.

"Likely." Lornysh twitched a shoulder to suggest he didn't know. Was that true? He'd been an army scout for the last few years, but before then… who knew what he'd done? Jev did not.

"And they care what's going on here? On my family's land? What do you mean important people? Why would any of us—" Jev touched his chest, then waved in the direction of the castle, "—be considered important to elves?"

Lornysh lifted a shoulder again. Why did Jev get the feeling he knew far more than he was saying?

Jev stared down at the bullet, trying to digest all the implications of it and of the body.

"Just to be clear," Rhi said into the silence, "the artifact we're looking for isn't here, right?"

"I do not sense it," Lornysh said.

"So, if that's the butler that took it out of the castle, does this mean someone took it from *him*? After shooting him?" She looked at Jev.

As if he knew anything. He didn't even want to accept that this *was* Corvel's body. He'd *liked* Corvel. The idea of him being heartlessly murdered on land where he should have been safe distressed Jev deeply.

"I suggest," Jev said, aware of Rhi watching him expectantly, "that we return to the castle and see if Zenia has learned anything."

Lornysh's expression never overflowed with emotion, but it grew even more guarded than usual.

Later, Jev would take him aside and explain that he trusted Zenia now. Even if he wasn't positive he should. She had made it clear where her loyalties lay, and even though he didn't object to the Water Order in general—interrogation sessions notwithstanding—he was skeptical whether they were the rightful keepers of whatever this artifact was. Had it truly been stolen from them? Or were they, like the Fifth Dragon guild, opportunists looking to claim it?

"Maybe someday somebody will tell me what this thing actually does," he muttered to himself.

As Jev headed for the path back, Cutter stood and asked, "Are we going to show him the cairn?"

"Cairn?" Jev asked.

Rhi, who had also been turning to leave, paused and lifted her eyebrows.

Lornysh spread his palm. "There weren't any identifying markings, and it would be unacceptable to disturb the rocks to seek clues from the bones."

"There weren't any identifying markings here either." Jev pointed to the skeletal remains, not believing the bullet counted as a marker. "And you didn't mind me poking through the bones."

"That man's spirit was never properly laid to rest. His ghost may haunt this small glen. Perhaps after your mystery is solved and you can with certainty name the owner of the bones, it would be appropriate to return to inter his remains."

"I can do that. But let's see this cairn, too, before we go."

Lornysh hesitated. "It is older than your mystery. There is little point in disturbing it."

"I won't disturb it. I'll look at it. Is that allowed?"

"He's getting in a snit over it because elves laid the rocks," Cutter said. "He wouldn't let me touch it either."

Lornysh sighed. "Yes, you may look. It's not hard to find."

Rhi looked like she wanted to head back to check on Zenia rather than traipsing farther up the stream, but she followed Jev and the others. He wouldn't have minded if she left. He had more questions for Lornysh but doubted his friend would speak openly with her around. Among all the other things he was wondering, he now wanted to know why elves had come onto his family's property and buried someone.

CHAPTER 16

ZYNDAR PRIME DHARROW ISN'T HERE?" Zenia asked.

"That's right, ma'am, and I don't have the authority to let you in." The guard glanced into the courtyard behind him, as if he was hoping someone would come over to back him up—or maybe take over the job of speaking to an inquisitor—but Zenia didn't see anyone walking through the area at the moment.

"You don't have the authority to keep me out, rather," she said. "I am here in the name of Archmage Sazshen, leader of the Order of the Blue Dragon temple in the capital. I am here to question the Dharrow family and its staff on her behalf."

"I…"

She could tell he didn't want to let her in but also that he worried about the ramifications of refusing her. Finally, he leaned into the small guard station built into the stone archway and rang a bell.

"Someone should come to speak with you," he said.

Should? They had better.

"Where is Zyndar Dharrow?" Even though she hadn't enjoyed chatting with the crusty man the day before—damn, had it only been a day?—he was a likely source of information. With the help of her dragon tear, she ought to be able to pry out his secrets.

"He was summoned early this morning to a meeting at Alderoth Castle and hasn't returned. Something about the coronation, we figured. Heard a lot of the zyndar primes were called. We expect him back any time though." The guard looked toward the dark sky. "Rumor has it the new king isn't much for drinking parties and orgies. I suppose he could grow into them. He's young, they say. I heard Jev served with him. I can't wait to talk to him, ask him all about Targyon. The whole castle and all the villagers are downright perplexed about him being named Abdor's heir."

If Zenia had wanted gossip on their new king, this man would have been easy to obtain answers from, even without magical influence, but that wasn't why she had come.

A dark-haired woman in her twenties appeared in the courtyard and waved for Zenia to enter. Zenia had seen her the day before. Jev's cousin, Wyleria. The same cousin Lornysh had apparently spoken with. She ought to be a decent resource and perhaps guide around the castle.

Zenia briefly reintroduced herself, then said, "What can you tell me of Jev's mother?"

She'd planned to ask first about the butler, but maybe she could surprise an answer out of the woman before she realized she was part of the investigation.

"Er, it's been a long time since she disappeared. She can't be suspected of any crime, surely."

"No, but your former butler is the last one believed to have seen the artifact stolen from the Water Order Temple." Zenia *hoped* it had been stolen. Sazshen had been vague about it. Vague about *everything*. "He seems to have been loyal to Jev's mother. Was she your aunt, or were you only related through marriage?"

A furrow creased Wyleria's forehead. "Yes, she was my aunt. Or *is*. We're not sure what happened to her. She may still be alive. Jev's mother is my mother's older sister, one of three. If you want information on her, our grandmother—*her* mother—might be the person to ask."

"Is that Visha?" Zenia remembered the babbling woman who had tried to foist that basket of sweets on Jev. He'd suggested she might be a good resource.

"Yes. She's lived here since before Jev was born. She makes clothes and creates all manner of tapestries. Many are hanging around the castle."

Zenia nodded, though she didn't care about the woman's artistic endeavors. "Where is she?"

"Usually in her rooms by evening. I can take you to her, but she's not... I mean, she's very sweet, but she's gotten to be simple, and she might not remember the significance of an inquisitor. Please be understanding with her."

"Of course." Zenia followed Wyleria across the courtyard and toward a set of exterior stairs that led to a well-lit balcony garden. The oak doors on either end of it had been painted blue with elaborate stencil art running up and down the planks. "Was she always that way?"

"No, only since she lost her daughter. Most of us believe Jev's mother went off to be with another man or maybe—" Wyleria lowered her voice and glanced around to ensure nobody was on the balcony with them, "—an elf prince. But Grandma Visha always seemed to believe her daughter had died. Maybe she's right and we're all wrong. It has been… golly, almost twenty years now? I was just a girl when it happened. One does suspect Jev's mother would have at least sent a letter if she were alive and well."

"Why do people think she ran off with an elf?" Zenia had heard plenty of stories revolving around that, perhaps because "elf princes" tended to be handsome. No matter how much humans in general had come to loathe the Taziir, it was impossible to deny their elegance and beauty as individuals.

"Oh, long ago, Dharrow Castle was known as a safe respite for elves. This was centuries ago, before the elves withdrew from our lands and before we decided starting wars with them was a good idea. Jev's mother read all the stories about them as a girl, I've heard. And people who are old enough to remember it say she wasn't pleased when her family arranged a marriage to Jev's father. Apparently, she'd had her heart set on finding a handsome elf. But I don't think anyone has any proof that she had one out there somewhere. It's just speculation. An explanation, I guess."

Wyleria shrugged, then knocked on one of the brightly stenciled doors.

"Why was your butler so close to Jev's mother?" Zenia asked.

"He came with her from her family's estate at the time of the marriage, and he'd known her since she'd been a girl. I'm not sure if she confided in him, but Jev's father occasionally lost his temper and snapped at him. My mother says he was jealous even though nobody believed Jev's mother was sleeping with the butler or anything like that. Corvel was old and stately even when I was a kid. He came that way,

I've heard, and never seemed to age, other than his hair going from gray to white over the years."

Wyleria knocked again. "Grandma Visha? We have a visitor who would like to speak with you."

A butler who never seemed to age sounded like someone with at least a little elven blood in his veins. The distinctive pointed ears rarely appeared once the blood was diluted down to a quarter or less, so it was harder to pick out those who merely had elven ancestors. These days, the thought of intermingling was considered horrendous, by both races reputedly. In previous centuries it hadn't been as taboo.

The door opened, and a plump woman with white hair pulled back into a bun stood there, a shirt dangling from one hand, a needle and thread in the other.

"My pardon," she—Visha—said. "I was in the middle of a project and couldn't quite find a way to set everything down without risking knots and a tangled mess. You know how frustrating that is!"

"Of course, Grandma. This is Inquisitor Cham. She has some questions revolving around Vastiun's death and the returning of his belongings. Do you have a moment?"

Zenia nodded to the woman, and also to Wyleria, glad she hadn't mentioned the artifact specifically.

"Vastiun's death? The poor boy. My grandson was such a warm, friendly lad. The founders haven't been kind to this family this past generation, I fear. Tea?"

Zenia started at the abrupt transition.

Wyleria merely smiled gently and said, "Please."

"I just had some brought up." Visha turned into a foyer with a fountain tinkling in the middle and doors to a bedroom, sitting room, and a lavatory leading away from it. "Come sit with me, please. What questions do you have? Oh, and there are lavender-gort thumbprints. You'll have to share with me. We baked them earlier today, but far too many. They're terribly delicious."

As Zenia and Wyleria trailed the woman into the sitting room, Zenia wondered if she would get anything useful from the woman. Visha draped the shirt she was repairing over the back of the sofa, then started to put the needle in a pin cushion but pricked her finger instead and let out a soft gasp of pain. She laid the needle on the table, sucked on her finger, then sat at the other end of the sofa in front of a tray of green-specked cookies and a pot of an aromatic floral tea. There was only one cup, but she rang a bell, and a servant soon appeared with two more.

Zenia knew the woman was old, but she couldn't help but shake her head at having a person employed for the sole means of fetching things. And answering to a ringing bell.

"I didn't know gort could be made into cookies," Wyleria said, taking a chair and smiling as the servant stopped to add logs to a fire burning in a hearth.

"The only way to get the little ones to eat their vegetables," Visha proclaimed. "Dara's boys were here earlier, you know. I do hope Jev will have some children now that he's back from that dreadful war. I'm certainly in favor of stamping out all elves meddling in human affairs, but really. Ten years. The prime of a man's life. So much to give up. Tea?"

"Yes, please," Wyleria said.

Zenia hadn't sat yet, but the women looked expectantly at her, so she headed toward a chair. She eyed another door that opened from the sitting room, this one off to the side of the fireplace. It was well-lit, showing all manner of weaving equipment and canvases on easels.

Zenia wouldn't have glanced twice at the crafts room, but she sensed magic somewhere inside of it. Something similar to her dragon tear. Maybe that was exactly what it was. It almost felt like a cluster of them. She remembered Jev's admission that zyndar families often kept some in vaults for promising children.

She drew upon the power of her own dragon tear, trying to augment her ability to sense the magical and to verify her suspicions. She was here looking for a magical artifact, after all. What if the butler hadn't taken it with him when he left? What if it remained in the castle?

But why would this old woman have such an item? It made much more sense that she, perhaps the oldest person living here, might guard the family's dragon tears.

"Cookies, dear?" Visha held the tray toward Zenia, frowning briefly toward the crafts room, but then smiling when Zenia met her eyes. "I'll be happy to show you some of my projects. Do you enjoy tapestries?"

"I like the ones in the temple," Zenia said, though she'd never looked closely at most of them. Aside from the one outside the lavatory that showed a dragon waist-deep in a lake and washing his armpits with some kind of mushroom sponge. Zenia was fairly certain dragons had neither waists nor armpits that stank, but she'd appreciated the humor of the art.

"Which temple are you from, dear?"

"The Temple of the Blue Dragon. I'm an inquisitor, and the archmage sent me to ask a few questions."

"Ah, the Water Order Temple. I did three tapestries for them several years ago. Do they still hang there? One is a playful one of a dragon. That's my favorite."

Even though Zenia wanted to get on with her questioning, she smiled, glad she could truthfully say, "I've seen that one. And I enjoy it."

"Is it hanging somewhere suitable to its majesty?" Visha asked, and Zenia couldn't tell if it was a joke. Maybe they were thinking of different tapestries.

"If it's the one I'm thinking of, it's on the wall between the men's and women's lavatories. Above the sign instructing the penitent to wash their feet before supper."

"That seems an appropriate place then." Visha's eyes twinkled.

Wyleria looked puzzled, and she sipped from her tea.

"I just have a few questions for you, Zyndari. Do you know anything about the relationship between the butler Corvel and your missing daughter? It seems he was quite loyal to her."

Wyleria's puzzled look did not fade—clearly, she didn't understand this line of questioning. Perhaps her puzzlement was founded. Maybe it led nowhere.

"The butler? Oh, I barely knew him."

Wyleria's brow furrowed more deeply. Zenia's might have furrowed too. Had Wyleria gotten her story wrong? If Corvel had come with Jev's mother when she'd married Heber, wouldn't that mean the butler had lived in her home—and in Visha's home—before then? Even if Visha had lived elsewhere, she'd been here since her daughter's marriage. Surely long enough to get to know a butler.

Frowning, Zenia opened her mouth to ask for clarification, but Visha spoke again first.

"I've not had any luck at all getting my tapestries into the Fire Temple. The archmage there told me that whimsy is completely inappropriate for his people. As if the Fire Dragon himself wasn't known to inhale beer and play chips with dwarves."

"Uhm, yes, Zyndari," Zenia said. "That's unfortunate. May I ask a question about—"

"Do you have any idea how I might sway him? I've sent cookies."

"Gort cookies?" Wyleria asked. "Perhaps there's a reason that didn't work."

"No, lemon-lavender cookies. They were delightful." Visha looked earnestly at Zenia. "I even have a tapestry on display in Alderoth Castle. My daughter's husband Heber arranged for it. Have you spoken to him yet about your questions?"

"No, but I will as soon as he returns. I was told he was meeting with the new king."

"Yes, I do hope the new king will follow in his uncle's footsteps in laying down the law against those pesky elves and keeping them out of our country. You can't trust anyone with points on his head. They tell our people nothing but lies. Accuse us of thieving. As if humans would want anything they have. What audacity. Do you like the cookies? The secret ingredient is almond extract."

Zenia drew upon her power and tried to gauge if the woman was deliberately trying to misdirect her, or if this was an example of the simpleness Wyleria had mentioned.

Visha's mind seemed scattered, and even with magic, Zenia struggled to grasp her motivations. There was a child-like quality to the thoughts that did come through, a concern about her tapestries, a determination to finish repairing that shirt, an eagerness to see Jev married with children, and—oh—should she try to guide Heber into arranging that?

Feeling her cheeks warm, Zenia leaned back in her seat and withdrew her mental probe. She told herself not to be distracted by thoughts of an arranged marriage for Jev, that it had nothing to do with her mission here.

"Do have some tea, dear," Visha said, sipping from her own cup. "It goes so well with the cookies. I had a dragon tear of my own many years ago, and I used it to guide me in baking. Sadly, it was given to my cousin when he went off to fight in the war. He's a cook too. He can make breads that increase a man's stamina and strength for a time. I can't say my cookies do that. They can increase the size of your waist if you're not careful." She chuckled at the joke.

Zenia forced herself to smile. It wasn't often that the inquisitor was the one thrown off in a questioning session, but she did feel that way. She decided to speak more with Wyleria and the servants around the castle for now. When Jev returned, she would ask him for permission to spend the night. She had a feeling it would be easier to sneak up here and search for clues—and take a look at the source of the magic she sensed—once Visha and the rest of the castle had gone to sleep.

Sneaking about like a burglar wasn't how she preferred to gather evidence, but it wouldn't be the first time she had done things that way.

Still, as they finished the evening snacks, and Wyleria led Zenia out of Visha's suite, Zenia couldn't help but look back over her shoulder and wonder if she'd been outmaneuvered by a senile old lady.

The six-foot-long and three-foot-high rock arrangement was far more artistically laid than Jev had imagined when Cutter called it a cairn. He could see it well since they hadn't had to travel far and the silver glow of the meeting stone still lit the area.

The granite stones had been cut and elaborately placed, each one fitting together like a piece in a puzzle. Nothing that he could see adhered them to each other, but they had not tumbled to the grass below, despite the age of the collection.

Oh, he wouldn't have been able to guess at the age based on the stones themselves, but they had been there long enough for moss to grow thickly on the north side, and dirt had gathered in the crevices on the top via the winds from numerous monsoon seasons. A few tufts of grass and a lone flower grew from between the stones. The cairn could have been built decades ago or centuries ago, but he agreed with Lornysh's assessment that it had been done before Corvel had left the castle.

"It is the grave of a friend," Lornysh said. "Not an enemy. You can see that more care was put into the placement of the stones than might otherwise have been done."

"Not bad stone-laying for an elf," Cutter said.

"There are rumors that long ago, elves were the ones to teach dwarves to work stone," Lornysh said.

"There are rumors that you wear your grammy's panties, too, but we don't put much stock in those."

Jev walked around the cairn. Even though the others had warned him there were no markers, he had to see for himself. All these revelations of elven meeting stones that were apparently monitored, along with the very existence of this place, had him questioning what he thought he'd known about his family history and this land.

He didn't spot any markings on the cairn, but by accident, he stepped on something in the grass, something solid enough that he felt it through the sole of his boot. He bent down and pushed the grass aside. The silver light glinted off something dull but something that definitely wasn't stone or earth.

He had to dig to pry it out of the dirt, then squatted down to stare at his finding. And to rub the dirt off it. A feeling of numbness crept over him. Another bullet.

"What did you find?" Lornysh walked over and squatted next to him.

Jev held it up toward the light. "It's the same make as the one that was in that skull. It looks older. Or at least like it's been out here longer."

"Yes."

"There are scratch marks. Almost like someone was trying to cut it?" Jev handed it to Lornysh, curious to get his opinion. He was good at tracking and finding clues that eluded others.

Cutter came over for a look, though Rhi merely folded her arms and hitched her hip against the cairn. Lornysh glared balefully at her for disturbing the resting place. She looked back toward the trail they'd blazed and didn't seem to notice the glare.

"Cut it *out*, I'd guess," Lornysh said.

"Er, out of a body?" Jev looked toward the cairn, but he also looked toward the trees in the area. Maybe someone had pried it out of a trunk after missing a shot? But only to cast it to the ground? Why bother?

"One of my people might have removed the item that killed a person if the person was a friend." Lornysh tilted his head toward the cairn.

Jev scraped his fingers through his beard again. He found this mystery, as Lornysh had called it, intriguing, and he would have loved to research more, but he feared nothing here would lead him to the artifact Zenia sought. And until he found that, or she did, the Water Order would dog his every step. He might not have objected to Zenia trailing him around indefinitely, but some lesser minion of the Order might be given the task if they didn't find the artifact soon. It was also possible the Order had the power to keep him from going about his duties, from restarting his life, until this was resolved.

"Maybe one day, I'll come back to this place and figure it all out," Jev said, "but for now, let's see if Zenia has learned anything back at the castle."

"You don't think the more recent death is important to all this?" Lornysh pointed toward the skeletal remains.

"It may very well be. I just don't know what it's telling us right now. Do you?"

Lornysh gave the cairn a long look, then said, "No."

"Are you sure?" Jev asked quietly, turning his back to Rhi.

Lornysh hesitated. "At this point, I have only guesses."

CHAPTER 17

A S ZENIA TRAILED WYLERIA THROUGH the castle, stopping to talk to anyone who remembered Corvel, she couldn't stop thinking of the magic she'd felt in Visha's suite. Had she made a mistake in giving up on her questions so early? Maybe she should have demanded to see the crafts room and whatever cubby or vault hid the magical items within. Except that it wasn't within her right as an inquisitor to demand to see a family's heirloom dragon tears.

A clatter of hooves drifted through a window that opened out onto the courtyard. Zenia paused to jog to it and peer out. Had Jev and the others returned? Had they found anything interesting?

From the third-story window, she spotted Heber riding in with two attendants.

"I need to talk to him," Zenia said, turning back toward Wyleria.

She waited in the hall and managed a smile, though she'd been yawning a moment ago. Growing weary of playing tour guide? As soon as Jev returned, Zenia would foist the duty onto him. And maybe they could check and see if Visha had gone to sleep and her crafts room might be investigated...

"We can meet him at the stable," Wyleria said. "This way."

The woman led the way down narrow interior stairs that Zenia hadn't seen before, but as soon as the scent of horses and straw wafted up from below, she trusted this was the right direction.

For some reason, the lanterns, which had been lit everywhere else around the castle, were out. She silently commanded her dragon tear to glow.

Wyleria glanced back as they descended from the third to the second floor. "That's handy."

"At times."

They reached a landing, and someone young called, "Wyleria?" from a side passage. A boy of seven or eight poked his head out, holding a lantern aloft. "Do you have a minute? Grammy Visha said I could ask *you* about lizards."

"Uhm." Wyleria paused, glanced at Zenia, then said, "I'm actually showing our guest around. I—"

"Go ahead," Zenia interrupted. She might have better luck questioning Heber without Wyleria watching. She anticipated having to be firm with him and that he might not have told his son everything. What if everything with the butler had been a misdirection and Jev's father had been the one to open that package years ago?

"All right," Wyleria said. "Thanks. The stable is down the stairs, around that bend, and through the door."

A whinny drifted to them from that direction.

"I think I can find it." Zenia waved and strode off as Wyleria followed the boy through the other exit.

Once again, the way was not lit. Zenia reached the bottom of the stairs, rounded the bend, and spotted light ahead through an open door. The stable scent, much stronger now, drifted to her nose.

Abruptly, the door ahead slammed shut, and a lock *snicked*. If not for her glowing gem, she would have been enclosed in darkness again.

Had Heber done that? Somehow anticipating her and not wanting to talk to her?

Well, it would take more than a closed door to stop her.

But before she reached it, a boom sounded, followed by a great cracking of stone. The noise came from all around her. The ground lurched, and she was pitched against a wall.

Rocks tumbled from the ceiling, one slamming into her shoulder. She cried out in pain, and fear surged through her limbs as more rocks clattered to the floor. There was nothing here to hide under.

Zenia whirled and sprinted back toward the stairs and the landing as more rocks pelted her. She hoped the whole castle wasn't coming down.

As she ran, words sprang into her mind.

Grammy Visha said I could ask you *about lizards.*

Had the grandmother sent that boy? To pull Wyleria away from danger? Danger she'd *known* about?

It seemed impossible that the old woman could have been responsible, fully or partially, but as Zenia clambered up the stairs with rock slabs slamming to the floor all around her, she knew she'd made a huge mistake.

* * *

As Lornysh led the way out of the woods, Jev was relieved when the castle came into sight. He didn't fear darkness or the night, but this night had been odd so far, and thinking of that eerie silver light glowing onto that cairn made him shiver in the salty sea breeze. Light glowing from an elven structure that had existed two miles from his family's castle for centuries and that he had somehow never known about.

But *someone* had known about it.

"Glad to see civilization," Rhi said.

She rode beside Jev, the horses picking routes over the dark, uneven ground and up toward the road.

"My father will be pleased you consider his castle an example of such," Jev said, though the banter was only a reflex. He wasn't in the mood for it. "I understand my mother called it old and drafty and a relic of a foregone era when she moved in."

"She must have loved him a great deal for her to have made such a sacrifice."

"It was an arranged marriage, actually."

"So, no love?"

"There might have been eventually. They seemed companionable enough when I was a boy." His parents had never yelled or argued that he recalled. Admittedly, he couldn't remember them smooching openly in front of him and Vastiun. Or cuddling. Or rushing up the stairs with arms linked on the way to make passionate love. But then, he'd hardly been looking for such things. Even now, it was hard not to find the idea of his parents having sex anything other than disturbing.

"Companionable. Let's hope your future wife gets more from you. A woman wants a man who can make her lady parts thrum and throb."

"By the dragon founders," Jev blurted. He was glad his horse was picking the way up the uneven slope. If he'd been the one walking, he would have pitched over at that comment. It wasn't that he hadn't heard about *throbbing* from time to time among the men in the army, but there was something alarming about a monk of one of the kingdom's religious orders discussing it.

"I'm sure they would agree," Rhi said blandly.

Lornysh guided his horse onto the road and did not look back at this conversation.

A boom rang out, startling Jev as much as Rhi's comment had. For a moment, his mind jumped back in time to the Battle of Terring Pass, and he was out in the snow with cannons blasting from the front line as elven defenders fired arrows from their perches high in the rocks.

"Are explosions typical in your castle?" Lornysh asked over his shoulder, sounding far calmer than Jev felt.

"No." Jev swore and urged his horse to top speed.

As he galloped over the drawbridge and into the courtyard, the thunks of rocks falling reached his ears. He didn't see the guards or stablehands or *anyone*. He slid off his horse, leaving it to stand on the flagstones and drink from the fountain, and raced for one of the back passageways.

The thuds had stopped, but raised voices made it to his ears, as well as the whinnies of scared horses.

"What happened?" he yelled as he ran. "Where is everyone?"

He didn't know who would answer, and he didn't care. Though he had no proof, he worried this had to do with Zenia. And with that cairn, the skeleton, and those bullets fresh in his mind, he worried further that it couldn't be anything good.

The back courtyard came into view, but the voices to one side drew him into another passageway.

"Jev?" someone called from the direction of the stables.

He ran outside, saw the building intact and the hands trying to quiet the horses. Neither appeared injured. A side door that led from the back of the main wing of the castle and to the stables stood open with people gathered around it. Rocks sprawled on the cobblestones at their feet.

More rocks—stone from the structure of the castle itself—were piled waist-high inside the doorway.

Jev pushed people aside in his rush to reach that doorway and figure out what had happened.

"Zyndar Jev," someone blurted. "What do we do?"

They were asking him? As if he knew. "What happened?"

"There was an explosion," someone with a young, squeaky voice yelled.

"It was just a collapse of some of the castle, not an explosion."

"No, you're wrong. There was a big boom! Someone attacked us. We should be getting guns!"

"You're not old enough to get a slingshot."

"I'll keep away invaders with my slingshot. I shot you in the butt once."

"Sssh, shh," a woman said, and one of the boys was slapped on the back of the head.

Jev barely noticed. He had reached the entrance, but he couldn't go in. In the doorway, the rock pile only rose to his waist, but just a few steps farther in, it rose to the ceiling. To what had *been* the ceiling. Jev peered up into darkness, grimacing. The hallway on the floor above had collapsed downward, bringing rugs and furniture and beams down along with the stone.

How had this happened? Random chance? He highly doubted it. The castle might be centuries old, but it was well-built, and ceilings didn't collapse at random.

"Was it just bad luck?" someone next to him whispered, one of the cook's assistants that had worked in the castle for twenty years. "My prediction for today—for those born under the air dragon's sign—said fortune doesn't like to be ignored. Did we... ignore something?"

"I agree with young Gherrod," someone said. "This wasn't an accident. What if that inquisitor sabotaged the castle?"

"She was asking all those questions, interrogating Jev's grandmother of all people. That's what the servants said. What if she didn't get the answers she wanted and brought down the wrath of the Blue Dragon?"

Jev spotted soot on some of the rocks near the bottom of the pile. He swiped his finger through it and sniffed.

"Someone set a charge," he said. "Deliberately."

"It *was* the inquisitor," someone said.

"No, she has no reason to blow up the castle. She—" His gut twisted as a thought sprang to mind. Did someone have a reason to blow *her* up? He lurched to his feet. "Where is she?" He tried to make his voice calm but panic threatened. Founders, what if she was under this mess?

He'd just started to like her, damn it. He didn't want to lose her. He'd lost far too many people he cared about over the years.

"That's what I was asking, Zyndar. What if she planted a charge and then ran off? Who's watching the gate?"

Someone cursed and sprinted around the building and toward the front gate.

"Hymar, Min," Jev said, picking out the names of people he recognized, people who had worked here the last time he'd been home. "Put together a team. I want this rubble cleared out. Is my father back yet?"

"I saw him ride in," someone said, "but he's not here now. I don't know where he went. He must have heard this."

"Clear the rubble. I'll come back to help after I check the other side."

Jev ran around and through another entrance, his heart pounding against his rib cage. How much of the ceiling and level above had collapsed? He hadn't been able to tell from outside.

"Jev!" came an alarmed cry, and Wyleria grabbed his arm as he jogged inside. "Your friend, the inquisitor—"

Jev returned the grip. "She wasn't under there, was she?"

Wyleria's already wide eyes grew wider. "I—I'm afraid she might be. I was guiding her, but then I was pulled to the side and—"

Jev released her and sprinted through the corridor and up the stairs so he could get to the other set that led down to the stable yard—presuming they hadn't been buried.

He ran into darkness. Someone hadn't lit the wall lanterns for the night. Or they had been lit earlier and someone had doused them.

Cursing, he ran back so he could grab a lit lantern from a wall. He came out on the second-floor landing but lurched to a stop before he'd taken more than two steps. Most of the landing was buried. That meant the stairs and more than thirty feet of corridor had been smothered in the rockfall.

He held the lantern up, searching the rubble, what he could see of it. Most of the corridor was blocked.

"Zenia?" he called, but he feared she wouldn't hear him if she was buried under all that. She wouldn't ever hear anything again.

He shook his head. It was too early to give up on her. She might not even be under there.

Jev glanced at Wyleria, at the way she'd covered her mouth with her hand as she stared at the rocks. Tears filmed her eyes with moisture. She seemed certain Zenia was under there. And dead.

Jev bit his lip. He wouldn't condemn her to that fate until he saw her body.

"Wyleria, go get some men to help me clear rocks from this side. And assign some of the women to search the castle for Zenia. She might not have—you didn't actually see the rocks crush her, right?" His voice cracked at the word crush, and he grimaced at himself.

"No, but she was going that way, and the time... there hadn't been enough time for her to get out and to the stables."

"All right, we'll clear out the rocks. Go get people." He hated giving his cousin orders but hoped she would understand his need right now. "Oh, and go see if there's an elf standing in the courtyard somewhere. Or outside. He was on horseback and might be lurking. He can sense magic, so he'll be able to tell if Zenia's dragon tear is under here. Or isn't." He hoped it wasn't. How far could Lornysh sense magic? He'd felt that meeting stone from who knew how far away.

"Lornysh?" Wyleria blurted. "If your father sees him—"

"I'll deal with him. Just go, please." Jev grabbed the first rock and hurled it into an empty spot on the landing.

"All right."

As she retreated, he threw another stone. Some of them were too large for one man to move, and even if they hadn't been, he realized this would take hours. He despaired of finding her before it was too late.

"No, I *will* find you," he vowed and hurled another stone away. "And I'll find whoever did this too."

He gritted his teeth, imagining pummeling someone into the ground, then grabbing a pistol and shooting that person. That anger fueled him as he poured his energy into moving the rubble.

CHAPTER 18

DAZED AND ACHING, ZENIA CRAWLED up the dark stairs. She didn't think she had any broken bones, but she hurt all over. She'd lost track of how many stones had fallen, pounding her in the back and shoulders. Somehow, she'd managed to keep her arms over her head and keep from taking any blows to it. She needed her head. Not that it took a lot of brain matter to figure out that she'd been duped by that old lady.

Why hadn't Zenia asserted her inquisitor authority and demanded to search that crafts room? Out of some notion that she should be respectful and polite because this was Jev's home? She'd sensed magic. She shouldn't have hesitated to investigate it.

Well, she wouldn't hesitate now.

Shouts floated up from the floors below, but the thick stone walls made the words impossible to understand. The rocks had stopped falling, their thunderous thuds no longer echoing in her skull. That didn't keep her from glancing into the darkness overhead often, afraid that more of the castle might come down atop her. She'd barely made it across that landing before the entire ceiling had collapsed, and she wanted nothing more than to find an exit and sprint outside.

Not that she could sprint anywhere now. Zenia grimaced as she continued resolutely upward, crawling more than walking, using her hands to guide her and also for support.

She rounded a bend, and a light came into view. A lantern on a landing. She'd reached the third floor. From here, she could go around the exterior of the main wing and back down to Visha's suite. She hoped

Visha was down there by the rockfall, making sure her dastardly work had been done, instead of sitting in her crafts room weaving a tapestry.

Not that Zenia would pause if she was. No matter how injured she was, she could handle an eighty-year-old woman. She *would* search that crafts room.

When she reached the balcony with the garden and heard voices in the courtyard below, she crouched low so she could cross without being seen. She thought she caught Wyleria's voice, a frantic note to it, and almost rose up to wave at her and let her know she had survived, but the grandmother could be down there too. And whoever the grandmother's ally was. Someone with a pistol, perhaps. Zenia doubted the old lady had been the one to set the charge that had brought down the ceiling.

The door to the suite wasn't locked.

"Finally, some luck."

Zenia opened it, slipped inside, and forced herself to stand upright. A swelling bruise on her spine protested mightily, and she planted a hand on the wall for support.

"We'll find a healer later," she whispered to her wounds.

As she crossed the sitting room, limping on a swollen knee, she tried not to think about how finding a healer would mean riding all the way back to the temple in the city. Maybe she could convince Jev to carry her. She snorted, imagining what Sazshen would say if she rode into the temple square in some man's arms. Especially the arms of a man she'd been sent to arrest two days earlier.

Zenia limped into the dark crafts room, grabbing a lantern from the wall by the fireplace. She pulled her dragon tear out from under her robe and gripped it, feeling its gentle warmth against her palm. She used its magic to guide her past looms and easels toward the far wall of the room. Three huge tapestries hung there, all featuring dragons. One red, one white, and one blue.

"No love for the earth dragon?" she whispered, looking toward the walls, thinking a tapestry holding a green dragon might be elsewhere, but she didn't see it.

Maybe Visha had been born under the air sign and didn't get along with those from the Earth Order.

Zenia's gem guided her to the center of the Air Dragon's tapestry. Wishing it had been the Water Dragon, which surely would have signaled success for her, Zenia pushed aside the heavy drapery. Nothing but bare stone lay beneath it. It looked like all the other stone on the walls.

More shouts sounded in the courtyard. Zenia wagered the castle inhabitants would start a search soon. How long did she have to snoop before someone found her?

She slid her hand over the stone wall, specifically the large rectangular stone the dragon tear's magic was guiding her toward. A vault or even a secret room had to be back there, but how could she access it? And should she barge right in if she could? It could be booby-trapped.

Something stabbed her finger, and she jerked back, the tapestry falling back into place. She almost dropped the lantern but managed to keep a hold on it, to use it to examine the blood welling from a precise prick of her fingertip.

Stone ground, and she stepped back farther. The tapestry stirred on the wall, and she expected a door of some kind to open. Instead, golden light glowed from the stones.

She stepped farther back, her butt smacking against a loom. Maybe this hadn't been a good idea. But she couldn't give up now. She wiped the blood from her finger and stared resolutely at the wall.

Mist swirled in the golden light, and a figure coalesced in front of the tapestry. Zenia's heartbeat pounded in her ears. This could only be dwarven or elven magic.

"You have been tested," the figure rumbled, the words seeming to sound inside Zenia's head instead of coming through her ears. It—he— pushed back a cowl to reveal a man's angular face, a neatly trimmed beard emphasizing the jawline. He reminded her of Jev. Some ancestor of his? "You are not of the Dharrow bloodline. Nor were you appointed as the current guardian. You may not enter the safe."

A shiver went up Zenia's spine as the apparition stared straight at her.

"Would any Dharrow be able to open it?" she asked, though she doubted the entity had been created to answer questions or have sentient thought. It probably delivered this message and nothing more.

"You are not of the Dharrow bloodline," it repeated. "You may not enter the safe."

"Right, I got that." Zenia rubbed her finger. She feared she would have to wait for Jev and hope the person or people with inimical intentions toward her didn't chance upon her first. "Though maybe…" She looked toward the sitting room. Jev's grandmother on his mother's side wouldn't have Dharrow blood, but if she'd been appointed as the current guardian, then her blood must open the safe too. Right?

"Wait here," she told the apparition.

Doubting it would listen, she gripped her lantern and hustled around the clutter and into the other room, hoping Visha hadn't put away her sewing project. More specifically, Zenia hoped the needle was still on the table. Ah yes, there it was. The woman must have hurried off to arrange that rockfall without tidying up. Or had it already been arranged? Had someone guessed Zenia would head that specific way toward the stable? It seemed hard to imagine, given all the entrances, exits, and hallways in the various wings of the castle. But she had made it clear she wanted to talk to Jev's father, and someone might have assumed he would go to the stable when he returned.

"Questions for later," Zenia muttered, picking up the needle.

She held the tip to her lantern, squinting. A hint of blood seemed to darken it, but it was hard to tell in the dim lighting. Even if it *was* stained, would dried blood work on that test?

When she returned to the crafts room, the apparition had faded, the glow disappearing. She pushed aside the tapestry again, careful not to touch the stone this time. The lantern clanked and scraped as she held it as close to the wall, to that particular stone, as she could. She spotted a hole, a hole so tiny it could have been mistaken for a pore in the stone. But she was certain that was where the needle or whatever had pricked her had originated.

"Let's see if this works," she murmured and poked the tip of the sewing needle into the hole.

It slid in an inch, then halted. A faint click sounded, like a spring releasing. Zenia let go and jumped back. The needle shot backward out of the hole and crossed half the room before *tinking* to the floor.

"I guess that was a rejection."

It had been a long shot.

Zenia waited for the apparition to appear, perhaps with more threatening words this time, but instead, a grating noise came from within the wall, like a gear turning. The stone next to the one with the pinhole slid out a couple of inches.

She lunged forward, afraid it would slide out all the way and crack to the floor. But it stopped there. Warily, she gripped the sides and pulled it out. The stone fit tightly in its nest, but she eased it out. As she stepped back to set it on the floor, a soft golden glow came from the hole in the wall. She peered into it, not getting too close lest some trap guarded the items inside. Was it enough that one had Dharrow blood, or would some greater test need to be passed? As old as his family was, hundreds of people in the kingdom must share blood with Jev.

She squinted into the glow, trying to pick out what lay back there. Dragon tears shouldn't glow, not when they weren't in contact with a wielder. She did pick out familiar oval-shaped gems lying on the bottom. Then there was also one whitish-yellow carved object…

"That's it," she whispered, reaching in. "Has to be."

Silently asking her own dragon tear for protection, she touched the ivory artifact, then drew her finger back. She waited to see if anything would happen.

Nothing.

A thud sounded, a nearby door shutting. Someone entering the suite?

Fearing she had run out of time, Zenia snatched the artifact out. She bent, intending to stuff the stone back into place, but white flashed before her eyes.

A gasp came from the doorway to the crafts room. She glimpsed a familiar white-haired bun before a vision sprang into her mind with the intensity of a mallet striking a gong.

Zenia's knees buckled. She sensed Visha walking into the room, but she was powerless to do anything about it. A scene played in her mind, as if she were in the middle of a stage full of actors, and she lost all awareness of her body and the outside world.

"Take this to the humans, Princess Yrellia. To someone of import, someone who will pay attention. I grow weary of suffering their soldiers, and it has become harder and harder to keep the young elves from enacting their plan, to cross the sea and use magic to attack the humans on their own soil, to devastate their kingdoms." The speaker, a gray-haired elf in white and silver robes, stood in front of a green backdrop, branches leafing out all around him, a platform of lace-like wood under his feet.

An elven woman sat cross-legged before him, her head bowed, her blonde hair partially hiding her face. "I will do as you say, Father."

She extended her hand, and he rested a trinket in it, a carved ivory trinket that had been imbued to speak the truth to any who would listen.

"It shares the history, the true history. The one that humans have chosen to forget. I did not believe it was so until I visited among them in disguise. Until I saw that none of their leaders remembered. Perhaps this war of theirs would end if they remembered the truth. If they accepted it."

"That they have been stealing the dragon tears from us for countless millennia? Almost since the days when the dwarves gave them to us for safekeeping?"

"A task I fear we have failed." The gray-haired elf sighed deeply. "And the dwarves won't let us forget it."

"They've stopped trying to annihilate each other with them."

"And now the humans use them to try to annihilate us." He waved for her to rise. "Take it to the Kor capital. It is that kingdom that leads the war on us. It is that king who must be swayed—or those with the power to influence him."

"I understand, Father." Yrellia closed her fingers around the carving and rose lithely without using her hands.

"It is no longer easy for us to walk in their cities. You may need to befriend one with the means to act as a liaison or guide for you."

"One of their nobility, perhaps?"

"Yes. We have had supporters among them in the past. Find such a person."

"I understand, Father. It will be done."

Pain splintered in Zenia's mind, and she lurched back to awareness as something was yanked from her fingers. She tried to lunge after it but realized she was on her back on the floor. She grasped only air, and then the darkness crept into her vision again.

As Jev tore chunks of stone from the rockfall and hurled them into a growing pile behind him, a hand came in from the side and gripped his shoulder.

He pulled away, afraid someone wanted to stop him. What if his father had come in and intended to order him to give up?

"Jev, she's not under there," Lornysh said, his familiar voice getting through the mindless rock-throwing haze he'd been in.

Lornysh looked down at Jev's hands, at his bleeding fingernails. He raised his eyebrows.

Did that mean Zenia hadn't been caught? That she was safe somewhere else?

"Is she alive?" Jev croaked, worried he was misinterpreting his friend.

"That I do not know yet, but I sense her dragon tear." Lornysh pointed upward and toward the center of the main wing.

"She wasn't caught?" Wyleria asked from behind Lornysh. They stood together on the landing. "Thank the founders. I was so sure..."

"Lead the way," Jev told Lornysh. "Please."

"Of course."

Lornysh headed for the nearest set of stairs. Jev started after him, but Wyleria squeezed his arm, making him pause.

"I found the elf out front, waiting with a dwarf, and I got him inside and through a door before anyone noticed, but we almost ran into Grandma Visha leading your father out into the courtyard. They were talking about I don't know what. We might not have long before he comes to check on this." She waved at the rockfall but also included Lornysh in the gesture.

"I'll deal with it." Jev knew his father would explode when he found an elf in his midst, but he didn't care. He had to find Zenia. That was all that mattered right now. Even if she hadn't been caught in that rockfall... if it had been meant for her, someone in the castle was after her. Someone who might try again as soon as he found her.

He ran up the stairs after Lornysh, catching up quickly. He had the urge to shove his friend along so he could move faster, but he doubted Lornysh wanted humans planting their hands on his butt. Judging by the way he paused at the next landing and tilted his head, he didn't know exactly where the dragon tear was. Shoving him wouldn't help.

A cry of pain came from somewhere ahead. A woman's cry.

Jev raced past Lornysh and sprinted through passages until he came out on his grandmother's garden balcony. The door to her suite stood open. He sprinted in and scoured the suite with his gaze.

"Zenia?" He couldn't imagine why she would be in his grandmother's rooms, but the cry had come from this direction and this level.

He poked his head into the dark crafts room and almost drew back right away, since no lanterns were lit, but Lornysh came up behind him and stopped him with a hand to his shoulder.

"It's in there." Lornysh peered into the dark. "As is she. On the floor behind the loom over there."

Jev couldn't see her, but he trusted his friend. He snatched a lantern off the wall and plunged in, almost tripping over an easel. He started to kick it out of the way, but a groan came from the back, and he forgot his irritation. He raced through the maze of projects and finally spotted Zenia as Lornysh had described her, on the floor. A lantern lying next to her must have gone out when she'd fallen.

"Zenia?" Jev dropped to his knees, set his lantern down, and touched her face. "Are you all right? What happened?"

He glanced around the room, puzzled about why she was in here and who or what would have attacked her.

"Here." Lornysh knelt by the wall a couple of feet away and swiped his finger through a scattering of sand or dust on the floor.

Jev stroked Zenia's hair as Lornysh stood, shifted a tapestry aside, and ran his fingers over the wall. One of the stones wasn't flush with the others. He drew it out and peered into a dark hole. Jev vaguely remembered the spot, remembered standing in this room when he had been six or seven and his father removing dragon tears to test him for aptitude with them. It was the secret niche he'd been thinking of when he'd mentioned heirloom gems to Iridium, but he hadn't seen the spot in decades.

"This was disturbed recently," Lornysh said. "It looks like there's a magical ward on it or a warning. But it wasn't reset the last time someone was in here."

"Did Zenia trigger something? Why didn't she wait for me?" Jev frowned down at her.

Her eyelids fluttered but did not yet open.

"Did you know someone was after you?" he murmured softly, answering his own question. She might not have thought she had much time.

"There are eight dragon tears in here in addition to the one she wears around her neck," Lornysh said. "I don't sense any other magic in the room, but…" He gazed toward one of the walls, his eyes growing distant.

"She took it from me," Zenia rasped, her green eyes finally open and looking up at them.

Jev read the pain in them and wished he had the power to heal her. A bruise darkened one of her cheekbones, and one of her eyes was swelling shut. If she'd been caught by any of those falling rocks, she would have more bruises under her robe.

"It was showing me… the past," Zenia said. "From the elves' eyes. I think it would have shown me more, but she took it from me."

"Who?" Jev asked.

"Visha."

"My *grandmother?*" As soon as his startled word came out, Jev realized he shouldn't have been so surprised. Grandmother was old, yes, but she was also the guardian of the dragon tears—and of another artifact inside that vault, it seemed. If she'd seen a stranger removing an item, of course she would have taken it back.

"She tried to kill me," Zenia whispered.

"Uh?" Jev looked up at Lornysh, as if his friend might advise him on how to respond. If Zenia had been hit on the head, she might be confused.

"She arranged the rockfall," Zenia continued earnestly. Her eyes were clear and didn't appear dazed or confused. "Or she had an accomplice. I'm sure of it. I made the mistake of looking toward the vault when we were talking. She saw me. I didn't realize that was enough for her to see me as a threat. Where did she go? She must have the artifact." Zenia struggled to sit up.

"Wait, just rest." Jev didn't want to force her to stay on the floor, but he also didn't want to encourage her to run off. She looked like she might pitch over if she tried to stand. "Lornysh will find the artifact."

Jev met his friend's eyes, expecting a sarcastic response or for him to point out that he might run into trouble if he strolled openly around the castle. But Lornysh nodded gravely and jogged out of the room.

"I must take it back to Sazshen," Zenia said. "And I wish to see the rest of the vision. To know what happened next. I shouldn't be curious about something that's not mine, I know, but I am."

"I think we all are at this point." Jev gathered her into his arms—she was halfway to her feet already—hoping to halt her attempt to sprint off without seeming like he was impeding her. "Come, sit on the couch. I know my grandmother has some poultices and some willow bark powder for tea. It'll help with the pain."

"I don't want tea, Jev. I want to find that artifact."

"I know, but Lornysh will do that. And you can lick the powder if you don't want to take time to make tea. Though I seem to remember it being bitter and disgusting."

"Lornysh will get it? And then disappear with it? What if—"

"He won't." Jev hoped he spoke the truth. He didn't think Lornysh would abscond with the artifact, but if it had something to do with the elves, then maybe he would consider his people the rightful owners.

After depositing Zenia on the couch, Jev made a stay-there motion with his hands and hoped she would. He hurried to the cabinet where his grandmother kept her healer's supplies.

Footsteps pounded on the floor outside the crafts room. Jev didn't see the poultices he had been thinking of but spotted a jar of the unctuous salve his mother and grandmother had slathered him and Vastiun with whenever they had been injured. He assumed it had medicinal qualities. He spotted the willow powder, grabbed it and the jar, then hurried to stand protectively over Zenia. She'd half risen, using the arm of the couch for support, and looked determined to rush away, no matter who was coming.

"Jev?" came Cutter's voice from the next room.

"In here."

Cutter and Rhi appeared in the doorway.

"Zenia, what happened?" Rhi demanded and rushed to the couch. She wrapped an arm around Zenia's shoulders, also appearing determined to keep her from hurrying off.

Good.

"A rockfall happened." Zenia didn't look like she wanted anyone stopping her. "To me. At least partially. I was lucky and ran fast enough to avoid it." She touched her shoulder and winced. "Most of it."

"A rockfall?" Cutter asked. "In a castle?"

"I saw soot." Jev sat on Zenia's other side. "Someone set a charge. It's downstairs on the way to the stable if you want to take a look at it."

"You do know how to get me excited." Cutter trotted out, his tools and weapons clanking on his belt.

Zenia gripped Rhi's arm. "Jev's grandmother is the one with the artifact. She may be running off to hide it. Will you find her? Please?"

"His grandmother? How old is she?"

"Not too old to hide an ivory carving." Zenia didn't mention again her suspicions about the rockfall, but her lips pressed together with disapproval. And pain.

Jev frowned. Could his grandmother truly have been responsible for the rockfall? It seemed so unlikely. His father was the one who hadn't been down there even though the staff had said he was in the castle. That had been odd. But Jev couldn't imagine his father sabotaging his own castle, not when he'd be the one who would feel responsible for leading the repairs later. If the old man wanted to get rid of an inquisitor, he'd be more likely to walk up and shoot her. Or challenge her to a duel.

Zenia, her face still tight with pain, lowered her hand.

"Let me spread some of this on your injuries." Jev held up the jar of salve he'd grabbed. "It might help with the pain until we can get you to a healer."

"Rhi?" Zenia asked, her gaze intent and locked onto the other woman. She didn't acknowledge Jev's offer.

Too focused. Like a hound pointed at a treed raccoon, unaware of anything else around it.

Rhi nodded. "I'll go look for her."

"Lornysh is already looking for her, so follow him if you see him. Apparently, he can sense magic—the artifact. Make sure—" Now Zenia glanced at Jev. Warily. "You know what to make sure, Rhi."

"Yes, ma'am. I'll get the bauble. You stay here and let your zyndar rub stuff on you." She saluted, then jogged out of the room.

"*My* zyndar?" Zenia mouthed and looked at Jev again, this time for more than a glance.

"I could be," he said. "You don't have one of your own yet, do you?"

"No, I've never wanted a zyndar." Zenia, perhaps realizing she'd done as much as she could for now, and that Rhi would do the work she needed done, finally let herself slump against the backrest of the couch.

"Not at all? We're terribly desirable." Jev removed the lid from the jar, nose wrinkling at the pungent tea-tree-oil scent. "Perhaps you should start a collection."

"A collection? One wouldn't be enough to satisfy me?"

"I suppose the right one could be. I've been told I'm satisfying. Admittedly, not for some time." He grimaced as an image of Naysha popped into his mind. He'd only meant to joke with Zenia, to take her mind off her pain, not to think of past romances.

"Because you've been away at war and there was nobody around to satisfy?"

"No women, at least." Jev smeared some of the goop onto his finger, then lightly touched it to the bruise on Zenia's cheek. "I've never been excited at the prospect of satisfying men or animals."

"Those being almost the same thing?"

"When it comes to what I'm willing to satisfy, yes."

She didn't wince at his touch. Heartened, he spread the stuff on, being as gentle as he could.

Shouts and bangs sounded elsewhere in the castle, the din muffled but audible within this central suite, but Zenia closed her eyes. Jev finished smoothing the salve over her cheek. Her nose wrinkled.

"I promise it's better than licking the willow bark powder," he said. "But not much."

She smiled faintly. "Did you find anything interesting following the elf into the wilds?"

"Interesting, yes. Explanatory, not really. I have more questions instead of fewer."

"That's often the way of investigations. You run in circles only to end up close to where you started."

"I apologize for not—I mean, I truly didn't know that artifact was located in the castle. I suspected the answers were here on my land somewhere but not quite that literally."

"I know."

"Do you want me to smear any of this salve elsewhere?" Jev held up the jar. "I can't see where all you're bruised under that robe."

"My knee is throbbing like a dwarf hammering away at a lucrative vein. And there are bruises all over my shoulders."

He waited since she hadn't said whether she wanted *him* to do anything about her aches, and he hated to presume, especially when he was no healer. But when she shifted on the cushion, her eyes tightened at the corners and a soft gasp escaped her lips. He slid off the couch and knelt beside her legs.

"Which knee hurts?" he asked.

"The giant swollen one."

He thought she might make him lift her hem to peek, but she touched her right leg. He did push her hem up, though he was careful not to intrude on her modesty. The knee *was* noticeably swollen and already turning blue.

"Thank you, Jev," she whispered as he rubbed some of the salve on it. "Is this what zyndars do if you collect them?"

"I'll happily rub anything you want." He decided this wasn't the time for a sexual leer and kept his focus on her knee.

"Sounds stimulating."

"It could be."

The faint smile ghosted across her lips again. He decided he would order the next member of the castle staff he saw to go into town and bring out a healer, someone with a dragon tear to lend magical power.

"Why aren't you married, Jev?" Zenia asked.

"There weren't a lot of options in Taziira." He did not allow himself to think of Naysha, though it was hard, since she had already intruded on his thoughts. Sometime, when the dust from all this settled, he would find out what had happened to her. He couldn't help but wonder about the man she had married, the children she'd had. He hoped that once he knew she was satisfied in her new life, he could let that particular ghost settle under a funeral cairn.

"That's the only reason? I've heard zyndar marriages are often arranged when they're young. And you…" Her eyes opened halfway, and she reached out and touched his hair. It was a whisper of a touch but enough to send a sensation of warmth through him. And enough to make him think about running his hand higher up her leg. "You're nice," she finished.

"Am I?" He pulled down her hem, covering her leg again.

"I expected you to be an arrogant ass. Because all zyndar I've met are."

"*All* of them? How many have you met?"

"Dozens."

"Hm. How many that had been away at war for years?"

"Only one."

"Maybe sleeping on your back in the mud and having elven guerrillas try to shoot you full of arrows rubs off some of the arrogance."

"Then your entire species should be sent off to war. Promptly. Every year."

"Species?" Though he was reluctant to disturb the hand that had come to rest in his hair, he rose to sit beside her on the couch again. She had mentioned other wounds. "You think we're something other than human?"

"Most zyndar seem to think they are. Superhuman."

"Hm." He might have made more of a defense for his fellow noblemen, but he remembered the story she'd shared of her past, of how she'd come to lose her mother. He couldn't make any excuses for that. For Zyndar Veran Morningfar. Jev would remember who had slighted her, and if he ever had the chance to pay the man a visit, he would flatten him with a punch. "Do you want me to treat the bruises on your shoulders?"

"Yes." Zenia shifted away from the backrest and turned sideways, pulling her hair forward over her shoulder. "It's warm and tingly, so I hope that means it's doing something."

"Me, too, but I guess if I can make a woman warm and tingly, that's partway to being satisfying."

She opened her robe via the ties on the front and let it slide off her shoulders. She wore a light chemise underneath, one that left her shoulders and arms bare. Had they been less bruised, he would have found the sight stimulating, but all he wanted to do was hug her and apologize for the injuries she'd received in his castle.

"Why aren't *you* married, Zenia?" he asked. "Surely, there are more options here in the city than in enemy forests."

"Maybe. But I chose to focus on my career." She bent her head forward as he gently smoothed salve on the angry lumps rising from her skin. A long moment passed before she quietly added, "And I may have, in choosing that career, become someone... I don't know. Untouchable. Or that people don't want to touch."

"Because you're an inquisitor?"

"Yes. People fear inquisitors. People always seem to feel guilty about things, and they hustle away from me like they think I'm going to drag them off to a dungeon for an interrogation."

Jev, remembering his *own* interrogation, could understand why people would have such notions. But she hadn't been the one to hurt him.

"You never feared me," she whispered, shifting on the couch again so she could see him.

"No," he agreed, making himself look into her eyes rather than down at her chest—the thin chemise did nothing to hide curves, and a naughty voice in the back of his mind suggested he should ask to inspect all of her for bruises. And apply salve as needed. Languidly. He shut the door firmly on that voice. "I hope it doesn't make you feel less fearsome, but after the things I've seen over the years, a human representative of the Water Order doesn't make my knees quake."

"Was it worth it?" she asked. "The war?"

He closed his eyes and took a breath. "I wish I could say it was, that it had all been worth it, that being there had meant something, but as captain of Gryphon Company, I knew a lot that went on behind the scenes. I knew we were there because of the king's paranoia, paranoia that may or may not have been founded. Even if it was, starting a war preemptively because of something you think might or might not come to pass is morally questionable at best."

"I'm sorry."

"Not your fault," he murmured, then opened his eyes, not wanting to dwell on a past he'd already spent far too much time dwelling on. Dwelling *in*. "*I'm* sorry my castle fell on you."

He smiled, hoping to change the subject. Or maybe they should finish up, and he could put some effort into finding her a real healer. Of course, he'd have to take his hand off her shoulder—odd how it had managed to stay there—and she would have to put her robe back on, the robe that pooled at her waist now. The pistol holstered in a slender feminine belt amused him, even though he'd known it was there. He wondered if she was cold with the robe halfway off. Maybe he could warm her up.

No, this wasn't the time. Lornysh ought to return any moment. Surely, an eighty-year-old woman couldn't keep away from him for long.

"You didn't do it," she said, lifting a hand to his face.

She stroked his cheek, and he realized he'd been looking down at her waist. And other things.

He lifted his gaze to meet hers, relishing her gentle touch. "Do you want me to beat up whoever did?"

He didn't truly think his grandmother had been responsible, but her face crinkled in a dubious expression, so maybe she did.

"We'll see what Rhi drags up for us to look at," Zenia said, drawing her hand from his cheek to his lips.

That felt nice. More than nice. Arousing. Though he'd rather have her lips on his lips. Would she be amenable to that? Probably not while she was injured. Perhaps later. He could invite her to the beach for the vacation he still hoped to have.

"I have to take the artifact back to Sazshen," Zenia said, apology in her tone.

Should he admit he hadn't been thinking of that at all and didn't particularly care right now? He knew why she was here. Nothing had changed, at least for him. Maybe she thought he believed his family had some claim on the artifact if it had been here in the vault all this time.

"I know," he said. "I won't stop you."

Some of the tension in her shoulders loosened. Relief. He hadn't realized how worried she was about it.

"Thank you." She hesitated, looking for something in his eyes, then leaned forward.

A testament to how out of practice he was with women, he didn't realize what she intended until her lips touched his. Fortunately, he remembered what to do after that. He fumbled the jar over to a table, then drew her gently into his arms, not wanting to hurt her but wanting to let her know that he appreciated the kiss. That he would be happy to be *her* zyndar.

Her fingers pushed through his hair and curled into the back of his scalp. Hot energy surged through him, and his thoughts of gentleness and appreciation shifted to something more passionate.

Until a gunshot cracked somewhere outside.

Zenia jerked back, and Jev bolted to his feet. More shots fired. Hells, was someone shooting at Lornysh? If so, it was his fault for sending him down there.

"I have to go," he blurted, extending an apologetic hand in a wave as he stepped past her toward the door.

"I'm going too."

"No, you should—"

"Go with you," she said firmly, pushing to her feet and tugging her robe over her shoulders.

She winced in pain, but she limped toward the doorway with the same determination she applied to every task.

Knowing the salve couldn't have done that much to help, he offered his arm. "We'll go together."

She hesitated, then relented, shifting closer to him. He wrapped his arm around her waist and slung her arm over his shoulders as they navigated toward the exit.

More shots fired, and Jev quickened his pace. Zenia didn't object.

He just hoped they wouldn't be too late.

CHAPTER 19

Z ENIA GRITTED HER TEETH AND kept up with Jev's
long strides as they ran out of the suite and into the balcony
garden overlooking the main courtyard. The main courtyard full
of people. She spotted Lornysh gripping Visha by the arm and taking
cover behind the fountain while men with rifles raced out of a doorway
and spread out. Two men with smoking weapons already stood pointing
them at—

"Rhi!" Zenia blurted.

Her blue gi flashed as she kicked and punched, trading blows with—
was that Heber Dharrow?

"Father!" Jev yelled, going rigid.

"*Why* are they fighting?" Zenia demanded, angling toward the steps
heading down.

"Don't shoot," Jev called to someone taking aim at Lornysh around
the statue in the fountain. "Wait here," he told Zenia and released her so
he could sprint away at full speed.

As if she would wait. She didn't know why Rhi was fighting with
the zyndar prime, but nothing good could come of it.

Jev sprang down the final steps and raced through the courtyard,
waving at men to lower their rifles or knocking them to the side if
the owners weren't quick enough to obey. He glanced at Lornysh but
sprinted to Rhi and his father.

As Zenia made her way down the stairs, irritated with her limp and
her wounds, Heber launched a flurry of punches at Rhi that would have
sent most people sprawling into the dirt. She weaved, ducked, blocked,

and returned the attack with a side kick. He tried to twist away, but she caught him in the hip. He staggered back. She didn't give him time to recover, and, an instant before Jev reached her and grabbed her from behind, she kicked his father again. Heber staggered back, bumped against the lip of the fountain, and tumbled into the water with a splash that silenced the courtyard.

The guards stared in slack-mouthed horror at seeing their master treated so. Though worried, Zenia trusted Rhi had a good reason for her actions. Since Jev had already stopped that fight, or at least half of it, Zenia hobbled around the fountain toward the other party of interest.

"Let me go, you pointy-eared bastard!" Jev's grandmother cried, trying to pull away from Lornysh while she flailed wildly with her fists.

He stood behind her, gripping her by the upper arms, and she didn't manage to connect. He didn't even seem troubled by her efforts. His cool gaze locked onto Zenia as she approached, and once again, she remembered the way he'd sprung from the rooftop to attack her and Rhi. And how effective he had been at that attack. Would he attempt to thwart her now?

"You!" Visha cried, spotting Zenia.

She stopped flailing, but she didn't lose any of her anger or indignation. She simply redirected it at Zenia.

"You thieving elf-kisser," she snarled. "This is all your fault. You came here to steal what's rightfully ours."

"It belongs to the Water Order," Zenia said.

"Actually, it does not," Lornysh said coolly.

Founders, Zenia had worried he would become part of the problem. She noticed that Visha had unclenched one of her fists but not the other.

Splashes sounded as Heber crawled out of the fountain on the other side of the statue.

"Father," Jev said. "We need to talk."

"You brought that elf into my home," his father said. "I'll box your ears in."

"Yes, that's what we need to talk about." Jev released Rhi with a stay-back gesture and approached his dripping father.

Rhi folded her arms over her chest but didn't attempt to attack the man again. Or had she merely been defending herself? No, Zenia had a feeling Jev's father had started the attack—lunging toward Lornysh, perhaps, to protect Visha. And Rhi had tried to intercept, at which point he'd turned on her.

"Also, I'd like to know what's happening and why there's gunfire inside our castle," Jev added.

"Inside *my* castle," Heber said. "You left for ten years. You came home and brought all this trouble with you. And that—" He thrust an angry arm toward Lornysh. "*That.*" He whirled toward his men. "I told you to shoot him."

"Not while my grandmother is standing next to him," Jev growled.

Fortunately, the men must have realized the elf had her, for none of them raised their rifles again. Heber scowled fiercely, water plastering his hair to his head.

Zenia captured Visha's closed fist. Belatedly, the woman tried to yank it away.

"I'm sorry, ma'am," Zenia said, though she wasn't, not when she suspected Visha of arranging to have that ceiling dropped on her. "But I was sent here to retrieve this."

"It belongs to my family. My grandson liberated it, and it's ours now, right and fair."

"Liberated it? More likely stole it," Lornysh said. "Or was handed it to hold temporarily."

"What do you know, Lorn?" Jev called over, frowning, a hand up toward his father, who looked like he wanted to plow through Jev, grab someone's rifle, and shoot Lornysh whether Visha stood next to him or not.

"Let's all calm down," Zenia said, willing her dragon tear to lend power to her words. "And figure out how exactly this artifact came to be here."

Zenia gazed into Visha's eyes, wanting the woman to let go so she wouldn't have to pry her fingers open.

Affected by the gem's power, Visha let her grip slacken. It was enough. Zenia extracted the ivory carving from her grasp.

She fought down a surge of triumph and the urge to grab the nearest horse and race back to the temple with it. She couldn't leave Jev with this mess, nor could she run off without Rhi. Jev had released her, but two of the castle guards had their rifles pointed in her direction, no doubt because she had been pummeling their master.

The artifact hummed with power in Zenia's hand, and white flashed around the edges of her vision. Did it want to foist another vision on her? Or a continuation of the last one?

"Not now," she whispered to it, willing it to understand. She dearly wanted to grasp all it had to offer her, but this wasn't the place to pass out. Last time, that hadn't gone well. She was lucky Visha hadn't smothered her with a tapestry while she'd been unconscious.

"Take whatever that thing is and get off my property," Heber ordered.

"No," Visha said, shaking her head and shaking off Zenia's influence. "That's the relic I told you about. It's ours."

"The Water Order is taking it into custody," Zenia said.

"But it belongs to neither of you," a new voice said from the castle entrance.

The guards whirled toward the speaker, a woman with long blonde hair in a dozen braids. Zenia gasped, for she recognized the woman— the elf princess?—from the vision the artifact had given her.

The elf lifted a hand, and the men with rifles lowered them again. Judging by the pained expressions on their faces, it was against their will.

Zenia shivered at the display of magic. She stepped back, tempted to hide the ivory carving behind her back, as if the elf wouldn't notice it then. But she could feel Lornysh looking at her, and the princess's gaze also turned in her direction.

Zenia walked around the fountain to stand by Jev, wanting his support and also not wanting to be close enough for Lornysh or the grandmother to reach her—and the artifact. Neither moved to follow her.

"What brings you to our fair castle?" Jev bowed toward the elf woman. "If it's word of my grandmother's cookies, we'll have to check the kitchen to see if there are any left. Also to make sure they aren't smothered with rock dust, as we've recently had an incident, and the kitchen isn't that far from the location."

The elf woman's gaze shifted toward him, her expression hard to scrutinize. Zenia doubted elves shared humans' senses of humor.

Jev spoke again, but this time, in one of the elven dialects. Zenia didn't know any of the words, only that the language had a beautiful lyrical quality unlike any of the human tongues and far different from the dwarven language.

The elf nodded slowly and replied in the same language.

Jev's father glowered, his fingers tightened in fists and his shoulders hunched. There weren't many kingdom subjects now with a reason to adore elves, but why did he have such distaste? Because he'd lost a son in the war against them? Was that Visha's reason for loathing them too? Or did it have to do with Jev's mother's disappearance?

"Interesting," Jev finally said after they had conversed for several moments.

He surveyed the people standing in the courtyard—more had filtered in through other doorways—and once again made a patting weapons-down motion toward the tense riflemen. Then he pointed to Zenia and told the princess, "It's not mine to give."

The elf's gaze returned to Zenia.

She lifted her chin. "It's not mine to give either. I was ordered to retrieve it and return it to the temple of the Water Order." She almost added that it rightfully belonged to the Water Order and had been stolen from a temple inquisitor years ago, but she wasn't certain of that anymore. She also hadn't figured out why Jev's younger brother would have taken it in the first place.

"So that its message may be hidden away once more?" the elf princess asked. "Your people should be, now more than ever, ready to hear the truth. Perhaps then they will not be so quick to embroil themselves—and my kind—in another war, a war where there was never anything to gain."

"Its message?" Jev asked.

The elf flicked a couple of fingers toward Zenia's clenched fist. The artifact grew warmer against her palm, and white light crept into her vision again.

Cursing, she dropped the artifact. She didn't want to, but she also didn't want to be knocked unconscious, not when the situation was tense and volatile.

But the vision found her, regardless.

"I thank you for guiding me through your countryside, friend human," the elf princess said, smiling at the man riding the horse beside hers. From a mountain perch miles inland, they looked out toward the sea and Korvann sprawling along the shore.

The human, a handsome man who looked a lot like Jev, grinned roguishly at her. "Friend human? Is that all I am to you?"

The princess's cheeks grew a shade pink. "I have enjoyed our journey to this point with you. Before I left the heartwoods, I hadn't realized humans were so vigorous."

The roguish grin grew broader. "Just some. When properly inspired."

"It's a shame I must return after I deliver this message." She looked down at her palm, at a familiar ivory tree-shaped artifact resting there.

"I suppose I wouldn't be welcome to visit."

"Not with your people currently invading the heartwoods, trying to kill mine. But perhaps if the message is heard and understood to be true…" She curled her fingers around the artifact and firmed her jaw. "It will be. I will not fail my father in this."

"I believe you." The man—Jev's brother?—leaned over and gripped her forearm. "Put up your hood. I can get you into the castle to see Prince Dazron—he'll have to do since the king is leading the war himself and since he wouldn't care anyway. Dazron is our main hope. The archmages of the Orders…"

"I'm told Earth and Air may be trusted and that they opposed the war, but that we must avoid Water and Fire."

"I'd prefer to avoid them all. The prince is known to be reasonable."

"Yes," the princess agreed, "and though he supports his father in public, he's privately spoken against the war and the way it is depleting your people's resources."

"Should I find it alarming that you know more about what the prince does privately than I do?"

"My people have ways." She smiled cryptically at him.

"Just so long as you haven't been investigating his vigor. He's married, you know."

"Really, Vastiun. You humans are so…"

"Appealingly unique and quirky?"

"You are quirky. Come." She nudged her horse into motion and raised the hood of her green cloak over her blonde hair. "We are not far now."

But as they rode down the hill, the road passed near a stand of trees. Dozens of men raced out from within, firing muskets and rifles. They were a ragtag bunch, appearing at first as bandits, but then two figures in blue rode out of the shadows on white horses. One wore the robe of an inquisitor and the other the attire of a monk. They sat astride the horses and watched as the bandits attacked the pair on the road.

The elf raised her hands, bringing some magic to bear, even as a dragon tear about her throat glowed a fierce golden. Jev's brother fired at the bandits, taking down several, but the inquisitor shouted something, and the men did not falter in their attack. They rushed at the elf. Vastiun jumped down from his horse, drawing a short sword and attacking in close quarters. A crude explosive went off, the force hurling Vastiun into the brush at the side of the road. The attackers focused on the elf princess instead of him. She realized she wouldn't drive back so many and whispered an enchantment, then hurled the artifact off the side of the mountain.

It floated out of sight and landed—the inquisitor did not see where. Vastiun, halfway to his feet again, gasped and grabbed the side of his head. As he bent over—in pain?—an arrow thudded into the princess's heart. Vastiun cried out in rage and swung his sword at the thugs, but there were too many. She crumpled to the road and died, the arrow protruding from her chest. The men beat Vastiun senseless, then, under the inquisitor's orders, ran down into the brush to hunt for the thrown artifact.

But they did not find it. Magic had hurled it farther than physical strength could.

When Vastiun woke, a vision burned in his mind, the resting place of the artifact. It was the last thing the princess had given him before dying.

With shaky limbs, he buried her in a cairn beside the road, then walked down the mountainside, magic drawing him to a place the others hadn't found. He picked up the artifact and stared at it, experiencing the vision it had been crafted to show.

It sprang back in time thousands of years and showed human after human sneaking into the Taziira heartwoods and stealing dragon tears, occasionally from the hordes of slumbering dragons, as so many of the stories told, but more often from the homes of peaceful elves. Sometimes, they murdered those inhabitants to ensure nobody followed them back to their homeland across the sea.

These adventurers all returned sharing tales of how they'd bravely won the dragon tears or had stolen them from unsuspecting dragons, *none of them mentioning the truth. Eventually, the elves took to the trees and made their homes difficult to find. Some of them sought revenge, leading humans to learn to fear their kind, but by the time the Era of Discovery came to a close, thousands of dragon tears had shifted into human hands. And as generations passed, humans forgot how they had come to have them and told stories of how the founders themselves had gifted them to the various human kingdoms.*

Only the elves remembered the truth.

The vision faded, and Zenia lurched upright with a gasp. She had fallen to the cobblestones. Had someone snatched the artifact while she was knocked out? No, she was lying right on top of it, the ivory carving digging into her hip. She pulled it out as she looked around for the elves or other threats.

Everyone in the courtyard lay crumpled on the cobblestones except for Lornysh and the elf princess. Or the woman Zenia had assumed was the elf princess from the original vision. The blonde female who'd died in the vision had looked so much like this person standing in front of her and looking at her.

"My twin sister," the elf said quietly, holding Zenia's gaze.

Zenia swallowed. With every human in the courtyard unconscious, the elf could have walked over and taken the artifact at any time.

"I wish to finish what she started, to make sure your people know the truth, that we are only your enemies because your people made us so. Humans coveted our magic, since they had none of their own, and took it by force. And the dragon tears were not even ours to give. We promised long ago to keep them for the dwarves who originally mined them from a rare vein imbued with magic. They used the gems against each other in a civil war that lasted centuries. Finally, their leaders rounded them all up and gave them to us so they could no longer use them against each other. They have been a mixed blessing for our people to say the least."

"Why should I believe you?" Zenia asked. "Or *this*." She thrust out the artifact.

On the cobblestones beside her, Jev groaned faintly. Elsewhere, a few other people also stirred.

"It is your choice to believe as you wish," the elf said, "but you should sense the truth in the Eye of Truth. It was given that name for a reason. It was created to show only truths and for those who partake in its visions to understand that."

"Magic could make me believe anything, I suppose." Unfortunately, Zenia found that she *did* believe the story. Sazshen herself was as much to blame as a carved piece of ivory. She'd been so evasive. Had she known exactly how the Order had acquired—no, *attempted* to acquire—the artifact? "Basically, your people want our people to know that we originally stole the dragon tears?"

"We do. My father believed that if you all knew, or at least if your leaders knew, then perhaps you would realize…"

"We should be asking forgiveness rather than trying to take over your continent and suborn your kind?" Jev asked, grimacing as he rose to his knees.

Had he heard the whole conversation?

Zenia touched his shoulder, wanting to know what he believed. His family was so tied up in all this. What did he think should be done?

"We do not require your contrition," the princess said.

Lornysh grunted. In disagreement? It was the first noise he'd made since Zenia woke. Visha lay crumpled next to him on the lip of the fountain, and she hadn't stirred yet.

The princess smiled knowingly at him but did not otherwise respond to him.

"And we do not ask that you return all the dragon tears, though there are some among us who have argued for that, yes. Argued that we take the war to your shores and recover all of them we can. They were only ever a small faction among us, but I believe your spies learned of their wishes and shared their words with your King Abdor. And that was all it took." The princess shook her head, her eyes holding an eternal sorrow that made her seem far older than she appeared. "All we hope for is a more restful peace going forward. If your leaders know the truth, perhaps it will ensure that."

As more people stirred in the courtyard, all seeming to have seen the vision and to understand the conversation going on, Zenia stared down at her fist, at her fingers closed around the artifact. It was still slightly warm, but it didn't seem to be oozing any magic now. No visions. No attempts to manipulate her.

"I think if you took it to our soon-to-be-king, Targyon, he would be willing to listen," Jev said, then lowered his voice. "If the Water Order allows it. It was clear to me—" he touched his temple, "—that they didn't want it to reach Prince Dazron five years ago. They may have decided humanity was better off not knowing its past. For their own good. Or for the status quo. I don't know."

Jev didn't look at Zenia, and she was glad. She did not want to see an accusation in his eyes. She hadn't known about any of this, but here she stood in her blue robe, clearly a representative of the Water Order.

"Your own family seems to have made a similar decision," Lornysh said, coming around the fountain and leaving Visha.

She was stirring now, frowning and lifting her head, and that made Zenia uneasy. Heber, too, had his eyes open, though he lay on his stomach, simply watching for now. Biding his time?

"To keep the truth hidden," Lornysh added.

Jev frowned. "Vastiun must have fled—joined the army and sailed overseas—to avoid the wrath of the Water Order. Maybe he feared he would never be able to get close to the prince once they realized he'd recovered the artifact. He told me none of this, not even when he lay dying in my arms. He simply mentioned the girl that he regretted losing." Jev lifted his eyebrows toward the elf princess.

"My sister was a lovely person."

"And then I, knowing nothing of the importance of the artifact, bundled it up with the rest of Vastiun's belongings and sent it home." Jev turned toward his father and also looked toward his grandmother. "What happened after that? Somebody knows. And was that Corvel's skeleton we found in the woods? Someone *shot* him. On our land."

Zenia expected the father to flinch or give away knowledge of the event, but it was Visha who clenched her jaw and glared defiantly over at Jev.

"I never saw his belongings, and I've no idea where your mother's butler went," Jev's father said.

Zenia almost nudged Jev to get him to look over at his grandmother, but his head turned in that direction without assistance. Her defiance didn't change. There was no shame in her eyes. She almost looked proud. By the founders, *she* hadn't trekked out to the meeting stone and shot the butler, had she? And if she had, why would she be proud of that?

"Grandmother?" Jev prompted.

"He was going to take it back to *them*." Visha pointed at Lornysh and also at the princess. "To some stinking elves. While we were at war with them. It was a betrayal. He betrayed his own people, and that's a crime deserving of a hanging or a shooting. The law says so. Kingdom and Order." She turned her defiant stare on Zenia, but only for a moment.

"You didn't do it," Jev said. "Follow him out there and shoot him? Surely not..."

If anything, Visha's expression grew more defiant. "You think I can't defend what's right? Boy, I fired at Ska invaders that came onto our property and thieved our horses during the Border Wars. You think I can't shoot when the law demands it? Or just when it's right? When people run off and become damn elf sympathizers? I did it before. I did it to my own blood." For the first time, her defiance slackened, and her voice developed a quaver. "You can't let your own blood betray the kingdom, betray you. No matter how much... I didn't mean to kill her though. Just a warning. She was going to leave her own boys to run off with *them*. It's not right. Not right. I didn't raise her like that. I didn't."

Zenia watched Jev's face as the words tumbled out, as the woman's self-righteous proclamations turned into a confession.

"The cairn," Jev said numbly, looking to Lornysh.

Though puzzled, Zenia didn't say anything. She had her own dilemma to consider.

But before she could return to pondering the carving in her hand, Visha faced her. "You going to arrest me for it, girl?"

Founders, was she supposed to? The woman had just confessed to not one but two murders. It was technically a kingdom matter, nothing to do with the Orders, but had she attempted a third murder?

"Did you try to crush me in that rockfall?" Zenia asked.

Jev winced. The accusation wasn't for him, but this was *his* grandmother. Would he try to take some of the blame? It wasn't his fault.

Visha glanced over at one of the armed guards, a man who pointedly did not look back. He studied the cobblestones at his feet and didn't meet anyone's eyes.

"I arranged it," Visha said. "You had no right to be here, no right to thieve what rightfully belongs to our family now. What's been locked up for five years and should stay locked up for five hundred. But I saw you looking. I knew what you were thinking and that you felt it with your own magic. I never thought an inquisitor would want to let out those elf lies, but they've got sympathizers everywhere. You never know."

Visha didn't realize that she and Zenia—or at least she and Sazshen—had been on the same side. They had both wanted to keep the truth locked away.

"And I was right, wasn't I?" Visha added. "First chance you got, you ran up there and stole it."

"I had orders from the archmage to retrieve it." Zenia couldn't help but feel guilty at having done exactly what the woman accused, but this was her mission, and her crimes were nothing compared to the ones Visha had perpetrated.

Jev stood still, his lips parted, looking as stunned as if someone had slammed a sledgehammer into his chest. Surprisingly, his father wore a similar expression. Zenia guessed he knew something about the artifact, but she wagered this was the first time he'd heard his wife had been murdered.

"Inquisitor Cham," the elf princess said. "The crimes that have occurred here have been human and are in your domain, save for one." She extended a slender finger, pointing at Zenia's fist. "Will you return the Eye of Truth to me? To my family? I will show it to your new king, and then I will take it to the other kingdoms and share this knowledge there, as well. If you relinquish the artifact. It was carved long ago by a relative of our family, so it is rightfully ours."

"Can't you just *tell* the king the truth?" Jev recovered from his shock enough to give Zenia a concerned look. Of all the people here, only he knew how much this mission meant to her. What she could potentially gain if she returned victorious and handed the artifact over to Sazshen.

"Not many humans are inclined to believe my people, especially right now," the princess said. "But the Eye of Truth was made long ago by a talented half-elf mage, a distant relative of mine, as I said. He lived as a hermit, trying to be neither a part of your world nor ours. Because of his neutrality and the power of truth he imbued in the carving, your leaders will be more inclined to believe the artifact than my lips. Inquisitor Cham?"

"Will you take it by force if I don't give it to you?" Zenia asked.

She rubbed her thumb over the artifact. If she believed all that had been shown to her today, she had to accept that returning it to the elves was the right thing to do. But if she did so—if she handed it over willingly—would Sazshen forgive her? Would she still consider Zenia as her successor? As the next archmage to lead the temple into the future?

No, not that last. If Zenia handed over the artifact to an elf, it would be more than failing to complete a mission. It would be choosing a side. Not the side Sazshen and the temple were currently allied with.

"I will not," the elf princess said. "I am a diplomat, not a warrior."

"I wish you'd said yes," Zenia said bleakly.

The elf tilted her head, curious. Jev shared Zenia's bleak expression. Yes, he understood. If she did her best to succeed but failed her mission, perhaps... perhaps that would be forgivable. But to turn her back on her mission...

"Maybe you can say you weren't given a choice," Jev murmured. "Would that be better?"

"Maybe. If it were true. But even if I were inclined to lie to the archmage... Well, you can't lie to an inquisitor."

"Ah."

Zenia opened her palm, offering the artifact to the princess. She wouldn't toss it or walk it over there. She couldn't go that far.

The elf lifted her hand, and the ivory carving floated away from Zenia, coming to rest in her palm.

Tears threatened, more of frustration than loss. Why couldn't the elf have taken the damn thing from her while she'd been unconscious? Why had she forced Zenia to choose? To make the choice that betrayed her mentor and everything she'd been for the last twenty years?

"I thank you, Inquisitor Cham." The princess shifted toward the fountain. "And I thank you—Lornysh is the name you're going by now?"

"Yes," he said, nothing inviting in his tone.

"I thank you for activating the meeting stone. We never expected a favor from you, not after the choices that were made."

"The choices that were *forced* to be made," Lornysh growled.

"You didn't have to join the humans and take up arms against us."

Lornysh switched to the elven language to give his angry retort. Jev must have understood, for his eyebrows twitched minutely, but he did not translate.

"Then why this help now?" the princess asked, still speaking in the kingdom tongue.

"In the end, peace is more desirable for all," Lornysh said.

"Said the mighty blood-letting warrior." The elf's expression grew bemused. "You are a puzzling *rysheria*."

"Yes."

The elves said nothing more to each other. The princess inclined her head toward Jev and Zenia, then turned and walked out into the night. She seemed to disappear before she passed over the drawbridge.

"Are you all right?" Jev whispered.

Zenia shook her head. "No."

He hesitated, then wrapped an arm around her shoulders. She leaned against him and closed her eyes, not wanting to deal with the world. Or the repercussions of her choice.

Hoofbeats sounded on the drawbridge, and she opened her eyes again. A rider in the king's blue, purple, and gold livery entered the courtyard.

"Zyndar Prime," he said, bowing from his horse to address Heber before turning his focus to Jev. "Zyndar Jevlain Dharrow?"

"Yes?" Jev asked, not lowering his arm from Zenia's shoulders.

"Excellent. I've been searching for you. You were last seen... many other places."

"Imagine that."

The rider slid off his horse and jogged over, pulling out a scroll with a purple seal on it. "Soon-to-be-crowned King Targyon requests you join him for breakfast tomorrow before the coronation."

"I would be happy to," Jev said.

The man offered the scroll and pulled out a compact writing kit. He unrolled it, unstoppered an ink bottle, slid a quill into it, and offered the implement to Jev.

"Signature required?"

"To make it official, Zyndar."

Jev signed for himself and added a plus one to the end.

"You're invited," he told Zenia as the rider accepted the scroll back, blowing gently on the ink.

"Is that allowed?" Zenia couldn't imagine being invited to the castle to have breakfast with the king, even the new king, who sounded less intimidating than the old one. Nor could she imagine cavalierly adding a guest to an invitation that hadn't offered the option.

"Absolutely. He owes me a few favors."

"The king owes you favors?"

"Lieutenant Targyon certainly does. I doubt being turned into a king will make him forget them."

Zenia wondered if she could find a healer and deliver her report to Sazshen in time for a breakfast meeting. Oh, how she dreaded making that report.

"It'll be fine," Jev said, watching her face. He lowered his voice to a murmur. "And it'll give you a reason to leave early tomorrow morning. In case reporting in to your superiors doesn't go well."

When had he learned how to read her face so well?

"They can't torture you if you're having breakfast with the king," he added.

Zenia sighed. Torture wasn't what she worried about. The future? That was another matter.

CHAPTER 20

J EV PACED ON THE PERFECTLY manicured brick drive that led through the massive gate at Alderoth Castle. The guards watched him blandly. He'd already shown them his invitation, so they knew he wasn't some panhandler, but one kept glancing pointedly at a clocktower inside the gate. Jev couldn't dally much longer.

Zenia hadn't accepted his invitation with glowing enthusiasm, and he couldn't fault her if she didn't come, but he would worry about her if she didn't. She hadn't seemed concerned by the idea of torture from the temple archmage, but *she* hadn't been the one in that cell, having her mind ripped to pieces. His brain still throbbed at the memory.

He hadn't been surprised in the least to learn the artifact belonged to the elves and that the Water Order had stolen it—attempted to steal it. But Zenia... Technically, she hadn't seemed that surprised either. But he believed she was a good, moral person—especially after he'd watched her hand over the artifact—and he doubted she'd known anything about her Order's history with the piece before she'd been given the assignment.

One of the guards cleared his throat. "Is that your date, Zyndar Dharrow?"

Jev had been staring down at the bricks as he paced. He jerked his head up and clapped his hand to his chest in relief when he spotted Zenia.

He started to grin and wave, but when he realized she wore a sedate beige dress instead of her blue robe, his grin faltered. Other than her brief stint with nudity, he hadn't seen her in anything but the inquisitor garb. True, he hadn't known her for long, but he felt certain she would wear her formal robe for a meeting with the king. *If* she were still an inquisitor.

She walked stiffly, but not as stiffly as the night before. He hoped the Order had let a healer work on her before kicking her out. Bleakly, he noticed that she no longer wore a chain around her neck. Had the archmage demanded she give her dragon tear back to the temple?

"Good morning, Jev," Zenia said, her eyes grave as she nodded at him.

"Are you all right?" he asked without preamble.

He wanted to wrap his arms around her and kiss her, but she didn't look like she wanted that. Besides, the guards might snicker.

Zenia drew a deep breath and let it out slowly. "I am no longer an inquisitor or in the employ of the Temple of the Blue Dragon."

"Founders' razor talons. Your archmage blamed you?"

"For not finding a way to bring in the artifact, yes. And even more for not trying in the end."

"It didn't belong to the Water Order. It never did."

Zenia spread her hands. "I'd rather not talk about it. I have some money saved so I won't be on the street. I'll figure out something."

"You're welcome at my home anytime." All the time, he added silently.

Her chin came up, some of her old fire in her eyes. "I won't accept charity," she said, perhaps more stiffly than she intended.

He almost joked and asked if she would accept a marriage proposal, but it was far too early for that. Besides, marrying her would have been difficult even before she broke into his family's vault and took something from it. Father would consider her a commoner, which was almost a worse crime. Not that *Jev* cared a whit about bloodlines, but his head ached at the idea of dealing with his family over it. Everything was already a riotous mess after his grandmother's revelations.

"I do thank you for the offer," Zenia added more softly. "I didn't say anything about your grandmother or share that part of the story with the archmage. Is she—what will you do?"

"Father, as zyndar prime, is responsible for everyone in the family and what gets reported to the watch offices. If anything. We're outside the city limits. What happens on rural zyndar property has historically been under the jurisdiction of the individual zyndar families. I will say I was very glad not to have to be the one to make any decisions regarding her. She should be shot for what she did, but how do you shoot someone who doesn't even grasp what's going on half the time?"

Jev had been angry—furious—last night when everything had settled down, and he'd realized the full implications, that his grandmother had *shot* his mother. Even though he'd been young when she disappeared, he'd never stopped caring for her and hoping she would return one day. No chance of that now.

"I'm not sure she's as demented as she lets on," Zenia said.

"Perhaps not, but could you stand an eighty-year-old woman up in front of a firing squad?"

"She did attempt to drop a castle on my head."

"Just the corner of the castle." Jev smiled, hoping to lighten her mood.

She snorted. In amusement? He wasn't sure.

"She *will* be punished. Father said so. I just don't think it will involve dungeons and firing squads. I'm guessing he'll exile her from the castle."

Zenia nodded.

"Zyndar?" One of the guards pointed at the clock tower.

"Yes, we're coming. My stomach is rumbling, and I can't remember the last time I sat down for a meal. It was biscuits on the ship over here, I think. We sat cross-legged on the deck and played chips." He shook his head at how much had happened in just a couple of days. That meal on the ship seemed like it had been weeks ago.

"Are your elf and dwarf friends staying around?" Zenia asked quietly as they headed into the castle.

"Lornysh is meditating in the woods somewhere, though he mentioned sneaking in later in the week to gauge the talent of the Korvann Symphony. Cutter is waiting for me to introduce him to Master Grindmor. You haven't heard anything new from her, have you?"

"No, but I've been preoccupied."

He grunted. "Me too."

"I've been wondering about something. What did your elf friend— Lornysh—say last night? When he answered the princess in Elvish."

The guards escorting them past the gardens, fountains, and statues of the grand courtyard looked curiously at Zenia. Jev waited until they'd been led inside and handed off to another set of guards to answer.

"Essentially, he said, 'You kicked me out. You're responsible for my actions.'"

"He worked with you in the army?"

"As a scout these last few years, yes. He's shot many of his own people." Jev wished their discussion had gone into more detail. He still wondered how his friend had come to be exiled.

They reached double doors leading into the great hall and were waved in. They didn't have to take more than a few steps before someone in blue and purple rose from a chair and stepped out to greet them. A familiar someone.

"I'm already sweating through my armpit guards, I sat down and wrinkled my silk trousers, and I'm so nervous I may wet myself."

Jev blinked at this greeting from Targyon, delivered as a sunbeam streamed through the vibrant stained-glass windows and spattered colored light onto him. Jev had been in the middle of sticking out his hand and offering congratulations.

"I hope that's not the opening line for your speech," he said.

Targyon grinned, though his eyes truly held a frantic—or maybe terrified—aspect, and grasped the offered hand. His palms were sweaty. Jev couldn't blame him, but since they still had almost two hours until the ceremony, he thought the nerves were premature. Targyon should wait until no more than ten minutes beforehand to sweat profusely and wet himself.

"Do you not think such candidness will endear me to my subjects?"

"I suppose it could make you seem personable. But they might not know how to deal with a personable king after Abdor." Jev looked over his shoulder. Zenia had walked in with him but had stopped a few steps back.

"Don't worry. Someone wrote a speech for me. It promises a complete lack of personableness. And personality." Targyon grimaced.

Though he probably wasn't supposed to presume to touch his monarch-to-be, especially when six dour-faced guards lined the nearby walls, Jev risked stepping forward and clapping Targyon on the shoulder.

"Be the man you want to be," he said, "not the man they think you should be."

"I'm not sure that's allowed." Bleakness mingled with the other daunted expressions in his eyes.

Jev frowned, wondering what Targyon had endured these last couple of days. He'd been so busy with his own problems that he had no idea. He wished he'd asked his father what had gone on at the meeting between Targyon, his advisors, the Order archmages, and many of the zyndar primes. But he'd been distracted by other matters last night.

"You're about to have power over half the kingdom," Jev said. "*You* get to say what's allowed. And you should be able to influence the other half of the kingdom too." He flicked his fingers toward one of the stained-glass windows that showed off the founding dragons, each in the color and element of the religious Order it represented.

"In theory, but that half put this half here." Targyon pointed at the window, then at his chest.

"Oh? Is that how it played out? Have you figured out if..." Jev hesitated, not certain he should insinuate his belief that foul play had caused the deaths of the princes.

Targyon got the gist anyway. "I've been trying to snoop, but I haven't had a moment to myself. Everyone wants to trail me around and fit me for clothing while teaching me etiquette. Jev, I was never supposed to have to know etiquette. That was for my older brothers who would have zyndar duties. I was—am—I'm supposed to just be a random sixth-born child that nobody cares about."

Jev groped for something encouraging to say. His reaction would be similar, though, if someone thrust the position onto him. And he was older and supposedly wiser than Targyon. At the least, he had seen more battles and had more scars. But it was a different kind of battle experience that would help a man here.

"If you set your mind to doing well," Jev said, "I'm positive you'll be more than competent at the job. The kingdom could use someone with a logical mind who isn't bloodthirsty. We've had enough war for a long time, and I wouldn't be surprised if the Orders chose you because they believe you have a kind soul and will seek to do what's best for the people, rather than worrying about making up threats where they don't exist and trying to foist our religiosity off on other races."

Targyon's mouth twisted. "I think they picked me because I'm young and they think they'll be able to manipulate me easily."

"If so, your awareness of that should make manipulation difficult."

"Seeing manipulation coming doesn't always mean you can avoid it. I don't know if I'm smart enough to outmaneuver all of them."

"No? You knew how to find edible and fermentable tubers in a foreign land, create a vodka still from rusty pots and pans out in the middle of a field, and make alcohol for the men. That's the hallmark of a clever mind."

"Knowing how to make booze?"

"Knowing that the men needed a morale booster."

"What does it say about humanity that alcohol is all it takes to make us happy?"

"Not *all*. Women are important too." Jev grinned, then looked back toward Zenia again. He lifted his hand in invitation, wanting to introduce her.

Targyon's mouth twisted into an even wryer expression as he watched her walk over. "I suppose I shouldn't have been so open in front of a high-ranking member of the Water Order." He rested his hand on his stomach and bowed deeply. "Inquisitor Cham. I read about a couple of your cases in the newspaper before I was shipped off to Taziira. It's an honor to meet someone who's done so much good work for the kingdom." Targyon lifted his head. "Though I must admit that when Jev checked the himself-plus-one box on his breakfast invitation, I didn't expect him to bring an inquisitor."

Jev grimaced, lamenting that Zenia would have to again explain how she'd lost her career.

Zenia stopped at his side. For a moment, nerves danced in her eyes— she hadn't likely expected Targyon to recognize her. But she masked her nerves and lifted her chin.

"You needn't worry about me sharing any of your words with others in the Order. I'm not an inquisitor any longer, Zyndar—er King—Targyon."

"Zyndar works. Or just Targyon. I have two more hours before anyone has to call me king or sire. I'm trying to enjoy my last free morning."

"Is that hard with soggy armpits?" Jev asked.

"It *is*. I should have waited until later to put on the formal clothing." Targyon tilted his head and regarded Zenia again. "You say you've quit your job?"

"I was asked to resign due to a choice I made to do..." She closed her eyes, her lips flattening. She had to be wondering if she'd made the correct choice, if it had truly been worth giving up her career.

"To do the right thing," Jev said firmly.

"I suppose," Zenia murmured. "For the moment, I'm unemployed. I don't know yet what I'll do tomorrow. Or the next day. Apply to the watch, I suppose, to become one of their detectives, though I'm not looking forward to starting at the bottom of their system. I have acquaintances there who I've shown up over the years, and they might enjoy zyndaring it over me."

"Zyndaring it?" Targyon asked. "I didn't know that was an expression."

"None of the soldiers ever used it around you?" Jev asked.

"No. They called me a librarian sometimes when they thought I wasn't paying attention. Also, when they knew I was."

"It's not quite the same."

"I'd like to hear more of this story of choices over breakfast." Targyon waved his hand at both of them. He didn't appear that in-the-dark about their oblique comments, and Jev wondered if he'd received some intelligence from someone about the artifact hunt. Or had the elf princess already visited him? "Will you follow me?" Targyon asked. "I can't promise you the company will be scintillating, but I can feed you well, especially compared to army rations."

"I'd be disappointed if the king's castle couldn't produce better than army rations. Who else will be at breakfast?" Jev wondered what company he referred to. The idea of having to make conversation with a bunch of Order representatives or crusty royal advisors made him grimace.

"Just me." Targyon grinned lopsidedly over his shoulder as he led them toward a passage on the far side of the great hall.

"Ah. It's not bad to have some self-effacing qualities, Targyon, but you may want to develop a confident kingly cloak that you can drape around yourself in public. Otherwise..." Jev didn't want to suggest Targyon would find himself the subject of manipulation attempts, since he'd already voiced that fear—and perhaps experienced that situation—but he did think a warning might help.

"I don't think I can get a cloak like that to fit."

"It's easy. Pretend you're an actor in one of those plays you like. An arrogant actor playing an arrogant role. Give your chin an upward tilt the way Zenia does."

Her step faltered. "I don't do that."

"Please, you're doing it now."

She adjusted her chin experimentally a couple of times, frowned thoughtfully as she considered the position, then elbowed him in the ribs.

"What was that for?" he asked.

"Zyndaring."

"Zyndaring? I suspect you do that far better than I."

"Hm, at least *some* of the company should be scintillating," Targyon said, watching their byplay over his shoulder.

A butler opened double doors for them, and Targyon led them into an alcove near the kitchen rather than to the grand dining hall Jev had been to several times for events. A table with three place settings waited next to tall windows that overlooked one of the castle's many gardens. A servant waited nearby, but the bodyguards stayed by the door. They would be out of earshot if the trio spoke quietly around the table.

Targyon gestured for Jev and Zenia to sit. It seemed this truly would be a private breakfast. Jev was surprised. He hadn't expected to be the sole person to have Targyon's ear on this very important morning for him.

"I hope you'll feel comfortable speaking here," Targyon said, then nodded to the servant.

The man disappeared through a swinging side door, and the scents of baking biscuits and gort being sautéed in garlic wafted out of the kitchen.

"Because I'd like to hear everything that happened with this Eye of Truth," Targyon said. "From a trusted source."

"Have you seen it yet?" Jev asked.

"I've seen it and held it. Its owner too."

"You held the elf princess?"

"No. I mean, I saw her. And held the carving. I—" His cheeks flushed, and he looked even younger than his twenty-two years.

Jev lifted an apologetic hand. He hadn't meant to fluster Targyon.

"We'll gladly share our version of the story." Jev held a chair out for Zenia, then slid into one next to her. "Zenia, it all started with you. Do you want to go first?"

"It all started with me? It all started with an elf woman and your brother, didn't it?"

"Technically, it started thousands of years ago."

"I saw the visions." Targyon didn't say what his opinion of them was. He sat, propped his elbows on the table, and rested his chin on his intertwined fingers. Waiting attentively for them to continue.

"I guess I'll start," Jev said. "And trust Zenia to elbow me and lift her chin haughtily if I go awry."

She elbowed him, smiling slightly.

Jev and Zenia spent the next hour—and an impressive seven courses of peach-jam-slathered biscuits, eggs and gort, smoked fish, and Jev couldn't remember what else—relaying the story.

Here and there, Targyon asked a question, but he mostly listened.

Finally, as activity picked up in the kitchen, and more people passed through the garden outside on their way to dress and prepare for the ceremony, Jev and Zenia wound down, finishing with the events of the night before. Jev was hesitant to explain his grandmother's role in everything, but leaving it out would be to leave too many questions unanswered. He reminded himself that this wasn't simply a friend he was talking to, not anymore. In an hour, this would be his new king, a man to whom he and hundreds of other zyndar would kneel and swear their fealty to later in the ceremony.

"Good," Targyon said in the end. "I appreciate your thoroughness. I almost asked you to write up a report, but you aren't my employee yet, so that seemed presumptuous."

"I believe kings are allowed to presume much from their zyndar." Jev licked frosting off a cinnamon bun, one of several recently delivered in a basket. He paused mid-lick. "What do you mean, *employee?*"

"You need a job. You're not a captain anymore. Your company has dissolved and your men have returned to your land where they're once again taking up plowshares."

"Yes, but I am my father's son. I have duties he'll expect me to…" Jev stopped. He didn't *want* to do those duties. Why was he making an excuse? "I mean, he's gotten along well enough without me for ten years, I suppose."

"I'm sure he'll need you as he gets older and can't take on as much himself, and I wouldn't presume to send you out of the city often or keep you so busy that you're not able to assist him."

"Send me out of the city?" Jev looked to Zenia.

She lifted the cinnamon bun she'd claimed in a don't-look-at-me manner. She'd been doing more than licking the baked good for she had a smudge of frosting on her nose.

Since Targyon was watching them, Jev resisted the urge to wipe it off for her, especially since his napkin wasn't the implement he would prefer to use.

"Your title will be Captain of the Crown Agents, and my world-traveling spies will report to you and bring back any missives or information they intercept. With your linguistics and intelligence-analyzing background, you should be ideal. And I can't think of anyone I would trust more to be in charge of that half of my spy network."

"You have a spy network?" Jev leaned back in his seat, trying to remember if he'd been aware of Abdor having such an organization. He supposed it was logical to assume the king had people independent of the army's intelligence gatherers.

"I've inherited one, yes. But Zyndar Garlok, the current captain, seems shifty and possibly blackmail-able by the criminal guilds. I'm told it's within my prerogative to hire new people."

"And promote them directly to the top?"

"Absolutely. But you won't be alone at the top. I believe it makes sense to have *two* captains, one in charge of foreign affairs and one to oversee domestic issues. Since you've been out of the city for ten years, you wouldn't be as qualified for that as someone who is currently and intimately acquainted with Korvann and its various organizations, legal and otherwise." Targyon smiled and looked at Zenia.

Her lips parted, and she lowered her bun to the plate. Except she missed the plate and dropped it on the lacy tablecloth beside it. She didn't seem to notice.

"You're offering to hire me, Sire?" Zenia must have decided they were close enough to the hour of the coronation to start using a majestic honorific.

"You did mention you're without employment. I would like to swoop you up before some other agency bids for your talents."

"Other agency? I can't imagine anyone would be eager to hire an inquisitor. I—"

Jev leaned over and poked her in the shoulder. "Don't tell him that or he won't offer much of a salary. Tell him that numerous agencies, including the Fifth Dragon, have already made offers and eagerly await confirmation that you'll work for them."

He didn't think she had a mouthful of cinnamon bun, but she managed to almost choke regardless. She looked incredulously at him. "You want me to lie to our new monarch?"

"He won't be crowned for another hour. It's perfectly acceptable to fudge the truth with some random zyndar kid who's barely in his twenties."

"Really," Targyon murmured.

Jev winked at him, then whispered, not quietly, to Zenia. "You want him to realize how valuable and desirable you are so he'll offer you a high salary."

"I had no idea zyndar were so schooled in the ways of job interviews," she said back.

"I'm a wise and worldly zyndar."

She flicked a few fingers at him and turned her attention to Targyon. "Sire, are you saying that you would like me to lead—co-lead—your intelligence network?"

"I am," Targyon said gravely.

It did not seem to be an off-the-cuff offer. Jev wondered if Targyon had known the full story, at least a version of it, before they showed up that morning. If so, he hadn't shown his chips beforehand. Jev had a feeling Targyon would be better at this new job than he thought.

"I believe you have the intelligence and integrity for the position, and I need people I can trust." Targyon nodded to Jev and lowered his voice. "Desperately."

"I'm honored," Zenia said. "And I accept."

"Excellent. Zyndar Dharrow?" Again, Targyon seemed grave. Formal.

Jev steepled his fingers. "As you point out, I am zyndar, so I don't think it's allowed for me to do anything *other* than accept."

"True, but I would prefer that you want the position, not that I strong-arm you into it."

"Strong-arm?" Jev waved at Targyon's sleeves. They both knew he was on the wiry side. He'd been downright scrawny when he first entered into service. Now he could pass as lean, but he would never beat Jev in an arm-wrestling contest.

"As a monarch, it would be within my right to use both of my arms against your one."

"Is that how it works?"

"Privileges of rank."

"Huh."

Targyon continued to gaze at him intently.

"I had planned to get terribly drunk and lounge around on the beach when I got back," Jev said. "Only a certain inquisitor's attempt to arrest me interrupted that noble dream."

"*Attempt?*" Zenia said. "I most certainly arrested you."

"True. It wasn't until fifteen minutes later that your grasp on me grew tenuous."

"Only because you had superhuman help."

"Lornysh will be pleased you used that adjective on him."

Jev scratched his jaw. He would take the position, as he'd said, simply because he was zyndar and Targyon was soon to be his monarch. And also because Targyon had turned into a friend out in the field. But did he truly want the job? Was he *qualified* for the job? After being out of the city—the entire country and continent—for so long?

Of course, he would have Zenia to lean on. The idea of working side by side with her pleased him. And maybe even titillated him. He supposed he shouldn't fantasize about them locking themselves in an office deep within the castle and joining forces to do untoward things on a stout desk. It would have been scandalous when she'd been his arresting officer, but now...

He scratched his jaw again. Now, what? They would be colleagues working in the same office every day. Would having a relationship be problematic? Potentially fraught? Then there was still the matter of social rank. If their relationship worked out and he wanted to marry her, what then? He was his father's only surviving son. As much as he would prefer to eschew all zyndar marriage traditions, his whole family would fight him if he proposed to a commoner.

"Are you hesitating because you truly don't want to do it?" Targyon said softly. "If that's the case, I don't want to make you. I thought you were good at your job in the military and might enjoy having a civilian equivalent. Technically, a government equivalent, I suppose, since this wouldn't be working in the private sector."

"No, I was hesitating because I was fantasizing about my future colleague." Jev decided not to mention the rest. It was something he and Zenia could figure out later. After they'd known each other for more than three days and been on a date.

"Zyndar Garlok?"

"No." Jev leered over at Zenia, though he was positive Targyon had only been teasing.

She arched her eyebrows. Whatever she'd been contemplating, it probably hadn't involved desks.

"That's good," Targyon said. "Garlok is old, pock-marked, and usually smells of that oddly-flavored chicle he chews. I assumed you could do better."

"I certainly hope so. I accept the job, Targyon. Sire." Jev offered his hand as he nodded.

"Excellent. And you can keep calling me Targyon. Except when I'm wearing the crown and holding the scepter and tilting my chin up officiously."

"Arrogantly." Jev smirked at Zenia.

"You're about to get another elbow in the side," she whispered.

"So long as you don't get the frosting that's all over your nose on me. I suspect professional dress and bathing will be required for this new job."

Zenia jerked a hand up to her nose, found the crusty now-dried frosting, and scraped furiously as she glared at him. He smiled innocently. It wasn't as if *he* had put it there.

"So long as you don't stink as much as you did when I met you, I'm sure normal dress will suffice," Zenia said.

"I'll endeavor to smell delightful."

Targyon leaned back in his chair as a servant appeared to clear the dishes and wordlessly offer Zenia a damp napkin. She scowled but accepted it.

"I suspect the Crown Agents Office is going to be a more interesting place to visit once you two are instated," Targyon said.

"It doesn't sound like Zyndar Garlok sets high standards to meet."

"No, I almost look forward to letting him go. Or suggesting his retirement, as I intend to put it. When will you two be ready to start? Tomorrow?"

"So soon?" Jev hadn't gotten his beach vacation yet. His chance to drunkenly do nothing while letting the sun scorch the skin that had grown pasty while traipsing through those sunless elven forests. And then having a beautiful woman rub aloe vera gel all over him. Would Zenia be amenable to that? Or would she call him a fool for sunburning himself? He would allow that if she did it *while* rubbing aloe vera gel on him.

"The day after tomorrow? Normally, I would be happy to give you a week or two to settle affairs and relax, but..." Targyon lowered his voice and made sure the servant had left and none of the bodyguards had strolled away from their posts by the far door. "I don't want to assume my position is approved by all. The first thing I'd like you two to research is what happened to my cousins. For that matter, was my uncle's death truly a battlefield accident in which the enemy overcame him, or was it planned?" Targyon's face grew grimmer than an elven funeral cairn.

"Ah." Jev had already wondered about the three cousins and heirs succumbing to the same disease of the blood in the same month, but he hadn't considered that foul play might have been involved in the king's death. Should he have? He hadn't been on the front lines for that battle, so he hadn't witnessed the man's fall.

He grimaced at all the work, all the interviews they would have to do, both of people in the city and also of soldiers in the army, to research that. But he caught Zenia's expression, her eyes gleaming with anticipation, and decided the work wouldn't be so bad. Especially since it wouldn't involve investigating his own family. It wouldn't be so personal, so uncomfortable. At least to him. It would be very personal and uncomfortable for Targyon, who must even now be wondering if he would go the way of his uncle and cousins if he didn't please the right people.

Jev leaned over and gripped his shoulder. "I understand. We'll get on it right away. Zenia is an expert at interrogating people, you know."

When he smiled over at her, he caught a wistful expression on her face. Was she thinking of the dragon tear she'd been forced to give back? And whether she would still be an *expert on interrogating people* without it?

Maybe so, but she lifted her chin and said, "Yes, I am."

"Excellent," Targyon said.

A door opened, and a castle steward leaned in. "King Targyon? If you've completed your meal, it's time to prepare for the coronation."

"I'm ready, Dodd." Targyon pushed himself to his feet, waving back the servant who rushed forward to pull out his chair. "As ready as is possible, I guess," he muttered, then gave Jev an army salute, open palm to the side of his forehead. He bowed to Zenia and headed off.

Not like a man going to the gallows, Jev told himself sturdily, but like a noble zyndar ready to serve his country and embark on a new career that would benefit the entire kingdom.

EPILOGUE

"Y OU ONLY GET ONE DAY off?" Rhi asked as she and Zenia picked their way down the path leading to a beach at the east end of the city and the docks.

Rafts and fishing boats floated in the delta nearby, and farther inland, the mangrove branches waved in the sea breeze. A white-tailed eagle sailed over the river, and Zenia took the lucky bird as a good sign for her new career.

"Isn't one day enough?" she asked. "It's not like I had other plans."

She did not admit it, but she would have preferred to start her job today and get to work on the king's problem. She was also eager to meet her new colleagues and see her office in the castle. In the castle! She had never expected to be invited up there, much less to be able to list it as her place of employment. As much as she would miss the familiarity of the Water Order Temple, and the tinkle of the great fountain in the square outside, she looked forward to this new challenge in her life.

"Some people would enjoy the time and celebrate the new job by taking their families out for a meal. I suppose you don't have much family, but you could take a lover out to dinner." Rhi wriggled her eyebrows at her.

She wore her typical blue gi since *she* hadn't been dismissed from the Order's service. Zenia hoped Rhi wouldn't get in trouble if she was seen walking with her. Strange to think that she might be considered a bad influence now, at least by some.

"I don't have a lover, so that would be difficult." Zenia searched the beach for Jev, wondering if *he* might one day be interested in assuming that position. There hadn't been much time for exploring romantic relationships yet, but he had kissed her... and nibbled her earlobe. Those seemed like the types of things a lover would do. But since she would only be interested in a lover who wanted to marry her, was there any point in speculating?

Zenia had seen far too many bastard children abandoned at the temple gates by unwed mothers who couldn't care for them to contemplate a simple fling. Even when people took precautions, children often came out of *flings*. Admittedly, she wouldn't exist if her mother hadn't slept with a zyndar man, but her childhood hadn't been the easiest. She wouldn't wish that on any children of her own.

"I suspect you could get one more easily now that you're not wearing that shield of a blue robe that terrifies men at a hundred paces."

Zenia looked down at her clothing, clothing that felt strange. She'd been so accustomed to wearing her robe that she'd usually even worn it on her days off. When she'd moved out of her room at the temple, leaving the handful of inquisitor robes behind, she'd found precious little casual clothing in the drawers. Today, she wore loose cotton trousers and a long-sleeved tunic with ties on the front, the garments flapping in the breeze as she and Rhi left the boardwalk and ventured onto the beach itself.

Warm sand slid between her feet and her sandals, making her wonder why Jev had dreamed of getting drunk down *here*. All manner of waterfront pubs with chairs and tables lined the boardwalk. Albeit, they were extremely crowded and noisy now. The first of the three days of holiday following the coronation were upon Korvann, and the whole city was celebrating. People's boisterousness might be as much due to the end of the war as the crowning of a new king.

"Ah, there's one now." Rhi pointed down the beach, past numerous people lounging in bathing clothing to a shirtless figure with a hat pulled over his face. Two brown ceramic jugs—empty or full?—of beer were stuck in the sand beside him, and the sun had already turned his chest pink.

From this distance, Zenia couldn't see the scars, but she knew they were there. They didn't detract from the fact that he had a very nice chest. She imagined running her fingers along its muscular contours, and her cheeks flushed as she reminded herself that she wasn't interested in flings. Besides, if his chest turned any redder, he wouldn't want it touched for days.

"One what?" Zenia asked.

"Lover. Potential lover. At the least, you can ask him to dinner."

"He doesn't appear to be conscious."

"This is true. Are you sure he invited you to come join him here?"

"Well, he told me where he'd be today." Zenia had not known if it had been an invitation or if he'd merely offered the information in case she needed to talk to him before they officially started their jobs.

Zenia's mind still boggled that she'd been hired by the king, that she'd sat down with him for a private breakfast in the castle. She'd always looked down her nose at zyndar and had thought herself indifferent to the pomp around royal celebrations and the royal family, but it had been surreal, nonetheless.

"He shouldn't mind when we plop down next to him then," Rhi said. "I'm invited, too, right?"

"I'm not positive I'm invited."

"You are. Trust me." Rhi grinned as they picked their way past families having picnics and swimmers drying off on towels. "If he didn't want you to come see him, he would have said he was busy doing zyndar things at his castle. He's probably dreaming of you coming up and kissing him right now. Well, perhaps not *right* now. His flag isn't at mast."

"Rhi!"

"What? You lie on your back on the beach in nothing but shorts, and people can see these things."

"Only people who look at other people's… *special* areas."

"Special areas? I'll tell him you think that part of him is special. I assure you, he'll be delighted."

Founders' horned heads, how had Zenia ever thought coming to the beach with Rhi would be a good idea?

Since Jev had that broad-brimmed floppy hat pulled over his face, he didn't see Zenia and Rhi approach. Zenia stopped in the sand beside him, letting herself look him over more openly than she had during that embarrassing search in front of Iridium. She couldn't lie. Even sunburned with empty beer jugs next to his hand, he looked…

"Scrumptious." Rhi slapped the end of her bo against one of his bare feet. "I approve of this man for you, former Inquisitor Cham."

Jev jerked, yanking his hat off and peering up at them. He looked like he'd been startled awake, and Zenia slapped Rhi on the arm. After so many years in Taziira, he probably envisioned elven attackers invading camp whenever he woke with a start.

"Sorry about that, Jev," Zenia said. "That's how monks greet people. By beating them with a big stick."

Jev recovered his equilibrium, set the hat aside, and propped himself on his elbows. "Oh?"

"Yes, I believe it's in the Old Codex of the Monk."

"Nah, weapons handling is covered in the New Codex," Rhi said.

"What *is* covered in the Old Codex?" Zenia tried to remember if Rhi or any other monk she'd worked with had referenced it.

"Being pious and celibate so best to serve the founders. Also, the importance of knowing your daily fortune and acting according to it so as best to ensure success."

"That's it?"

"Just about. The Old Codex was more of a pamphlet carved onto stone tablets than a book. There were a lot of pictures. People didn't read that well back then, and paper hadn't gotten trendy yet."

People still didn't read well, at least when it came to the general population. Those who worked for the Orders were all educated. It occurred to Zenia that, even though she hadn't gotten the position of archmage and influencer over the way of the Water Order that she'd hoped for, she might one day come to know the king well enough to have some influence on him. The rumors said Targyon loved science and books of all kinds. Maybe a simple suggestion would be all it took for him to render education mandatory in the kingdom.

"You're celibate?" Jev asked Rhi.

They hadn't conversed often but apparently often enough for him to guess that Rhi's midnight poetry-reading activities weren't as sedate as she suggested.

"She's as celibate as she is pious," Zenia offered.

Rhi smiled. Piously.

"I'm going to go establish law and order among those shirtless gentlemen playing with the ball down by the water." Rhi pointed at two teams of bare-chested brawny young men whose physiques suggested they worked hard at jobs involving intense labor. They played hard too. Rhi wasn't the only woman gazing in their direction.

"Are they being disorderly?" Jev asked.

"Not yet, but it's only a matter of time. I may have to beat one of them with my bo." She winked at them and wandered off.

"To think, *I* was the one kicked out of the temple," Zenia said.

Jev scooted over on the blanket he'd brought out and patted the spot next to him. "Will your new position take the sting out of that? I know you lost more than just a job."

Zenia settled cross-legged next to him. She noticed a couple of young women on nearby towels scowling at her. Had they been ogling Jev with speculation? She would think the ball-playing men more entertaining subjects, at least at the moment, but if one wanted someone more mature, someone a little scarred, Jev did have appeal.

"It'll take a while to get used to it," Zenia said, "but I'm looking forward to it. And I'm eager to start on our first case."

"I am too. I'm worried about Targyon, and I'm glad we'll be close in case he needs advice. Or a protector." His eyes grew steely with determination. He was quick to grin and make sarcastic comments, but he clearly had a serious side.

Zenia looked forward to seeing more of his sides.

"But I'm determined to enjoy my day off first." Jev smiled, the steeliness fading. He pulled one of the jugs out of the sand and offered it to her. "Drink?"

"Inquisitors don't dull their senses by imbibing alcohol."

"But you're not an inquisitor anymore."

"I wouldn't think crown agents should dull their senses either."

"Are you sure? I haven't seen the handbook yet."

"*Is* there a handbook?" Zenia asked.

"I don't know."

"If there's not, we could write one. A collaborative project."

Jev wrinkled his nose. "Will you be offended if I hope there's already one in the office?"

"I'm amenable to following an existing handbook, so long as it's cohesive and well-organized."

"I can see working with you will be a wild experience."

"I doubt the new king wants wildness in his spy network. He seems like the type to approve of organization and handbooks."

"I know that's true."

"Excellent." Zenia beamed approval at him.

Jev shook his head and tilted the jug back for a drink. But he paused before it touched his lips, his eyebrows arching as he looked past Zenia's shoulder.

A sturdy bearded figure in coveralls, boots, and a leather apron strode across the beach. A few other sets of eyebrows rose as Master Arkura Grindmor approached Jev and Zenia with a determined set to her jaw.

"She doesn't look like she found her tools, does she?" Zenia asked, disappointed. She'd hoped she might have helped the dwarf—and also cleverly deduced Iridium's hiding spot.

"She looks like she ate a tool for lunch and has indigestion."

Zenia rose to her feet, dusting off sand, so she could bow her head respectfully.

"Look at this." Arkura said without preamble, pulling a hammer out of her belt, the shaft made from some black material and the head glinting in the sunlight like a jewel. Or a diamond?

"You found them?" Jev sounded surprised.

"*One* of them." Arkura jammed the hammer back through her belt. "Lying in saltwater like a discarded sardine tin. If my tools could rust, they'd be covered in the stuff. I'm going to knock that woman's head off the next time I see her."

"Iridium?" Zenia asked.

"Yes. *After* I get the location of the rest of my tools from her. I only found the hammer because some clod let it fall out, then didn't notice."

"Was it in one of the pumping stations?"

"Yes, you guessed right. And I'd thank you for that, but I'm so frustrated I could shave a bearded dragon. The tools had been there. You could tell. There was a rusty mark on the ground in the shape of my toolbox. It's not made of diamond, you see. It can rust. Now, I'll have to build a new one. When I get the rest of my tools back." She glowered at Zenia, then propped her fists on her hips and shifted the glower to Jev.

"You're saying I should send my friend Cutter to your workshop to start searching for them?" Jev asked mildly.

"I'm appalled he's not already there." Arkura looked at the position of the sun in the sky. She didn't point out that Jev—and Zenia—owed her a favor, but she didn't need to.

"I'll go look for him now." Jev stood so he could shake sand off his blanket and fold it up. "And if he has any trouble with the quest, I should be able to help from my new position."

"I don't care what position you assume, but I want my tools back." Arkura whirled and stomped back the way she had come.

"Since she was kind enough to rescue us, I'm not going to point out what a grump she is," Jev said.

"Or that she didn't address you as Zyndar Dharrow and bow obsequiously?"

"I'm just happy she didn't point out that my beard is even farther from my balls now than it was when she first met me."

A young woman who happened to be walking past as he made that comment threw Jev a startled look.

"If I were still an inquisitor, I could fine you for talking about your reproductive anatomy in public," Zenia said.

"I *know* there's not a law about that."

"You've been gone for ten years. The law evolves over time."

He squinted at her. "I haven't yet learned how to tell when you're joking and when you're being serious."

"Working together should be interesting then."

"Of that I have no doubt."

THE END

Printed in Great Britain
by Amazon